CRITICAL LUCRE

MW00625644

Debut novel of the
EPSILON Sci-Fi Thriller series

BRIAN H. ROBERTS

Crimson Lucre is a work of fiction. Names, characters, businesses, organizations, places, events, and incidents are the product of the author's imagination or are used fictitiously. Any resemblance to actual events, locales, organizations, or persons, living or dead, is entirely coincidental.

Developmental Editor, Sandra Haven
Copy Editor, Dylan Garity
Cover Design, Daniel Schmelling

ISBN paperback 978-1-7369921-0-4
ISBN ebook 978-1-7369921-1-1

ONE ELEVEN PRESS

To Carole Roberts, who taught me to master and love the English language. Thanks Mom.

To Joel Berman, who introduced me to the miracle of creative writing as a student at Sunset Junior High.

CHAPTER 1

Dallas's eyes fluttered open. Bewildering flashes of light. A piercing alarm. Panicked, he bolted upright, only to bang his head against an unseen barrier inches above his face. Nausea wracked his body from head to toe. Only the aspiration tube in his throat saved him from drowning on his meager stomach contents.

The convulsions subsided, and he self-assessed. *Arms and legs restrained. No pain beyond this killer headache.* As he lay there, confusion transitioned to clarity. *Call for help.* He fingered the call button taped to his left palm and pressed it.

He heard the snap of mechanical clasps releasing. Presently, his sleep tube opened like a clamshell, and he felt the touch of the medical attendant on his chest. "Sir, I'll have you out of your sleep tube in five minutes."

The attendant removed the electrodes that sprouted from Dallas's body like puppet strings run amuck. Their constant signals ordered his muscles to contract while he slept, preventing the otherwise certain muscular atrophy. Next, IV tubes were slipped from both forearms and his groin, and the sites expertly bandaged to prevent bleeding and infection. An fMRI cap was lifted from his head. As EKG leads were torn from his chest, Dallas let out a stifled cry around the tubes in his throat. He glared at the attendant, continuing the muffled, guttural curses for another fifteen seconds. Once they ceased, the tubes were withdrawn. "You know the protocol is to remove the tubes from my throat *first* before you remove the pads from my chest," he accused the attendant. His voice was raspy, and his words slurred, but his eyes flashed his irritation.

"Yes, sir. But when I followed protocol last time, you cast aspersions on my mother's lineage, and threatened my eternal soul."

Dallas rolled his eyes but said nothing more. He knew the attendant's programming precluded harm to any human. But given his ongoing experiences with Robbie, Dallas entertained deep suspicions that this AI had somehow concluded that he was not.

The attendant reached in and released the restraints on Dallas's arms, legs, and waist. At last, Dallas floated free. He inventoried his musculature. His five-foot-eight, 160-pound frame came out of stasis more or less in the same condition it had entered nine months ago. He knew from previous experience that his complexion was pallid, with the exception of his freckles, which covered his cheeks, forehead, and shoulders. His wavy, strawberry blond hair was still in a tight crewcut. Curiously, hair and nails did not grow during stasis.

The attendant helped Dallas into his flight suit while he still floated within the confines of the open sleep tube. Once dressed, Dallas grasped the edge of his tube and pulled himself upright. He took in the cylindrical command module cabin from fore to aft. A screen on the command console across from his sleep tube flashed in synchrony with the audible alarm. Four more sleep tubes further aft exhibited various stages of reanimation. Except for the incessant alarm, everything was as he remembered from when he went under.

He pulled his way to the pilot's seat and touched the screen. The alarm stopped. Navigational readouts continued to scroll. Dallas read the telemetry on the screen. "Robbie, this indicates we're more than five degrees outside our trajectory window. How is that possible?"

"Sir, I am not synced to the mainframe. My current in-flight programming priority is servicing the sleep tubes and returning the occupants to operational status."

The sound of retching emanated from one of the other sleep tubes. Robbie wheeled silently, then stopped beside it in preparation for another wakeup protocol. Dallas turned to the console and began scrolling through the navigational readouts.

One by one, the four other team members gathered around Dallas's station. LaDonna Pleasant arrived first. As the mission flight surgeon, she normally awakened before the others, except during active alarms, like now. Of all the crew members, LaDonna always came out of a sleep tube the hardest. At forty-six, her age was a contributing factor. Along with her bloodshot eyes, her ebony skin was visibly green. She was a vigorous woman, yet she always left a sleep tube looking frail. She grated at the ironic reminders from the crew about the mission doctor being the sickest of all.

LaDonna supervised Robbie when he was in medical mode. So now she multitasked, keeping a wary eye on Robbie's activities while also looking over Dallas's shoulder. "Dallas, why are you up first?"

"We experienced an onboard alarm. We're off course. I'm confirming the heading given by our navigational system with good old-fashioned celestial navigation. You got a lucky star, Doc? Based on what I'm seeing, we could use it."

"If the stars are so lucky, then why do I feel like this?" She pointed both index fingers at her green-tinged, bloodshot-eyed visage.

"Fine, then pick any star. We've got several hundred in our database I can reference. I just need a third star bearing to complete this calculation."

"Vega. Sounds like 'Vegas.' Will that do?"

"Vega it is." Dallas manipulated a joystick on the navigation console to center the star within crosshairs on his monitor. The crosshairs flashed briefly, recording the star's bearing. A second later, the celestial navigation algorithm flashed a position on-screen. It matched the position given by the onboard navigational system, confirming they were indeed off course. Following protocol, Dallas immediately selected three more stars.

LaDonna eyed Robbie from her position near Dallas. She wanted to give direct oversight to the assistant, but she was still in no condition to do so. Rubbing her bloodshot eyes, she turned back to observe Dallas. "Next time I go into stasis, I'm upping my anti-nausea IV."

"Won't that put you to sleep?"

"Nothing would please me more than to sleep through my awakening." She chuckled at her own joke, but Dallas remained fixed on his navigation console.

The next floating in behind Dallas was Dave Caraway, the mission geologist. Before being hired by EPSILON, the huge high-tech firm known mostly for manufacturing autonomous vehicles, Dave had spent his career working for a Canadian mining consortium, prospecting and developing rare earth element mineral fields in the ever-expanding Canadian arctic. The seventeen rare earth elements were vital for the production of electronics of all kinds—everything from cell phones to smart medical and scientific equipment, to autonomous vehicles and robotics.

China had cornered and held the rare earth elements market on Earth early in the century. As demand increased, China used their monopoly to leverage concessions out of Western companies, often obtaining technology and intellectual property rights they could not otherwise obtain by espionage. As worldwide rare earth elements availability dwindled, Western companies engaged in bidding wars, driving up prices. EPSILON had refused to accede to China's demands, instead paying a premium for the limited Canadian-sourced rare earth elements. But most Western manufacturers knuckled under to China's coercion. They simply did not have the resources to take on the eight-hundred-pound Chinese panda.

Like other competing private ventures into space, EPSILON intended to mine rare earth element minerals on Mars and the asteroids, process them *in situ*, and ship them back to Earth. Any Western company that broke China's stranglehold stood to reap untold billions of dollars. When

NASA rovers discovered rare earth elements on Mars ten years earlier, it set off a space-faring corporate gold rush of interplanetary proportions.

"Top o' the mornin' to ye!" Dave affected his best Irish brogue and a chipper disposition. But he, like LaDonna before him, was largely ignored by Dallas. He affected a flinch when LaDonna turned toward him. Her obvious discomfiture proved too tempting a target for his sarcasm to pass up. "Gotta hand it to you, Doc. You really know how to light up a room."

She flashed an angry stare at him, unable to muster up a comeback.

Dallas responded in defense of his not-yet-fully-functional flight surgeon, "Dave, you do remember your next physical is due this month? Not a good idea to insult the hand that wears the vinyl glove."

Dave suppressed the urge to retort with a smart-ass comeback. He had surrendered his manhood to the tender mercies of the mission flight surgeon during previous physical exams and had no desire to expose his family jewels to her if she had a score to settle.

After another five minutes, Luis Alvarez, the mission robotics/mechanical engineer, joined them. Luis looked himself over. He had preserved his original muscled weight through stasis, a fact the bodybuilder was enormously proud of. But at the sight of Robbie, he set vanity aside. "Robbie, little buddy! How you doin'? I've missed you!" As he exited his sleep tube, Luis gave Robbie an affectionate pat near the AI's face screen.

"I'm doing well, Luis. Thank you for your concern."

Dallas chimed in, "Luis, it creeps me out the way you two carry on. It's like the two of you grew up together as kids, swingin' on the tire swing, jumpin' in the old swimmin' hole, playin' hooky from school. It's just not natural."

Luis made his way to the group clustered around Dallas. "What's all the excitement? Did Dave break something again?"

"Looks like Robbie took us for a joy ride while we were all asleep." Dave had peered over Dallas's shoulder long enough to determine that they were off course, and that Dallas was confirming their position by running multiple iterations of the celestial navigation algorithm.

Luis jumped to Robbie's defense. "Rock nerd, what you talkin' about? Robbie would never do that to me. I think you messed up navigation with all that snoring in your sleep."

The exchange prompted a response from Dallas. "We're not lost. We're off course. To be precise, we're off course by over a million miles. I'm backing up our given position and vector with multiple celestial fixes. If *Prospector* is off course as much as the navigational system indicates, it could take us weeks to backtrack to Mars."

LaDonna broke the stunned silence. "*Prospector* was provisioned with food rations for seven days. We ate one day's worth before we entered hibernation. Dallas, I'm deeply concerned about the prospect of the crew reentering sleep so soon after reanimation just to get back to Mars. The required medical expertise is beyond what Robbie alone can provide, if I'm incapacitated."

Dallas and the crew were all aware of the risks multiple sleep-wake cycles posed. LaDonna had explained to them during mission training that early test subjects had experienced organ failure undergoing frequent cycles. Two subjects had died. Subsequent research reduced the side effects for a single cycle. But the side effects returned when cycles followed each other in rapid succession. Mission planning provided rations for a brief recovery period in Mars orbit of up to six days before descent to the surface. The entire mission provided a fifteen-month gap between cycles. If the mission were ever scrubbed, requiring back-to-back sleep-wake cycles, a specialized medical team would rendezvous with *Prospector* once it was back in Earth orbit to supervise the critical reanimation.

Medical ethicists considered the risks of hibernation a fair trade-off for the reduced risk of long-term cosmic radiation damage. NASA required the procedure as a precondition for the lease of a DeepStar booster, as was the case with EPSILON for its Prospector program.

The last crew member joining the group behind Dallas was the electrical/software engineer, Allie O'Donnell. At thirty-five, she was the youngest of the crew, and always came out of a sleep tube looking like she had just woken from a power nap. Athletically built, she kept her straight blond hair short in a pixie-style haircut. Her brown eyes were clear and bright. Her prominent cheekbones and chin radiated the faintest suggestion of a rosy glow. Allie was considered by most to be attractive, even without makeup, which she wore on only the rarest of occasions (space flight was not one of them). Much to the chagrin of her crewmates, she commanded the largest social media following. When awake, she usually spent about an hour a day posting and interacting with her followers. "Can't a girl get any beauty sleep around here?"

The lack of response drew Allie to the cluster of crewmates huddled around the navigation station. She quickly saw by the ashen faces gathered around Dallas that something was wrong. Luis filled her in. "We're over a million miles off course."

Allie floated the rest of the way to Luis's side. "Not the greeting from you that I was expecting." She poked him playfully in the ribs. Her mischievous smile quickly faded when she noted the man's serious countenance.

Dallas caught her arrival in his peripheral vision. "Allie, patch me in to SaMMCon."

"Right away, Flash." Allie pulled herself into the seat at the communication console beside Dallas.

The crew made a habit of addressing Dallas Gordon by his naval aviator nickname. Dallas had earned the moniker early on in his flight training in the navy. With his flight trainer seated behind him in his T-34 Turbomentor, Dallas had spent three hours flawlessly executing every maneuver he was commanded to do. At the end of their flight session, the trainer had directed Dallas back to base: "Bring her home to the barn, son."

To which Dallas replied, "In a flash, sir."

All intra-aircraft communication was monitored by a naval ground controller at Naval Air Station Corpus Christi, where Dallas's T-34 was based. So, in the finest naval tradition, this privileged conversation between flight instructor and trainee had been readily shared with anyone willing to listen. Dallas was boisterously greeted by the ground crew after landing.

"Nice flight, Flash!"

"We'll have you refueled in a flash, Flash!"

"Hey Flash Gordon, can I have your baby?"

Dallas had doubted the sincerity of that last request, considering he was quite certain his chief mechanic at the time was a lesbian and already in a relationship.

He wasn't especially thrilled with the nickname. Way too corny. But naval flight trainees seldom, if ever, got to pick their own. By the time he earned the rank of Lieutenant Commander, he wore his moniker as proudly as his many combat medals earned flying an F-35 during the Iranian War. Only right now, he didn't feel like the invincible fictional Flash Gordon from the previous century.

Allie pulled herself to the communication console and booted up her screen. She was unsure if the nausea she felt was due to the lingering effects of hibernation or the news she had just awakened to.

CHAPTER 2

Ann Waters felt something was wrong. As flight operations director (FOD) for EPSILON's Santa Maria Mission Control (SaMMCon), Ann readily viewed the entire flight control room. The capsule communication officer (CapCom), Evan Griffin, had adjusted his headset as if he were having difficulty hearing. He then sat forward in his chair, assuming a posture of heightened alert.

Ann got up from her FOD flight control station at the back center of the room and approached Evan's CapCom station, positioning herself beside Evan to his right. Evan immediately switched from his headset to his speaker. "… experienced a nav alarm upon awakening. Nav control indicates Prospector 1 is five degrees outside of target trajectory. Reentered reference stars four times into nav program per procedure. Texting calculations for FDO analysis."

"Evan, do you have the text version?"

"Yes, Ma'am. It's on my screen."

Within the mission control room, the flight control stations were arranged in three rows, all facing a pair of large screens mounted on the front wall. Each flight station had numerous smaller screens and keyboards. The two big screens in the front of the room were mounted above three doors that led to conference rooms, staff offices, and a small staff lunchroom. The flight control room floor was recessed twelve feet below a bank of observation windows at the back of the room. Any activity in the flight control room occurred in full view of any visitors in the public lobby.

Monica Gonzalez stepped from her flight control station and positioned herself behind Evan to view his screen. Shorter and heavier, Monica acted as a surrogate mother to Ann, who had lost both her parents while she was attending college. At fifty-eight, Monica was Ann's senior by nineteen years, but readily served under the younger flight operations director. Ann appreciated the good humor and friendship she found in Monica's company outside the workplace. But at this moment, Ann appreciated all the more Monica's analytical instincts as the mission flight dynamics officer (FDO).

Monica closely studied Evan's screen. Evan scrolled through four sets of calculations on his monitor. He was not a mathematician, but he knew that each described a spiral trajectory from Earth outward to Mars. If they were consistent with the orbital dynamics flight path laid out by Monica at the start of the mission, Prospector's path would intersect the orbit of Mars at the same time that the actual planet arrived.

Monica spoke aloud absently, as if what she was seeing made no sense to her. Ann noted a strong Spanish accent, as she always did when Monica was so engrossed. "The warning message at the end of each calculation indicates that Prospector 1's velocity exceeds flight parameters."

Looking now at Ann, she spoke with more conviction in her voice, the accent now less obvious. "If true, it means the spacecraft has already crossed Mars's orbit. Prospector is over a million miles outside of Mars's orbit and almost equally farther ahead than they should be. Given Prospector's current flight vector, orbital insertion is not possible."

Portia Knox, the program flight surgeon, inserted herself into the conversation. "Ann, if Monica can't get Prospector 1 into Mars orbit within six days, I'll have to scrub the mission. We can't allow the crew to starve before they attempt a landing, and I won't allow a second hibernation cycle without a medical team present for the waking. Which means they would need to head back to Earth where reanimation can be properly monitored."

Without looking at her program flight surgeon, Ann pressed Monica, "Can you insert Prospector 1 into Mars orbit within six days? We've come so close to being the first to put boots on Mars. I'd hate to see someone else leapfrog us. It could cost us control of the claims we've already staked. Ten years of unmanned prospecting, five years spent assembling Prospector Base—it could all be for nothing."

Monica consoled Ann as best she could. "It all depends on how quickly we can reverse course and brake at 100-percent thrust. If I can't slow Prospector 1 down enough, Mars will pass them by before I can insert them into orbit. It could take weeks for them to catch back up."

By now, the entire SaMMCon staff had stopped their normal activities, focusing intently on the conversation at the CapCom station. Ann returned her attention to her FDO. "Monica, why haven't I been notified that Prospector was off course?"

"Miss Ann, all of the telemetry Drew has forwarded to me shows Prospector is perfectly on course."

Ann quickly redirected her attention to her guidance and navigation control engineer (GNC). "Drew, when is the last time you provided the nav stat report to Monica to review?"

Drew responded in his laconic Southern drawl, "Ma'am, I gave Monica this mornin's summary ninety minutes ago."

Feeling guilty for throwing a coworker under the bus, Monica mustered to his defense, "It's true, Miss Ann. I finished my review twenty minutes ago and put it in your inbox. Prospector's heading was nominal."

Ann had reviewed the report just before she left her station for this very conversation. She turned around to address Cliff Sherman, the integrated communications officer. "Cliff, is it possible that Prospector's position is at odds with their telemetry?"

Cliff monitored all communications and instrument telemetry. Unable to make eye contact over his monitor, the man stood, his waist-length dreadlocks swinging as he rose. He was the only one in the room wearing long sleeves—at the insistence of Human Resources, to cover potentially questionable tattoos. "Ann, the same nav program Commander Gordon used to fix their position runs in the background and transmits their positional data. The telemetry report was routed through the GNC and the FDO, and is sitting on your desk. I can't explain the discrepancy with the info I've got."

Drew spoke up. "Ma'am, I'd like to review the navigational software code. Maybe there's a clue there as to what's goin' on."

Ann stood silent for a moment, processing everything she had just heard. Snapping off instructions rapid-fire, she started with the CapCom control station. "Evan, send a message back to Prospector 1. Tell them 'message received' and to stand by for further instructions. Then send a copy of the audio file and the text message to the FDO and the GNC—and cc me."

Ann pivoted to address Monica. "Your highest priority is finding a solution that will safely insert Prospector 1 into a Mars orbit. Use the nav calcs Evan just forwarded to you as the basis for their current vector."

Lastly, she turned to the GNC, halfway down the row from the FDO station. "Drew, ping Prospector and get a copy of the nav program code. Take it to the nav team and have them comb through it. We need to know what we're dealing with, and how reliable the shipboard nav system is."

Ann raised her voice to be heard throughout the room. "While you're working on your assignments, I'll speak with Ajay to see if NASA can confirm Prospector 1's position and vector. We send no solution to Prospector 1 until I know which to trust—the telemetry, or the onboard navigation."

Ann briskly walked to the back row of flight op stations and turned toward the NASA rep station. Even though EPSILON was a private corporation, they, like all organizations that aspired to exploit the resources on Mars, had adopted NASA terminology and operating procedures. NASA had transitioned from its original model, as a government agency that owned and operated its own fleet of spacecraft, to a regulatory agency model like the FAA. NASA promulgated rules and standards that space-faring enterprises adhered to.

The DeepStar nuclear ion propulsion unit EPSILON used was leased from NASA. NASA had the budget and nuclear permitting authority to develop the technology, based on its previous NASA Evolutionary Xenon Thruster (NEXT) project. Components were fabricated on Earth, then launched into orbit where they were assembled. To date, four had been constructed. All four had been leased. Two firms—EPSILON and BMAC—had ambitious missions to establish mining bases on Mars and within the asteroid belt. EPSILON's entire Prospector program depended on the leased NASA booster. NASA's remaining two units were leased to private firms to deploy solar weather observatories, deep space telescopes, and communications relays midway between Earth and Mars.

Ann's boss, Mission Director Malcom McDowell, was already deep in conversation with Ajay Kumar, the NASA representative. Just as Monica Gonzales fulfilled the emotional role of "mother" to Ann, the mission director was much like a father to her—or maybe an older brother. It was Malcom McDowell who'd recruited Ann after she earned her PhD, and who'd promoted Ann to flight director nine years later.

The taller and heavier African American from Chicago stood back a bit from the diminutive Bombay native, out of respect for the latter's personal space. "Ajay, how much time will it take NASA to establish speed and vector?"

Ajay replied in his thick Hindi accent, "Malcom, the NASA Infrared Telescope Facility on Mauna Kea is positioned to be able to see Prospector right now. I should have your information in two hours."

Not to be delayed by NASA bureaucracy, Malcom pressed, "Can you make it one hour?"

Ajay diplomatically raised an eyebrow. "The astronomers need time to position the telescope. Then they need to get two measurements far enough apart for the answer to not be affected by any rounding errors. They will input the measurements into their mainframe and transmit the results directly to me. If you want an independent check, that will add more time."

Malcom capitulated, "Alright. Two hours it is. But time is of the essence. If we're five degrees off heading, and a million miles from Mars insertion, we have no time to spare."

Ajay extended an olive branch to the disconsolate mission director. "I understand, Malcom. I'll do everything I can to get this to you quickly."

"Thank you, Ajay. I'll give our finance department a heads-up that they can expect a surprise bill from ITFM."

Turning to Ann, Malcom gave her a deadline. "Tell Monica to provide her solution within two hours. If NASA backs up the accuracy of the calculated position, I want her solution transmitted to Prospector ASAP. If our telemetry is right, then we have an even bigger problem. We won't know how to effect a course correction until the nav team can confirm the reliability of the onboard guidance system."

The knot in the pit of Ann's stomach twisted a bit tighter upon hearing Malcom's assessment. It was the same as her own, but hearing it spoken out loud magnified her perception of the menace to the mission, and to the crew. "I'll work with FDO and GNC. We'll be ready to transmit in two hours."

Malcom gestured with a thumb at the bank of glass that separated the public lobby from the flight control room as he walked toward the mission public information officer station. "In the meantime, I'll work with Alice to prepare a statement for the press. The sharks should be smelling blood by now."

CHAPTER 3

Ajay Kumar opened his email as soon as it arrived. He scanned through the message from ITFM Mauna Kea and noted that the position and vector were consistent with those provided by Prospector 1 two hours ago. He quickly forwarded the email to Malcom McDowell and cc'd Ann Waters. Then he rose from his chair and walked over to Ann's station. "Ann, ITMF has verified Prospector's position and vector."

She had already opened the email and was reading through the message. "Thanks, Ajay."

Ann quickly forwarded the message to Monica, Drew, and Steve Chan, the booster. Steve supervised the DeepStar thruster propelling the Prospector Command Module to Mars and back, as well as the structural integrity of the spacecraft itself. He'd worked for the NASA contractor that had developed the DeepStar thruster before he was pirated by EPSILON five years ago. He found both companies equally stressful to work for, but EPSILON paid him so much more, it more than covered the cost of his anxiety medications. Who said money couldn't buy you happiness?

Ann walked to the front row of flight operation stations for an impromptu meeting. "Everyone, NASA just confirmed that the onboard nav readout is correct. Telemetry from Prospector 1 is incorrect. We proceed on the assumption that the anomaly is limited to telemetry."

Ann faced her CapCom. "Evan, send Monica's first solution to Commander Gordon. Given the eighteen-minute transmission time, that gives him about forty minutes to program Monica's parameters into the onboard nav and reorient the spacecraft for the revised vector."

Monica's solutions required Prospector 1 to rotate nearly 180 degrees. Prospector 1 was an elongated cylinder, composed of its DeepStar nuclear ion propulsion thruster, the Command Module crew cabin (which contained the sleep tubes and the onboard instruments), and the Descent/Ascent Vehicle. It looked like a silver-colored pencil that had not been sharpened.

By reversing direction, Prospector would essentially be "putting on the brakes." The slowing spacecraft would drop back toward Mars's orbital path, allowing Mars to "catch up" to the spacecraft, enabling orbital insertion. The difference in Monica's solutions was that the first solution assumed 95 percent thrust for braking, providing the crew an opportunity to adjust course if required. It had a sixty-minute window to implement. The second solution assumed 100-percent braking thrust but provided them with ninety minutes before they needed to initiate the maneuver.

Ann walked over to the booster station. "Steve, will Prospector be able to withstand the strain?"

Steve's voice quavered, his anxiety getting the better of him. "Ann, Prospector wasn't designed to turn 180 degrees in space. The primary forces it was designed for run along its longitudinal axis. It was never intended to resist the kind of torque that long-term steering thruster deployment would introduce."

Ann lowered the intensity of her voice and placed a reassuring hand on her booster. "Steve, will Monica's maneuver work?"

He took a deep breath and slowly exhaled. "I completed the structural analysis as you requested. If the thrusters are fired at full power, there's a strong possibility Prospector 1 could bow slightly in the middle, setting up a harmonic resonance. Prospector would look like a hula dancer, rhythmically swaying at its 'waist.' This motion has two consequences, both bad.

"Once set in motion, the perpendicular wobble lessens the accuracy of the spacecraft's response to navigational commands. The other consequence is the introduction of stress fatigue at the point where the Command Module attaches to the booster. The bad news is, missing Mars orbital insertion would mean scrubbing the mission. The worse news is, Prospector 1 could approach Mars too closely, burning up in the atmosphere. Or it could break apart from the stress fatigue. Either way, we lose the spacecraft." He looked her in the eyes, his voice now steady. "And the crew."

Ann cupped her face in her hands, eyes closed tightly. "Can't we reduce thruster output for the turn?"

Steve responded, "Engaging fore and aft steering thrusters at half power to initiate and then to terminate the turn should dampen any vibration. But it adds to the overall time to complete the maneuver. It will take thirty-one minutes to complete the turn using half thrust."

Ann did a quick calculation in her head. *It will take Dallas about half an hour to manually input Monica's numbers into the onboard guidance, another half hour to execute the turn, plus the original eighteen minutes for the transmission with the instructions to reach him in the first place. Total time: roughly eighty minutes. Not enough time.*

"Evan, belay my order. Send Monica's *second* solution. That will give Commander Gordon about ten minutes to spare to execute the maneuver."

She turned to her FDO. "Monica, work up a third solution in case they run into any delays implementing."

"Miss Ann, I based the second solution on the latest time possible to initiate the new vector. If initiated any later, even at full thrust, Mars will pass Prospector before she can intersect the planet's orbital path."

"Evan—"

"Message with second solution on its way, Ann."

Ann felt the blood draining from her head. She breathed deeply twice to regain her composure, then once more after she determined that no one had noticed. "Thanks, Evan. I have no desire to greet the crew with a medical team because we had to scrub the mission."

Now came the waiting. The lives of Dallas and the others hung on whether the message arrived in enough time, whether Dallas could input the new plan and execute it, whether the craft could handle the vibration without …

She shook off the fear that gnawed at her gut. Looking around the room, she saw everyone concentrating, silence echoing her own worries. Ann noted that Drew was not at his station. She walked toward the conference room, where the GNC and the nav team were pouring over the onboard nav program code. It would be another hour and fifty minutes before she would know if Prospector had successfully completed its about-face maneuver. In the meantime, she wanted to know why this crisis had happened in the first place.

CHAPTER 4

Allie flinched involuntarily when the comm notification went off. In the crew cabin's zero-gravity environment, it was technically impossible to "jump," at least as one would experience it on Earth. In zero-G, one's hands and feet tended to be floating freely, so there was nothing to push off from. She yelled loudly enough to be heard at any location within the crew cabin, "New vector solution from SaMMCon."

Dallas turned his head toward her. They were oriented upside-down with respect to each other, him being at the opposite end of the cabin. "Patch it through to my console, Allie."

He pulled himself toward his console chair, grabbed the nearest chair arm and deftly rolled over his own arm, and came to rest in the sitting position. He secured himself and rotated the chair toward his workstation. Dallas winked at Allie, seated beside him. "I would have taken up parkour back on Earth if I had known it was this easy."

After settling in, his brow furrowed. He read through the message twice, speaking to no one in particular, "Looks like we have one shot to get Prospector turned around to intersect Mars."

He addressed his robotics/mechanical engineer, "Luis, prep Robbie to confirm the accuracy of my entries into guidance control."

Luis looked up from his AI assistant, closing the anterior access panel. "I already set him to flight assistant mode, Flash."

Dallas rubbed his chest gingerly. "Good. At least I know he won't attempt to rip off any EKG leads when I'm not looking.

Robbie, come here and confirm the accuracy of my manual entries into guidance control."

Robbie held his position. "Yes, sir. May I position myself to observe your entries from over your shoulder?"

"Yes, Robbie. But stay back at least a meter." Dallas continued under his breath, "After you broke protocol during my awakening, I'm not about to trust you within arm's length, especially from behind."

Robbie operated on a central track that was recessed into the "floor," or rather what served as the point of reference for the floor. In zero gravity, the crew referenced aft, port, up, and down with respect to that floor. The track ran the full length of the crew cabin, providing positive maneuvering for the 340-pound attendant. Once at the desired location within the length of the cabin, Robbie could extend off the floor with what amounted to a built-in scissor lift.

The crew bore silent witness while Dallas and Robbie spoke softly to each other as Dallas typed commands and numbers into guidance control. Robbie spoke at his usual volume once they finished. "Sir, you have accurately entered all vector change commands and parameters into guidance control."

After a brief pause, Robbie spoke again, "Commander, based on my own internal calculations, this maneuver could threaten the structural integrity of—"

"Shut up, Robbie. I'm perfectly aware of the capabilities of this vessel."

"Yes, Commander."

Dallas looked up to see worry written on each crew member's face. "As Robbie has so graciously alluded to, in twenty-three minutes Prospector will perform an 'about-face' so we can decelerate enough to intercept Mars as it catches back up to us.

"We will rotate 173 degrees to port. Rotation will take thirty-one minutes. Thrusters will fire at half-thrust one minute and nineteen seconds to initiate, and again to brake. The booster will resume full thrust until we achieve orbital insertion in roughly 140 hours.

"If we miss this opportunity for orbital insertion, my orders are to return this ship to Earth. SaMMCon doesn't want us risking an unsupervised sleep cycle just to play tag with Mars." Dallas paused long enough to look each crew member in the eye. "I don't know about you all, but I don't give a damn about the bonus for a successful landing. I just want to be the first human to stand on another planet and wave to the folks back home. Who wants to join me?"

The responses came from all around. "I do!" … "Count me in!" … "Yea, baby!" … "Let's do it!"

Twenty-three minutes later, Dallas shut down the booster. The gentle tug to aft stopped. What had previously been microgravity became true zero gravity. Everyone floated freely in the center of the cabin.

Dallas reached for the joysticks that controlled the thrusters. "Engaging thrusters."

Everyone gently floated against the aft side of the cabin. Hearts raced and ears strained as telltale creaks and groans indicated stress to the hull. The faint susurration of propellant igniting and expanding through the nozzle of each thruster filled the silences in between. No one spoke.

After one minute and nineteen seconds, the soft shush stopped. The microgravity ceased. The hull quieted. Everyone floated back out into the center of the cabin. Luis grinned, Allie closed her eyes as if in a prayer of gratitude, and the others finally exhaled. Step one: check. They had initiated the turn, and the hull still remained intact. For now, anyway. The next second, their faces crinkled as each registered what loomed next: step two, and another hull-straining, structure-bursting possibility.

Dallas barked out orders, "System checks due in twenty-seven minutes: Allie—communication. Luis—full diagnostic on Robbie. LaDonna—sleep tube readiness. Dave—secure every free-floating item." It was make-work, but Dallas did not want his team obsessing on their upcoming second dance with fate.

At the end of twenty-seven minutes, the opposing thrusters ignited. The next minute and nineteen seconds would be critical. The hull had complained at the abuse it took to turn it in the first place. Could it handle such a second maneuver without tearing itself apart and disgorging its human contents into empty space? Pulses throbbed against ten eardrums. Everyone drifted to the port side of the cabin as the vessel's rotation slowed down and finally stopped.

The cabin lay still and silent. Primary propulsion restarted. The crew felt the familiar tug to aft and let out a collective sigh of relief.

Dallas reviewed the navigational readouts and let out a long, slow breath through pursed lips. "Our vector coincides with our predicted flight path. Ladies and gentlemen, we're going to Mars. No extra charge for taking the scenic route on today's tour."

Dave responded, "Take your time, Flash. We're all paid by the hour." Unlike the rest of the crew, whose income would accumulate and wait for their return, his paychecks were deposited into a joint account. His wife Sage routinely withdrew funds to manage the household and put the two boys through hockey lessons for the two-and-a-half-year mission duration. "With the money we're making on this adventure, Sage is hoping we'll be gone for an extra year or two. Hell, I'll be able to retire *and* put the boys through college."

Luis had smuggled half a dozen golf-ball-sized foam balls on board with his personal effects. He let one fly at Dave. "Take that, Rock Nerd!"

The foam ball caromed off Dave's head and drifted on toward Dallas, who made an effortless right-handed catch. He quickly changed the subject. "Everyone, we have less than 140 hours for our pre-orbital checklists. I want the DV locked and loaded, and the Command Module prepped for return to auto mode for recall to Earth."

Dallas lightly tossed the foam ball back to Dave, then swiveled around to his console. *Step one: check. Step two: check. But we're approaching Mars now from a different vector than originally planned. Let's hope we make it through step three.*

CHAPTER 5

"I just checked the web news. Prospector successfully corrected its course. They'll achieve orbit around Mars in less than six days. For what I'm paying you, they should have been halfway to Jupiter by now." The CEO stood with his arms folded, revealing a gold Audemars Piguet watch. He struggled to not wrinkle his nose at the software engineer's body odor. It was so strong it overpowered the greasy French fry smell emanating from the paper bag beside the keyboard.

The engineer slammed the paper soft drink cup down so hard on his work surface that a small fountain of cola squirted up and out of the straw. "Look, I told you from the beginning, there would be limits to what systems I could access. We both agreed that fucking with the guidance control was our best chance to delay the mission long enough for your needs."

Undeterred by the engineer's petulance, the CEO pressed him, "This doesn't give me enough time. Is there anything else you can do to stop Prospector?"

The engineer visibly calmed himself. Several crumbs dropped into his lap as he stroked his unkempt beard. "If I know Ann Waters, she'll have her nav team go through the guidance control code with a fine-toothed comb. Sooner or later, they'll figure it out. And when they do, she'll order a complete overwrite of not only the nav files, but the entire onboard mainframe."

The CEO pressed further, "What about the DV?"

The engineer leaned back, clasping his hands behind his hoodie. "I'm two steps ahead of you, dude. It will take the GNC hours to upload the software overwrite. Even if they only overwrite the guidance code, that will take a good half hour. That gives us enough time to transmit our data package for the

Descent/Ascent Vehicle guidance control in tandem with their signal. My Trojan horse will embed into the mainframe root drive. It won't infect the landing guidance program until the Command Module mainframe communicates with the DV during the countdown to separation. In the meantime, the DV has been in sleep mode and won't wake up until they perform their pre-orbital checklist. Even if EPSILON checks out the DV files after it wakes up, there won't be anything for them to find."

The CEO warmed to the engineer's proposal. "I hope you can do better than five degrees off-course this time."

The engineer leaned forward, typing on his keyboard. His monitor filled with code, and he pointed to it, knowing full well his employer could only see undecipherable hieroglyphics. "Oh, I'll do much better than that. As you can see, the entire guidance control program will shut down just as the DV reaches the atmosphere. By the time Gordon figures it out, they will have burned out like a meteor, or cratered into the surface."

The CEO overlooked the obvious slight by his underling. "Have you completed writing your code?"

"Yep. It's set to transmit as soon as EPSILON uploads their software package." The software engineer leaned back in his chair, hands once again clasped behind his head, and flashed a smug grin at the CEO.

The CEO weakly smiled back. He had endured the engineer's outrageous demands for money, high-end houses, and whores for months. It would be his greatest pleasure to have all this unpleasantness cleaned up prior to the Board meeting next month. He expected to have his black hole fully staffed with his own software engineers by then. Once fully operational, his facility would function at a fraction of the cost of this freelance asshole.

"Well done. I'll leave you to your work. Please alert me once your package has been delivered."

The CEO spun on his heels and briskly exited the room.

CHAPTER 6

Drew Usher announced the results of the Navigation Team's investigation in his syrupy Southern drawl. "We found extra code lines in both the guidance and nav system files. The extra code contained a simple instruction to boost thrust from 75 to 85 percent. The nav code replaced its measured position telemetry with a position calculated mathematically from the original flight path formula. We found the same code changes on both the Command Module hard drive and its weekly onboard backup."

Ann presided at the head of the conference table. She and Drew were joined by Monica Gonzales, Steve Chau, and Cliff Sherman, as well as Descent/Ascent Vehicle Control Officer (Control) Susan Bailey, Network Officer John Carpenter, Autotronics Corporation Representative Roger Wheeler, and Program Flight Surgeon Portia Knox. Susan monitored guidance, navigation, and propulsion control for the reusable Descent/Ascent Vehicle, just as Drew monitored those same functions for the Command Module of Prospector. Roger monitored the Autotronics RBI version 3.4, otherwise known to everyone as Robbie. Dr. Knox, like LaDonna Pleasant, was a flight surgeon. She interacted with LaDonna, and at times Robbie, regarding all matters regarding the crew's health and welfare.

Drew continued, "The last backup occurred five days prior to the crew's awakening. We know the guidance program was clean at launch, because our prelaunch copy is clean. So the extra code had to be introduced sometime between launch and day 270."

Monica spoke next. "Assuming the 10-percent increase in thrust accounts entirely for the difference in Prospector's position, I calculated when the booster output increased. According to my calculations, the increased thrust initiated at 22:15 hours on day 253."

Ann was running on three hours of sleep. It was catching up with her. She sat with her eyes closed, massaging her temples with her index and middle fingers. "So Prospector was infected with a virus?"

All heads around the table nodded in agreement.

Eyes opened, Ann continued, "I see two scenarios for how this could happen. One, it was manually introduced via some sort of thumb drive or memory card. Or two, it was uploaded in one of our transmissions from SaMMCon. We know the crew were all in stasis on day 253. What about Robbie? Could he have introduced a virus into the mainframe?"

Ann looked to Roger. Roger Wheeler was an avid marathon runner, a wiry though balding man in his late fifties. He managed the delivery and monitored the operations of all the RBI units sold to EPSILON. He, like the NASA rep, always wore a suit and tie. His gold cufflinks flashed as he reached into a briefcase on the floor beside his chair and pulled out a file folder. He read aloud from a printed email from Autotronics, "Starting from day 270, we are working our way back toward launch from there. We've detected no illicit activities to or from this RBI unit as far back as two weeks from the incident. We're convinced our unit did not participate in any illicit activity onboard, but we will continue to evaluate as far back as launch to verify that."

Ann addressed John Carpenter. "John, is it possible one of the crew cell phones could transmit a virus?"

As network officer, John monitored the overall communications system that maintained contact with Prospector. The system consisted of a string of transceivers positioned around the equator and linked to SaMMCon. This arrangement ensured that no transmission to or from Prospector would be blocked just because SaMMCon was on the wrong side of the Earth. It also ensured that the Moon was never able to fully block out line of sight when it was positioned between Earth and the spacecraft. "No, Ann. We've accounted for every call to Prospector. Each authorized phone uses EPSILON-256 encryption, just like the rest of our system. They can't be spoofed."

The data encryption technology used by the crew's smartphones was the same technology EPSILON used to protect its millions of autonomous vehicles. In a limited sense, it was possible to "call" individual members of Prospector's crew. When a designated cell phone on Earth called one of the astronauts' smartphones, the transmission was routed directly to the mission server. The signal was decrypted from the wireless company's format and re-encrypted using EPSILON's proprietary algorithms. Each crew member designated up to five phone numbers of family or friends. Aside from a twenty-minute delay between transmission and reception, it allowed loved ones to transmit talk, text, and video back and forth with their astronaut. Ann possessed one in her capacity as FOD. Any member of the general public would only receive an "out of service" message if they tried to dial their favorite astronaut.

John went on, "Frankly, our data encryption and sender authentication is the best in the world. There are over thirty million EPSILON AVs in use, and not one documented hacking incident. No other AV manufacturer comes close to our security record."

Ann exhaled slowly. "Cliff, is there any evidence this virus could have been introduced internally?"

"No way, Ann. Even if you jacked a USB drive into your workstation, our firewall would detect any malicious code. Our IT people are reviewing the firewall activity logs. They've found nothing so far, and don't expect to find anything out of the ordinary."

Ann sighed. *We don't have a clue except knowing some unknown source has messed up a multi-billion-dollar command module with malicious code. If that could be done ...*

She turned her attention to Susan Bailey. "Susan, what about the integrity of the DV software?"

"A copy from the DV hard drive was transmitted to us yesterday when it was activated. The nav team and IT team have both confirmed the software is not corrupted."

The knot in Ann's stomach loosened ever so slightly. However the malware had been introduced, at least the damage had been limited to the primary navigation and guidance control programs. The Descent/Ascent Vehicle, possibly by virtue of being asleep, had been spared.

After dismissing the meeting, Ann headed out to her car parked in the employee lot. With the advent of autonomous vehicles, fewer and fewer people actually owned cars. That same trend applied even more so to the tech-savvy employees of EPSILON. Ridesharing had become the new normal.

Ann pressed her key fob and her car chirped happily. She slid in behind the steering wheel and gripped it, her hands at ten and two, and called up her playlist. It was an impressive compilation of the greatest blues performers of all time. She never tired of it. With her hectic schedule, it took her weeks to play through the entire list.

As much as car ownership was an anomaly, seeing a car on the road with a steering wheel was even more so. Ann's autonomous vehicle was one of EPSILON's earliest models, the kind that still had a steering wheel. In its day, the wheel had helped skittish new adopters of AV technology to accept and trust it. A steering wheel acted like a security blanket of sorts—a driver could just drop out of autonomous mode and drive manually if they felt safer doing so.

In Ann's case, she loved the feeling of control, maneuvering over a ton of machinery as she willed. The stars were out tonight, twinkling feebly through the scattered light from Santa Maria in the humid coastal air.

It was still warm, warmer than usual for the Southern California coast in early September. She drove with the windows down and the AC off, the wind blowing her shoulder-length blond hair wildly. She headed north on Highway 101 to her home in Pismo Beach, a twenty-five-minute drive.

Ann had chosen a small two-bedroom bungalow midway between the beach and Highway 1, near the south end of town. The neighborhood was slowly gentrifying. One by one, neighbors sold out to developers. They tore down the original housing stock dating back to the 1930s, replacing them with townhouses and duplexes. Small apartment condos rose on consolidated lots.

In spite of the neighborhood turnover, Ann still loved it there. Beach access was a mere two blocks away. She still loved to surf. Her father had taught her how when she was twelve, and the family lived in Palo Alto. Surfing always brought her back to those happy times on the beach at Half Moon Bay. A nearby gym with a climbing wall satisfied her other sporting love.

It was while grieving the loss of her parents that Ann found her second sport: traditional rock climbing. The summer after graduation, she signed up for a six-week climbing course through Outdoor Leadership School. She loved the open-ended problem solving required to find and execute a climbing route, to properly set anchors for her belay line. Her newfound skills meshed well with her undergraduate degree in aeronautical engineering. She also found that she was equally adept at leadership, honing that skill set whenever it was her turn to lead a climbing party.

Over the six weeks, she developed an affinity with one of her instructors, a serious-minded strawberry blond named Dallas Gordon. He convinced her to become an instructor for the fall class sessions in the Wind River Mountains of Wyoming. She did, of course, under the condition that she would be on his instruction team. After the fall course, they spent the winter and spring teaching climbing in Patagonia, then returned to the Wind River Mountains the following summer.

Along the way, they fell in love. But when September came, they parted ways—she to pursue a PhD in Nuclear

Electric Ion Propulsion at Stanford, he to attend Naval Aviation Officer Candidate School in Pensacola, Florida.

Ann pulled into her carport, rolled up her car windows, and shut off the ignition. She unlocked the kitchen door and stepped inside. Ann missed Dallas the most when her house was dark and silent, as it was now.

"Play blues playlist." The soundtrack resumed playing from the living room speakers where it left off when she shut off her car. Ann tossed her key fob on the nearby kitchen table.

She'd seen Dallas again several times within the past three years. The aerospace community was a small one, and it almost became inevitable that such convergences would occur. But they said nothing that was not related to their roles. She had caught him looking at her a few times. But he always averted his gaze before their eyes could meet. She really didn't know if he still had feelings for her after twelve years had passed.

Ann collapsed into bed. While inconclusive, the news shared at the late evening meeting gave her more hope for the success of the Prospector 1 mission than she had felt for the past two days. As she lay on her back, Ann thought of the events of the coming day: 5 a.m. at the climbing gym, report to SaMMCon by 7 a.m. to oversee Prospector's orbital insertion around Mars (scheduled for 10 a.m.), and the Descent/Ascent Vehicle touchdown six hours after that.

EPSILON's owner had installed a champagne cooler in a back corner of the flight control room and stocked it with a couple dozen bottles of Dom Pérignon 2025, more than enough for one bottle for each flight control position, and for an epic hangover the following day. *Hope he stocked the cooler with cans of energy drink. Gonna need it for the day after.* With that thought, Ann fell asleep.

CHAPTER 7

"Incoming transmission," Evan Griffin announced, then sent the communication to the PA system.

"SaMMCon, this is Prospector. We have achieved orbital insertion around Mars. Velocity is three point five zero five kilometers per second, altitude is two-five-zero kilometers. Commencing DV separation and descent to landing site in T-minus six hours and three minutes. Our next transmission will be from inside the DV."

Cheers erupted from the SaMMCon staff. Visitors and press members alike jumped and cheered behind the windows surrounding the flight control room on three sides.

But the Dom Pérignon sat untouched in the cooler. Achieving a stable orbit around Mars with a human crew was a historic first; preparing for the descent and safe landing of the two-and-a-half-ton Descent/Ascent Vehicle in six hours required everyone's complete focus.

Ann sensed the relief in Dallas's voice even though he was speaking from roughly two hundred million miles away, essentially from the far side of the solar system. She wiped her sweaty palms on her pants as she pushed back her chair to stand. She circulated among the flight control stations, offering a mix of congratulations and status inquiries. She stopped first at the INCO station. "Cliff, telemetry update, please."

"Telemetry is loud and clear from both the Command Module and from the DV. Communications links are a 'go'."

Ann next stopped at the Flight Activities Officer station. Mark Stoddard offered his assessment without being prompted. "Telemetry confirms that pre-descent crew status is nominal."

She next stopped at John's network station. John, too, fed Ann what she needed to know. "All orbital and ground stations are online. No anticipated line-of-sight interruptions during the landing.

"Ann, our IT people just confirmed there were no rogue transmissions on the network between launch and the beginning of the flight path anomaly."

Ann alternated between relief and annoyance at the news. John confirmed the integrity of the mission communication system. But that still did not explain what had happened to send the spacecraft off course twenty-two days ago.

"Thanks for the update, John. I appreciate that you, Drew, and IT burned a lot of midnight oil combing through the data to correlate transmissions with sources."

Ann stepped between John's station and the Autotronics rep station to reach the front row of flight control stations. She paused at the control station, silently placing a hand on Susan Bailey's right shoulder. Susan responded to her prompt. "DV guidance, navigation, and propulsion control are all nominal, Ann. Commander Gordon will be sending flight vector confirmation in their next transmission."

Ann ordered the additional step in the pre-separation checklist with the acquiescence of the procedures officer. Tonya Gates and her team had developed the array of mission checklists for flight, descent, and base operations over the past five years. The crew trained on the procedures until they could perform all checklists in their sleep, though it was standard procedure to use the written checklists. She recently added the navigational check to ensure the Descent/Ascent Vehicle was not affected in the same way as the Command Module had been.

Ann next landed at the GNC station. Drew poured over the Prospector navigational telemetry streaming down his monitor. He paused long enough to indulge his pride. "Our software update is working perfectly. Commander Gordon's verbal report coincides with our orbital telemetry." Ann found Drew's laconic Southern drawl comforting, as always.

Ann walked over to Monica Gonzales to engage her FDO "Nice work, Monica. According to the telemetry I've just seen, Prospector didn't even need to engage any thrusters to drop into Mars orbit.

Monica beamed. She loved seeing her computations executed so flawlessly. "Thank you, Miss Ann. I don't even have to modify the descent path. Commander Gordon executed the flight path to orbit so perfectly."

Ann bypassed the CapCom station and settled behind the program flight surgeon, Portia Knox.

"Ann, I could have reported the instant Prospector went into orbit." Ann raised an eyebrow, but Portia continued without a pause, "To the last person, every crew member's blood pressure measurably dropped about thirty seconds before Commander Gordon's last transmission. All crew vitals indicate readiness for descent."

With a smile, Ann turned toward Steve Chan at the booster station. "What have you got for me, Steve?"

"Ann, the nuclear reactor is stable at 5 percent. Propellant feedstock shut down. Electrical power generation is nominal for system maintenance. Prospector 1 Command Module is in stable orbit until recalled to Earth for refurbishment as Prospector 2."

Ann turned back to the CapCom station, which she had deliberately saved for last.

"Evan, I'll have one of those jelly donuts now."

Even as dark as his skin was, Ann could see he was embarrassed. Ever since his promotion to the CapCom position on the Prospector team three years ago, he had secretly indulged himself with half a dozen jelly-filled donuts every day. Evan could see Ann's workstation reflected in his monitor screen and was careful to only open his drawer when he thought she wasn't looking. He turned to his left, accusing his suspected betrayer. "Dr. Knox, did you rat me out? I thought that we had an agreement."

But Portia threw up her hands in denial. "Don't look at me, young man. I've relied on you for my sugar fix for months."

Ann had been aware of Evan's "habit" for well over a year. "I skipped breakfast on my way to work from the climbing gym. Besides, you owe me for all the keyboard cleaning and maintenance for the past two years."

Evan flushed even redder. He reverently pulled open the drawer beside his chair. Ann reached into the open box inside his drawer. Three jelly donuts were nestled inside. Ann picked one that looked like it might be raspberry, then patted Evan on the shoulder, smiling to herself as she slowly walked back to her own station at the back of the room. *To the victor go the spoils.*

Ann sat down and reviewed the streaming telemetry and the reports being generated by her staff, nibbling her prize between swigs of cold coffee from a cup already on her desk. She had poured it when she first arrived hours ago. *Not bad. He must be getting these from the donut shop on Main Street.*

CHAPTER 8

The last to enter the Descent/Ascent Vehicle, Luis floated himself in feet-first, and stopped with both hands on the round frame surrounding the hatch. He braced his left arm, and with his right arm pulled the round hatch toward himself until it seated on the frame. He torqued the foot-long handle clockwise, the latches engaging with a soft click. He pushed himself to the last vacant seat, cinching down his lap belt and the double shoulder harness that crossed his chest in an "X" pattern. "I hate wearing this pressure suit. It makes my butt look too big." He looked across at Allie, waiting for a reaction. At age thirty-six, Luis prided himself on having a Body Mass Index of only 18 for his 189-pound frame.

"If you kept your head out of your butt, it would probably fit you just fine."

As the rest of the crew laughed, Luis smiled, having accomplished his mission. Luis had been a child prodigy, graduating from MIT in three years with a double major in Robotics and Mechanical Engineering. His minor, at least according to his friends, was in smart-ass humor. He adjusted his safety harnesses.

Dallas finalized his pre-separation checklist as Luis settled into his seat. He, like the other crew members, wore his surface pressure suit, helmet visor locked shut, in the event of cabin pressure loss during reentry. The suit materials were lighter, stronger, and less bulky than those used by NASA astronauts during the Apollo and Space Shuttle eras. To the casual observer, the suits looked about the same, but they came with significant communications capabilities. Smartphones fit into a charging pocket on the left sleeve were wirelessly linked to a built-in headset in the helmet. The phones transmitted in dual mode, either line-of-sight like a walkie-talkie, or via Wi-Fi within the Descent/Ascent Vehicle and at the base on the surface below.

The interior of the Descent/Ascent Vehicle cabin was circular, with a flat floor in the fore position relative to the Command Module, which would become "down" once they landed. Five seats were radially arranged around the floor, against the cabin wall, facing inward to the center. Robbie occupied the center of the floor, secured with a latching mechanism. He had traded his track wheel, which remained in the Command Module, for a set of hard rubber tracks. He looked like a miniature excavator, with four arms instead of one.

The cabin the crew occupied rested on a chemical propellant booster. The booster would be used for this entry into Mars's atmosphere, then would propel them back into orbit after twelve months. The Lander Module, positioned at the very front of the Descent/Ascent Vehicle, fit like a ring around the booster nozzle. It possessed three retractable legs that deployed for touchdown on the Martian surface. The Lander Module held the Descent/Ascent Vehicle upright during the long refueling process. Then it would remain behind when the Ascent Vehicle lifted off for its docking maneuver with the Prospector 2 Command Module. The abandoned metal and parts would be cannibalized—valuable resources for future missions.

During descent, the booster would not ignite until the craft was at an altitude of ten kilometers, after the heat shield had been ejected. The Descent/Ascent Vehicle would slow down when it entered the upper atmosphere, first from friction on the heat shield, then with a series of parachutes. Its parachutes served a dual purpose. They not only slowed down the landing module, they also served to maintain its alignment, keeping the craft from tumbling and burning up through its hypersonic descent, and keeping the vehicle vertical until it touched down.

Dallas radioed SaMMCon for the last time prior to touchdown. "SaMMCon, this is Prospector 1 DV. Pre-separation checklist is complete. Commencing separation sequence. We'll see you on the other side."

In spite of the years of training, it felt odd to him knowing SaMMCon would not actually receive his transmission for another twenty minutes. They would be on their final landing approach before the signal reached Earth. With that, he switched off his comm link and grabbed two joysticks located on a console that lay across his lap, attached to both of his armrests. "Opening docking latches." A soft whir sounded as small servos retracted the docking latches.

"Maneuvering away from Command Module with thrusters." Small thrusters pointed aft fired in short, half-second bursts. The Prospector 1 Descent/Ascent Vehicle eased away from the Command Module.

With a few more bursts from laterally aimed thrusters, the craft drifted to the side. A third set of thrusters aimed forward engaged, and the Descent/Ascent Vehicle began to slow. The Command Module passed it by, and the vehicle began to descend. Its slowing velocity allowed Martian gravity to have its way.

Within five minutes, the heat shield began to glow, signaling the beginning of radio blackout. The crew felt their bodies sag downward into their seats as the Descent/Ascent Vehicle decelerated in earnest. The cabin shook as the craft slammed into ever-denser atmospheric gas. In spite of the buffeting, Dallas breathed easy, glad to leave behind the attempted sabotage.

CHAPTER 9

Ann read the descent telemetry streaming from the just-separated Descent/Ascent Vehicle. She reminded herself to be patient regarding the twenty-minute communication delay across 200 million miles. The twelve-minute descent to the surface had taken place eight minutes ago. But the all-clear transmission from Dallas would not arrive for another twelve. A commotion to her right in the row of flight control stations immediately in front of her caught her attention. She looked up to see John Carpenter approaching her, face pale, his eyes wide as saucers.

He positioned himself between Ann and the mission control director, whose station was to her immediate right. Ann stood so she could look at John over the top of her monitor as he spoke to her. "The Network Team just reported something." Before either Ann or Malcom McDowell could speak, he continued, "After they combed through our network communication files, they requested files from NASA's solar weather stations."

NASA stationed five solar weather observatories midway between the orbits of Earth and Mars. Roughly equidistant from each other, they chased each other as they circled the sun, like painted horses on a giant carousel. These observatories were critical. They informed astronauts outside of Earth's protective magnetosphere of approaching spikes in the solar flux. The information gave astronauts time to shelter within the protective shielding of their spacecraft, or, if located on the surface of Mars, within their base.

While not designed to monitor communications, the satellites maintained a file of all radio signals. The satellites used the file for reference as they separated out signals that originated from the sun from other nearby signal sources that might trigger a false alarm. The file ran in a continuous week-long loop. Fresh data erased anything older than a week.

John continued, "An hour ago, NASA found a signal operating on our frequency and using our encryption. But it didn't match anything that originated from our network. They had our IT team review the code. Ann, it's a Trojan horse with a kill switch for the DV guidance control system. The DV is entering the atmosphere without guidance control. We just now figured it out."

Ann's knuckles turned white as she gripped the corners of her station. The Descent/Ascent Vehicle was equipped for a manual descent, but it was a risky contingency at best. Dallas had trained for such a contingency. But his success rate was spotty. Once the craft started to tumble, the G-forces rendered the controls impossible to operate. Dallas rarely brought the craft back under control during flight simulations. Everyone on the SaMMCon team knew that a loss of digital guidance control meant the catastrophic loss of the vehicle.

Ann willed herself to the front of the Flight Control Room. She steadied herself against Monica's monitor as she addressed the room. "Everyone, we've just learned that the DV guidance control has been compromised." Thirteen faces stared back in wide-eyed disbelief. "We don't yet know the source of the transmission."

She looked directly at John for confirmation. He quickly nodded his head. Ann continued, "But we know that malware was transmitted to the DV to kill guidance control. Due to the twenty-minute signal delay—the DV is already on its final approach sequence. It's already too late to transmit an abort. We won't know its status until the scheduled all-safe transmission reaches us twelve minutes from now."

As Ann's announcement sank in, there was a collective retroactive resolve to will the Descent/Ascent Vehicle safely to the surface. All heads turned back to their respective monitors, shoulders hunched forward in heightened attention, hoping against all odds for the safety of their comrades.

Ann returned to her seat and sat down. She gripped the edge of her workstation to keep her hands from trembling. With nothing else to do, she stared intensely at the stream of guidance control telemetry displayed on her monitor.

The telemetry scrolled on for another seven minutes, then abruptly stopped. Ann lived the next five minutes in slow motion, waiting for the all-safe signal from the crew.

CHAPTER 10

"Luis, I show no indicator light that the first parachute deployed. Does your console indicate deployment?" Dallas's voice had an odd vibrato quality from the violent shaking that the crew was experiencing.

"No indication of deployment, Flash." Luis's vibrato matched Dallas's.

The cabin pitched violently from side to side. The G-forces caused heads to snap with each pitch. Dallas shouted above the mounting cacophony in the cabin, "Chute should have deployed by now, switching to manual control."

He reached vainly for the button to release the first parachute, but his hands snapped away wildly from the constantly shifting G-forces. Every time he strained to position his fingers to press the button, they were swept away.

The cabin temperature rose. Each time the Descent/Ascent Vehicle pitched sideways, the unprotected surface scorched in the searing friction of hypersonic speed. As the cylindrical vehicle tumbled, the pink glow of reentry flashed brightest as it aligned broadside to the direction of descent. Breakup was imminent.

Dallas sensed his peripheral vision narrowing as unconsciousness neared. Allie and Dave, seated directly across from him, were flopping like space-suited rag dolls within their seat restraints. With one final effort, Dallas clasped both hands together and yelled to summon all his strength. He slammed his clenched fists on what he hoped was the release button.

The parachute released with an audible pop. The Descent/Ascent Vehicle snapped back into heat-shield-forward position. Dallas felt his body press toward the floor.

The helmets worn by the rag dolls seated across from him rolled forward and settled onto their chests.

"Hope EPSILON stashed a good supply of airsick bags on this airliner."

An experienced pilot, LaDonna resisted blacking out. Her voice reassured Dallas. He responded to her humor, "On behalf of the flight crew, thank you for flying the friendly skies."

Dallas turned to Luis, who was seated to his right. "Luis, are you still with us?"

"Present and accounted for." Luis's voice was still slurred. Dallas worried his mechanical engineer was still disoriented from the effects of high G-forces.

Per his training, Dallas spoke his intentions aloud: "The second chute should have deployed fifteen seconds ago; deploying second chute now."

Another pop, and the crew sank further into their seats. Dallas refocused on his mechanical engineer. "Luis, can you use your arms?"

"Yes, I'm not hurt." Luis spoke more clearly this time.

"Good. Our rate of descent is much too fast for our altitude. We need to shed weight, or we'll auger in." In the stress of the moment, Dallas reverted to his naval aviator jargon. After a brief pause, Dallas resumed, "When I deploy the final descent chute, release the Lander Module, then deploy the booster on my command."

"Release the Lander Module?" Luis was clear-headed enough to disbelieve what Dallas told him.

Dallas restated his logic, "At our rate of descent, even with full booster output, we'll hit so hard we'll just be a grease spot on the ground."

"But we'll have no legs to land with." Luis made a good point. The Lander Module came equipped with extendable legs that deployed as the booster ignited. Without them, the Descent/Ascent Vehicle would fall over on touch-down, even with the softest of landings.

Dallas responded with greater urgency, "Luis, if we don't do this, death is certain. Deploying final descent chute." Dallas punched one more button on his control console, then looked squarely at Luis. "Release the Lander Module."

Setting his misgivings aside, Luis punched a button on his laptop console. The soft whine of servos was nearly drowned out by the din in the cabin. The clasps securing the Lander Module to the rest of the vehicle released, and the crew sank even further into their seats. As the Lander Module fell away, the load on the parachute cords eased. Dallas grasped the two joysticks on his laptop console. Luis rushed through the booster pre-ignition sequence. "Ready for ignition on your command."

Dallas paid close attention to the altitude reading on his console. "Altitude six kilometers. Ignite booster. Prepare to cut power on my command."

Luis pressed the ignition button, and the cabin roared and shook. Everyone sank further still into their seats. Once again, arm movement was laborious. White-hot flame and steam erupted from the booster nozzle. Dallas struggled to steer the craft using the lateral thrusters without computer control, as the booster braked their descent more rapidly. Dropping the Lander Module mid-descent was a risky gambit. With the reduced mass, the booster thrust could rocket the Descent/Ascent Vehicle upward. The slackened parachute cords would burn up in the searing heat of the booster exhaust. Without the parachute, the fine control required for a soft landing was gone. Crash landing was inevitable. Dallas carefully monitored their rate of descent, knowing he walked a tightrope, bearing the lives of his crew on his shoulders.

Dallas shouted above the booster's roar, "Altitude four kilometers." Twenty seconds later, "Altitude two kilometers." Both Allie and Dave raised their heads. Twenty seconds later, "Altitude one thousand meters." Dallas fought to maintain vertical alignment as the craft descended. "Altitude five hundred meters." The cabin shook so violently it blurred vision.

"Altitude three hundred meters … altitude two hundred meters … altitude one hundred fifty meters …" The craft was threatening to ascend before reaching the ground. "Altitude one hundred twenty meters. Luis, kill the engine and sequence to reburn."

The cabin fell silent. Luis hurriedly reran through the pre-ignition sequence, rushing even faster as the craft reaccelerated toward the ground. Dallas resumed counting down their elevation. "One hundred meters … eighty meters … forty meters." Dallas shook the cramps out of his fingers, then grasped the joysticks. He shouted at Luis, "Ten meters … ignite engines!"

Luis slammed the ignition button. The cabin shook as the booster again roared to life.

Dallas screamed one final command, "Kill engines!"

As Luis did so, the craft touched down hard, crumpling the booster nozzle cowling, its crunch echoing through Dallas's brain. The room began to tip, then stopped suddenly with another nerve-racking crunch.

The Descent/Ascent Vehicle had come to rest at an 80-degree angle against a boulder the size of a house. Dallas commanded his wide-eyed crew, "Everyone stay seated." The command was not necessary. White knuckles and hunched shoulders betrayed the common knowledge that the ordeal was not yet over.

Within seconds, a metallic scraping sound started and then stopped. A longer screech followed as the cylindrical Descent/Ascent Vehicle half rolled, half slid off the boulder. It smashed to the ground with a jarring crunch, then began rolling down a slight side hill. All interior lights flickered then extinguished. The craft came to rest against a smaller boulder after a quarter-turn. Five seconds later, the emergency lights flickered on.

Dave and Allie lay on their backs, facing up at Dallas. He remained motionless until he was assured the vehicle was stable, then spoke. "Allie and Dave, assess for injuries. Can you exit your seats?" With the vehicle on its side, and all of them restrained around its perimeter in their seats, only Dave and Allie were in a position to release themselves easily.

"My neck is sore, but I'm okay." Allie was woozy after what felt to her like the spin cycle of a washing machine. She slowly stood and flexed her neck from side to side.

LaDonna, fastened to her seat above Allie, noted that she winced whenever she flexed her neck to her left. She worried that Allie might have suffered whiplash during the violent descent. "Allie, can you nod your head back and forth?"

Allie did so, but with obvious discomfort. LaDonna looked to Dave. "Dave, please examine Allie's neck for any swelling, especially along her spine."

Dave turned to Allie so he could examine her neck. He gently moved his gloved thumb and forefinger up and down her neck a few times, then worked outward using both hands. Allie flinched when he found a small knot on the side of her neck. He reported what he found to the flight surgeon. "Nothing on her spine, Doc. She's got a knot on her neck. Oh wait, that's her head!"

Allie swatted at her insulter, but winced in pain, missing her target.

LaDonna redirected herself to Allie. "It's probably just a strained muscle. I can give you something for the pain after I'm down."

Allie wound up a second time. This blow landed on Dave's upper arm. Dallas reasserted himself. "Allie, knock it off. Assist Dave and get Doc down."

Hostilities immediately ceased. Together, Dave and Allie moved to Dallas's left. Dave supported LaDonna's weight while Allie unfastened the restraints. Dave assisted LaDonna down to Allie's seat. Ladonna placed one foot on the back of the seat and the other on the storage locker beside it, then stood under her own power. She briefly examined Allie's neck and confirmed her muscle strain diagnosis.

Dallas waited until the examination was over. "Alright, all three of you, assist Luis."

Dave and LaDonna positioned themselves under Luis, who outweighed LaDonna by about seventy-five pounds. Luis lowered himself out of his seat after Allie unfastened his restraints.

Dallas continued instructing from his seat, "Okay, Luis and Dave, support Allie so she can reach up and unfasten my restraints. Allie, keep to my side. I'm going to grip my shoulder restraints and swing myself down once I'm free."

Luis and Dave stood side by side off to Dallas's right. Allie stood with one foot on Luis's thigh and the other on Dave's. They each supported a leg, so she wouldn't lose her balance as she unclipped Dallas. She leaned across him to unfasten the far-side clips first, then straightened up to unfasten the near-side clips. Dallas gripped his shoulder straps above where they crossed his chest. He swung free when Allie was finished.

Dallas dropped the final two feet and stood on the locker between Dave's and Allie's seats. Luis slapped Dallas's back. "You did it! You finally beat the simulator! First time you crash-landed the DV, and we survived." Everyone unsuccessfully stifled laughter. They recalled how every time Dallas had crashed the DV on manual pilot simulation, they had all joked that they had used up another life, like it was a multi-million-dollar video game.

Dallas gave Luis the evil eye, then burst out laughing. When he finally composed himself, he turned to Robbie, who was still fastened to his dock on the floor. "Robbie, lower yourself to our level."

Robbie reached down and gripped one arm on Dave's seat, and one on Allie's. Then he pivoted his treads and rolled his way down to the locker positioned in between. Dallas addressed his mission assistant. "Robbie, can you assess our position, or do you need to be outside to get a strong enough MGPS signal?"

To facilitate both manned and unmanned missions, NASA operated a small constellation of GPS satellites that orbited Mars. After accessing the signal, Robbie responded, "Commander, the signal is weak, but useable. We overshot the planned landing zone at Prospector Base by approximately sixty-five kilometers to the southeast. This places us approximately ten kilometers outside the limits of my digital terrain mapping. However, based on stored orbital digital photographs, I believe we are on the floor of an unnamed, eighteen-kilometer-wide crater, near its southeast wall."

Allie pulled her smartphone out of the sleeve pocket in her suit and read the display. Their phones were linked to the main radio onboard the Descent/Ascent Vehicle, which had sufficient signal strength to reach the constellation of communications satellites, or the Prospector Command Module orbiting overhead. Either facility relayed their transmission to SaMMCon. She looked up at Dallas. "No connection. The impact damaged the radio. Dallas, we're on our own until we reach Prospector Base."

Dave voiced the next obvious question. "How long will that take?"

Dallas mused over his answer. "Given the terrain we have to traverse, we'll be lucky to make twenty kilometers a day."

All eyes looked uneasily back and forth to each other around the cabin. Dave brought his gaze back to Dallas. "Do we even have enough oxygen to travel three days?"

CHAPTER 11

"Cliff, any signal from the DV?" Ann knew the answer. She saw the same lack of data on her monitor that Cliff Sherman did.

Cliff was barely audible. "Just white noise, Ann."

Ann pushed herself away from her station and slowly walked to the front of the flight control room. All eyes in the two rows of operator stations followed her there. Many were streaming tears.

The back row was huddled together, discussing in hushed tones the composition of a press statement. Malcom, Ajay, and Alice stopped briefly to listen as Ann addressed the room, "Transmission from Prospector 1 DV is five minutes overdue. The DV may have experienced catastrophic failure during entry. It's also possible that they landed safely but with some damage. In that case, it may mean equipment failure resulting in a loss of telemetry. If that is true, they may need our help."

Ann focused on her CapCom. "Evan, transmit every five minutes. Message is that SaMMCon is not receiving Prospector 1's transmission. We have commenced searching and will assist once we reestablish contact."

Ann turned to her INCO. "Cliff, monitor for signals from the DV and from Prospector Base."

Monica's cheeks were streaked with tears. Ann placed a hand on her shoulder, speaking softly, as much to console herself as her FDO. "Monica, calculate a landing field based on various degrees of descent control."

Ann returned to her previous volume. "The rest of us, start searching for the DV."

Ann raised her voice even higher to be heard at the back of the room, "Ajay, can NASA reposition all satellites with video capability?"

"Ann, all NASA video sats are at your disposal. We'll steer our sats for better coverage when we receive your landing field coordinates."

Ann redirected her gaze to the front two rows. "Anyone not assigned a task aids in the visual search. I'll be parsing out NASA's imagery to you all. Let's find our lost landing team."

The mission director, the NASA representative, and the mission public affairs officer resumed their huddle at the back of the room. Malcom cast a furtive glance up at the families, VIPs, and press in the lobby pressed against the glass wall. Hundreds of pairs of horrified eyes stared back, disturbed by the day's events, but too morbidly curious to turn away.

Ann walked back to her station, waiting for Ajay to finish his meeting and forward links for NASA's most recent video to her.

CHAPTER 12

"We're agreed. We travel fifteen kilometers due north to access the crater wall at its shortest height, on the north side. That route also allows us to skirt the central mountain on the crater floor. Once out of the crater, we travel northwesterly at bearing N 58° 00' 00" W for a distance of forty-five kilometers to a saddle in the ridge above Prospector Base. From there, we travel due north another fifteen kilometers, traversing downslope to base. This route adds ten kilometers to our travel distance but avoids the worst terrain obstacles."

Dallas looked up from the mapping displayed on Robbie's screen at the circle of anxious faces that surrounded him. He spoke in ragged breaths. In the time since they had crash-landed, the cabin had steadily lost air pressure. The pressure gauge read 57 kiloPascals (kPa), the equivalent of standing on top of a fifteen-thousand-foot-high mountain back on Earth.

EPSILON had carefully considered where to site its base for prospecting rare earth element minerals on Mars. They selected the Hellas impact crater in Mars's southern hemisphere. The center of the crater was at roughly 40° S latitude, comparable to the latitude of Sydney, Australia on Earth. Formed by a massive asteroid impact roughly four billion years ago, Hellas measured 2,300 kilometers across. In fact, it was the largest readily visible impact crater on Mars, so large that it was the first high albedo region to be accurately identified by astronomers in the nineteenth century.

Hellas was roughly four kilometers deep, two and a half times the depth of Earth's Grand Canyon. When it was formed, the energy released was so great that it re-melted the underlying mantle. Such re-melting created prime conditions for the concentration of rare earth elements. The entire floor of the crater, known as Hellas Planitia, was once a sea of magma. Today, after billions of years of weathering, only the northwest quadrant was exposed. In that area, the mean elevation was about nine kilometers below the Mars datum, making it the lowest place on the planet's surface. The remainder of the basin floor was buried under one to two kilometers of wind-deposited dust, which also covered vast glaciers.

Being the lowest area on Mars also meant having the highest atmospheric pressure, 1.24 kPa. The relatively high atmospheric pressure offered two benefits not found elsewhere on the planet. The first was a relatively mild temperature profile. During the southern hemispheric summer, daytime air temperatures could climb above freezing at mid-day. Daytime soil temperatures could reach a balmy 75° F. Nights were still cold, of course—minus 50° F in summer, and down to minus 140° F on a winter night. The relatively mild temperatures meant less energy required to heat habitats and pressure suits.

Hellas's relatively high atmospheric pressure was also above the triple point of water. Hellas was unique on all of Mars in its ability to maintain water in its liquid phase when temperatures exceeded the melting point, and to maintain ice when the temperature was below freezing. As a result, glaciers were a common feature of Hellas Planitia. They clung to south-facing slopes or lay buried under the ubiquitous Martian dust on the basin floor. Unlike any other place at this latitude, water was almost as abundant here as it was in the Martian polar regions—but under conditions more suited to human habitation.

For humans, water meant life and industry. It could be readily electrolyzed into oxygen and hydrogen, providing air to breathe, providing fuel for fuel cells to generate electricity, and providing fuel to power ascent boosters to transport refined rare earth elements to Martian orbit for the journey to Earth.

Dallas struggled to inhale the thinning air. "We have fifteen air canisters between us. If we're lucky, it will be just enough to reach Prospector Base in three days. Any delays, and we'll run out of air.

He turned to Luis. "We'll need climbing gear to get out of this crater. According to Robbie, the crater wall where we'll exit is composed of three tiers of two-to-three-hundred-foot cliffs with intervening thirty-degree slopes of about the same height."

Luis had busied himself inventorying their climbing gear while Dallas and Robbie conferred over the route to Prospector Base. "We have three two-hundred-foot lengths of ten-millimeter dynamic rope. And we each have our own harnesses, carabiners, anchors, ascenders, rappelling brakes, and runners."

Despite its name, Hellas Planitia was anything but level. Four billion years of plate tectonics, volcanism, meteor impacts, and crustal contraction had created a chaotic terrain of craters, fault block ridges, and grabens. EPSILON had recognized early in its mission development that Prospector crew members must be skilled climbers to negotiate the terrain. Given the route they had to travel to reach safety, it would take every bit of training Dallas had provided his team back on Earth.

EPSILON had tapped into his climbing expertise when they hired him. Dallas had been a climbing instructor after he earned his master's degree in Aeronautical Engineering from the University of Washington. He had an early start; his father taught him to climb when he was fourteen. At eighteen, he led a climbing party up the difficult Liberty Ridge route to summit Mt. Rainier. He climbed all through college and graduate school, landing a job as a climbing instructor with the Outdoor Leadership School. Which also led him to meet Ann. That had been thirteen years ago, and although much had changed in his life, two things remained: his love of climbing and his feelings for Ann. Right now, he needed to concentrate on climbing while ignoring the aching realization that she, and all the flight control team at SaMMCon, remained in the dark about their survival. A survival that still hung in the balance.

Dallas glanced at his landing party. He had led a six-month climbing training with the other four members of the Prospector 1 landing party. It had been arduous. He adjusted his climbing techniques to adapt to wearing a pressure suit. Numerous pieces of climbing hardware were specially adapted to be used with a gloved hand, especially locking carabiners. A locking carabiner locked and unlocked with the twist of a threaded nut located on the end of the spring gate. When the gate was in the closed position, the nut threaded over the end of the gate, preventing it from inadvertently opening if it came in contact with rock or a body part. But threading and unthreading small diameter nuts with gloves proved cumbersome at best. They tested several design alternatives, but these invariably involved enlarging the diameter of the nut. The designs worked better with gloves, but they introduced unacceptable wear on the ropes that rubbed against them. So, the team practiced using standard locking 'biners' with gloved hands. After months of practice, it took twice the usual time. But it was safer than a rope failure in the middle of a rappel or ascent.

Luis closed Allie's pack. "Flash, we're all geared up and ready to go."

Everyone wore their packs over their suits. The packs were enormous. Each contained two canisters of oxygen. One canister connected to the suit with a quick connect fitting built into the inside of the pack. The packs also carried a small fuel cell that powered the heating system built into their suits, all the climbing gear Luis had inventoried, and an emergency one-person thermoshelter. They welcomed the low Martian gravity. What weighed 120 pounds on Earth only weighed forty-five pounds on Mars, a tolerable load for the three male crew members. To trim pack weight for the smaller women, Luis stowed their spare oxygen bottles with the other five bottles carried by Robbie.

Dallas confirmed the landing party was properly outfitted with their helmets on.

"Okay, Luis. Equalize the cabin to ambient pressure."

Everyone manipulated their jaws to pop their ears. When the cabin pressure stabilized to the near-vacuum outside, Luis reefed counterclockwise on the hatch handle. A shaft of pale orange light beamed into the cabin from outside. It looked like sunset, when in reality it was midday. A gentle wind blew a small cloud of dust in through the open hatch, creating a swirling dance of tiny floaters that shimmered in the pale beam.

Dallas crawled out on all fours through the three-foot diameter hatch. He stood up erect after he allowed everyone else a clear path out. "Hmm. So much for the culmination of mankind's greatest journey. Maybe I can still use my catch-phrase when we reach Prospector Base."

Dallas chuckled to himself and slowly turned, fully taking in the view. Behind him, the crippled Descent/Ascent Vehicle lay on its side, looking like a discarded aluminum beer can. It was stained red with Martian dust and partially crushed as if some giant frat boy had clumsily squeezed the can too hard during a chugging contest. Above the fallen vehicle loomed a thirty-foot-diameter boulder. The boulder was stained a rusty red from dust, except for an arc of metallic scratches where the Descent/Ascent Vehicle had slid off its face on its way to the ground. The vehicle had come to rest near the bottom of a three-hundred-foot-high talus slope. Above that loomed a twelve-hundred-foot cliff that arced around them, forming a giant ring eighteen kilometers across.

The top of rim on the far side of the crater was barely visible above the horizon. On Mars, the horizon was a mere 3.7 kilometers away, enhancing the illusion of distance for humans used to a 5.1-kilometer horizon. The rim was completely obscured where it was hidden behind the central mountain. The central mountain looked like a collection of spires on a medieval castle conjured up by a mad wizard.

The mid-day sun shone with a pale orange light. At the horizon, the sky was a hazy butterscotch, but looking upward, it grew progressively black. A gentle breeze blew out of the northwest, the prevailing wind direction at this latitude.

Dallas wished he had the luxury of time to absorb everything he saw. He was, after all, the first human to step foot on Mars. It was the culmination of human longing since Galileo first trained his now-famous telescope on the planet in 1609. But his excitement was tempered by their tenuous position. Prospector Base lay seventy-five kilometers away by their chosen route, but it felt to Dallas like it might as well have been on the far side of Mars.

Dave emerged last from the ascent module, followed closely by Robbie. As he straightened up, he exclaimed in mock disappointment, "Hey! Where's the beach? My recruiter promised a lounge chair and unlimited tropical drinks with umbrellas!"

"Damn! I forgot something." Luis crawled back inside the hatch and reemerged thirty seconds later holding a small cloth bag. It contained half a dozen foam balls. He intended to use them to express his disdain for Dave, or any other crew member who he deemed deserved it. Not wanting to lose any foam balls in the out of doors, Luis swatted the bag across Dave's chest.

Dallas growled, "Luis, that's thirty fewer seconds of O_2 to get to base."

"Then let's get out of here, Flash."

Allie quickly stowed Luis's precious cargo in his pack for him.

Dallas pulled out his smartphone and tapped his visor app. A thin vertical line appeared in the center of his visor's field of view. He tapped in the bearing and distance they needed to go on this first leg of their trek. The bearing the vertical line represented now appeared in his field of view. He turned his head back and forth in the general direction he knew they needed to go. Whenever the line on his visor crossed over their intended direction of travel, the line and the numerical bearing flashed a bright red. He found a large boulder maybe a kilometer ahead that lay in their path, and struck out for it. Four other figures garbed in white pressure suits and a tracked vehicle the size of a home dishwasher fell in line behind him as he walked due north. The rust-colored dust they stirred up as they walked slowly drifted behind them to the southeast.

CHAPTER 13

Ann rubbed her temples. Two large, wall-mounted screens at the front of the flight control room displayed a satellite composite photo of the entire Hellas Planitia. A small red "X" in the northwest quadrant of the basin marked the location of Prospector Base. Roughly ten kilometers southeast of the base lay an elongated yellow ellipse, its long axis oriented northwest-to-southeast. The ellipse defined the area Monica calculated as the most probable landing location for the stricken Descent/Ascent Vehicle. She assumed a range of time during the descent when the parachutes might have manually deployed to slow the Descent/Ascent Vehicle enough for a survivable landing.

The search area was immense. The ellipse major axis was 150 kilometers long, and the minor axis was 30 kilometers. Total area was 14,100 square kilometers, and it still only represented a 60-percent probability that the Descent/Ascent Vehicle had come down inside of it.

Worry creased Ann's forehead, *What if it came down outside this area? If they came down outside of this search area, they'll be long dead by the time we eliminate the initial search area...if they survived at all.*

NASA sent a dozen links to satellite photos that needed to be reviewed by Ann's team; Ajay constantly added to the list. Ann had yet to prioritize which areas within the search ellipse to have her team review first.

Ann conferred with her FDO. "Monica, let's go over your assumptions one more time."

Monica stood beside Ann's workstation, presenting the background that went into her search area calculations. "Miss Ann, I took the mass of the DV and calculated a ballistic reentry based on their assumed speed of two kilometers per second at transmission termination. Then I subjected that trajectory to a chaos algorithm to account for the effects of air resistance on the DV. Then I assumed successful parachute deployment sequence at different times past time zero in one-second increments."

Ann scrunched her eyes shut in frustration. "So what you're saying is that this ellipse only represents a probable landing location regardless of crash survivability."

Monica's tone bordered on defensive. "Not true, Miss Ann. The closer you are to the base, the higher up the parachutes deployed prior to landing, and the lower the landing velocity and the more survivable the impact."

Ann opened her eyes and reexamined the ellipse. "So their best chance at surviving the landing lies at the northwest terminus of the ellipse?"

Monica's face brightened. "Yes, Miss Ann!"

Ann began to forward selected satellite video to various team members. She stood to address the room. "Listen up, everybody! The closer the DV came down to Prospector Base, the greater the chance they survived the landing. Begin your searches in the northwest of each search area that I forward to you, working your way progressively to the southeast."

Ann gave out enough satellite imagery to cover roughly 80 percent of the northwest half of the ellipse—just enough to task every person occupying the first two rows of flight control stations. The missing imagery was a swath roughly sixty to ninety kilometers from the northwest tip of the search area. Ajay had NASA tweaking the polar orbits of their nearest observational satellites to cover that area. Their cameras were not the highest quality—resolution was about two square meters—but they were readily available, and there were a lot of them.

Another notification popped up on her screen—Ajay announcing another link. Ann opened it up. It covered roughly the northwest half of the missing search area. She started a search herself, intending to forward the imagery to the first available staff member.

Ann scrolled back and forth in a southwest-to-northeast pattern. Even at this resolution, the terrain of Hellas Planitia was incredibly chaotic. The magma created a jumble of frozen lava flows, punctuated by pressure ridges and the occasional volcanic cone. Four billion years of asteroid impacts left regolith scattered everywhere. It filled in valleys. It coated all but the steepest slopes. She noted pennants of windblown sand and dust oriented on the southeast side of most boulders. The base of each pennant matched the width of whatever object they clung to and trailed away to a point to the southeast. Eventually, she recognized that the length of the pennant was proportional to the height of the boulder.

Ann's search included a large-impact crater. Only the southeast half of the crater lay within the imagery. She noted the central mountain was a collection of sharp peaks, their saw-toothed shadows stark against the crater floor to the south. Her search path continued in a northeasterly direction to the crater wall. It was a steep cliff, steeper than seventy degrees, except for a kilometer-wide section that was terraced. That section was composed of three shorter cliffs, with flatter slopes in between. Then her search continued over the seemingly endless magma fields of Hellas Planitia north of the crater.

Ann used a one-kilometer-wide grid pattern. On her ninth pass, she covered the very southeast portion of that large-impact crater. She paused to observe an object that was more reflective than the surrounding material. *Too small to be the DV.*

She moved on to the northeast and was about to pass out of the crater for the last time. *Wait, there was no sand dune beside that object.*

She backed up her search for a second look. Ann zoomed in as best she could on the low-resolution imagery. The object shone with a white luster but appeared only about two-thirds the length of the Descent/Ascent Vehicle. The lack of resolution made it impossible to see any lettering.

EPSILON's enigmatic owner had insisted on two-foot-high block letters spelling out the company name on all EPSILON spacecraft and facilities. It wasn't about vanity. It wasn't so the company could identify a crashed spacecraft.

According to the U.N. Space Law Treaties and Principles, once EPSILON (or anyone else, for that matter) placed Prospector Base on Hellas Planitia, other entities had to maintain adequate distance so as not to 'interfere' with EPSILON's operations there. Hence, the large block letters on everything EPSILON, so there could be no mistake whose facilities occupied this portion of Mars.

Ann transferred the image from her computer monitor to one of the two wall-mounted screens in the front of the room. She addressed the group. "Does anybody recognize what mission this object might belong to?"

She added a second "X" to the image of Monica's elliptical search area on the second screen. Ann's "X" was roughly sixty-five kilometers southeast of the "X" that marked Prospector Base and was within half a kilometer of the central axis of the search ellipse.

Malcom McDowell responded, "Ann, I'm overlaying a plot of every known mission to Hellas. Here are EPSILON's six unmanned exploratory missions." Six more red X's appeared onscreen. Five of them were hundreds of kilometers from the search area. The fifth overlaid the location of Prospector Base.

He continued, "BMAC landed three missions within Hellas Basin." Three blue X's appeared. The nearest was roughly 150 kilometers southwest of Ann's.

Ann queried, "Malcom, what about NASA missions?"

A green "X" appeared about a thousand kilometers to the east. NASA had landed a weather station there ten years ago. Ann addressed the room again, "Any thoughts on what we're looking at here? Whatever this is, it hasn't been here long enough to accumulate a sand dune."

Susan Bailey spoke up first. "Ann, this object is too reflective to be a boulder of native material, even if it was just blasted from a nearby impact. The overall dimensions of this object more-or-less match the dimensions of the Descent/Ascent Vehicle—minus the Lander Module."

She used her mouse curser to circle a dark smudge at one end of the object. "See that dark shape on this end? This is smaller than our two-meter resolution, so it's not clear, but it could be the DV booster nozzle. If it is the DV, it appears to have landed intact, even though it's lying on its side."

A murmur arose as heads around the room nodded in agreement.

Ann quickly copied the coordinates and sent them to Ajay Kumar. "Ajay, how soon can you maneuver a sat with a high-res camera over these coordinates?"

"Give me five minutes to find out, Ann," Ajay responded as he forwarded the coordinates to NASA's Mars satellite flight control group.

He picked up his phone and started an animated conversation with the NASA Administrator. Shortly, he hung up and spoke to Ann. "NASA's 2025 Reconnaissance Orbiter will be over your coordinates in six hours."

"Thanks, Ajay."

Ann turned and slowly walked back to her flight control station. A somber Evan Griffin was waiting for her. "Ann, I'm continuing to hail the DV, but without success. Do you want me to stop?"

Ann thought for a moment. "No, Evan. For all we know, the landing party is receiving what you are transmitting, just unable to send messages out. I want them to know we're making every effort to reach them."

Ann sat back down at her station, the knot in her stomach clenched tight as a vise. *This is going to be the longest six hours of my life.*

CHAPTER 14

Ann put the 2025 RO imagery on the right-hand wall-mounted screen. What appeared so ambiguous in the MGPS imagery was now clear. Objects as small as six inches in diameter were visible.

Susan Bailey voiced what all could see. "Look at the EPSILON logo! It's scratched, but clearly legible."

Alarm marked Drew Usher's drawl. "The hatch is open! Do you think the impact jarred it open?" The crumpled thruster nozzle was clearly visible. So were the scratches and dents from impacting the large boulder just uphill.

"The thruster nozzle looks crumpled, but striations radiate out from this point here." Susan Baily circled a spot on the screen just uphill from the nozzle's location. "The booster was firing when the ascent vehicle touched down. The DV had a controlled landing, then fell over."

Ann panned out a bit, taking in the surrounding terrain. "This double line on the ground originates at the open hatch, then travels due north." She scrolled north over the crater floor, following the line. She continued, "This could be tracks from the RBI unit."

Portia Knox spoke up, "I don't see any footprints. Did anybody exit the capsule?" As the program flight surgeon, she anxiously searched the screen for footprints. Footprints would not only prove that the landing party had survived, they might also provide clues on the crew's condition.

Ann used her cursor to point out lighter-colored marks that occurred at regular intervals of about a meter. "These might be footprints. But it's hard to tell. They're at the limits of the imagery resolution. I'm going to follow Robbie's tracks. Any crew member should show up clearly with this high resolution."

Ann panned out farther. The line remained visible, because its bearing remained consistent. She scrolled about ten kilometers north until the line terminated. She zoomed in to the point at the end of the line. Five white ovals and a silver rectangle resolved into view. A cheer erupted from the Flight Control Room. Dr. Knox spoke again. "Those little white bumps projecting from the ovals must be arms or legs. The crew are all walking!"

Steve Chan spoke next. "Why are they traveling due north? Shouldn't they be moving northwest, in the direction of Prospector Base?"

Ann zoomed out to the full extent of the imagery that they had of the crater, enough so the southeast half of the crater was fully visible. "A direct bearing to the base wouldn't be the fastest route. By traveling north, they avoid the central mountain. And when I was scanning on my search grid, I noted this."

She panned to the northeast quadrant of the crater, speaking as she zoomed about halfway back in. "The perimeter of this crater is a massive cliff in every location except this."

Her cursor circled a section of the crater wall that was laid back at a less extreme angle. "This section is about a kilometer wide. It appears to be terraced. See, the shorter shadows cast by three shorter cliffs here, here, and here." Ann's cursor fell on three concentric dark lines within this break in the crater wall.

Portia Knox spoke up again. "So, assuming they make a beeline for Prospector Base after they get out of the crater, how long will it take them?"

Ann zoomed out and added in older imagery to complete the terrain between the 2025 RO imagery and Prospector Base. Then she snapped a line running from the base to the gap in the crater wall the Prospector crew was heading for. She turned on a measuring tool and highlighted the line with her cursor. "It's just under fifty-eight kilometers."

Portia continued her line of questioning. "How long will it take them to travel that distance?"

"It's hard to estimate. They've made excellent time so far. But they still have to climb out of the crater. Then they'll have to scale this ridgeline and descend into the valley where the base is located on the other side. Maybe about four days."

Susan Baily deduced Portia Knox's line of reasoning. She'd developed and monitored the equipment inventory in the Descent/Ascent Vehicle. "The DV cabin comes equipped with three oxygen canisters for each crew member. Each canister holds twenty-four hours' worth of oxygen. Ann, they only have three days of air."

Ann walked over to Ajay Kumar's NASA Representative station. He looked up as she spoke. "Ajay, can you keep your RO satellite orbiting over the crew's location so we can monitor their progress?"

"Yes. Keep providing me updated coordinates to aim for with each pass. The administrator granted EPSILON full access to RO for the duration of this crisis."

Ann walked to the front of the room and turned to face the rows of flight directors. She addressed the group, "We've got to find a way to communicate with our landing party."

She pointed up and behind herself in the general direction of the right-hand monitor. "If we can communicate, then we can scout the path of least resistance for them. We must help them avoid obstacles that could delay them in any way, starting with the best location to climb up out of the crater. Evan, you're point to reestablish contact with them. They'll have their smartphones with them for their own comm lines and for their smart visors. But without the DV, they have no way to uplink to the Command Module. There has to be something we can use that transmits on their frequency. I'll scout routes for you to pass on once you figure out how."

CHAPTER 15

The landing party had traveled about ten kilometers according to Dallas's visor MGPS readout. He read the time display on the upper left of this visor—5:03 p.m. local Sol time. A Martian Sol was almost forty minutes longer than an Earth day. All Prospector computers, including the crew's smartphones, automatically compensated so that a Martian day was divided up into exactly twenty-four "hours." Nobody noticed that a Martian hour was about a minute and a half longer than an Earth hour.

Given their mid-day start, they made good progress. The terraced cliffs were a mere five kilometers away now. Dallas started laying out optimum climbing routes in his head. But it would be nearly dusk by the time they reached the base of the first cliff.

For the past couple of hours, a steady wind had blown out of the northwest. Dallas suspected convection currents powered by solar heating of the crater floor boosted the velocity. They made good progress, but the breeze lifted the lighter dust on the surface into a cloud about six inches deep. Everyone could see the ground through this shifting false surface, but it was disorienting. Each foot created a small eddy. When anyone picked up a foot as they walked, the eddy traveled away to the southeast. The false sense of motion it created was disorienting. Everyone learned to focus on the horizon to avoid motion sickness.

A pair of dust devils silently crossed their path about a kilometer ahead. Less than thirty meters wide, they ascended to an amazing height. It was difficult to assess, but Dallas estimated they were taller than the crater walls that surrounded them. He recalled the time when he was stationed at China

Lake Naval Weapons Center in the California Mohave Desert. He was there for F-35 flight training and went into the nearby town of Ridgecrest on a weekend pass. As he sat eating pizza and beer with a group of other pilots at an outdoor table, a dust devil skirted around them, just missing them. The wind blew a few napkins around and elicited a few laughs from the naval pilot trainees. It crossed the business loop of US 395 as they laughed and entered a lumber yard across the street from the pizza joint where they sat. To their amazement, two-by-fours tossed around like matchsticks. Sheets of plywood blew about as easily as the napkins they had just collected from the sidewalk. Dust whirled everywhere. They heard screams from within the maelstrom across the street.

Dallas and his fellow pilots dropped their pizza and dashed across the four-lane street, dodging cars as they went. When they arrived, the dust devil had moved on, but it had left the lumber yard in shambles. They found one employee sporting a goose egg on his forehead. He had foolishly tried to hold a stack of half-inch plywood down. A pair of customers had had the presence of mind to drop to the ground and cover their heads. Other than a coating of dust, they were fine. Dallas and another pilot named David dashed back across the street and retrieved a bucket of ice from the restaurant. The grateful lumber yard manager filled a plastic bag with the ice and had his employee hold it to his forehead in the employee lunchroom.

When the pilots all returned to their cold pizza, the conversation for the rest of the meal revolved around their utter amazement at the power of the wind they'd just witnessed. Dallas never forgot the experience.

He warily eyed the dust devils that drifted in the wind on all sides all day long as they walked. *I wonder how strong the convective winds are here?*

Aside from these occasional Martian denizens, the astronauts walked completely alone. Everyone felt the loneliness of the utter desolation, more empty than any desert on Earth. As they tired from the walking, the silence magnified the effect of isolation. It weighed on everyone's resolve.

Dallas knew the wind would subside soon. But cold air would soon drain onto the crater floor from the surrounding highlands. The weather app on his phone predicted a nighttime temperature of minus 60° F. The temperature had already dropped down into the single digits. He was glad for the heated suits, but he was concerned the fuel cells would not last the full duration of their trip. Colder temperatures depleted more quickly the compressed hydrogen and oxygen that the fuel cells catalyzed into electrical power to run the suit heaters. *We have to find shelter soon.*

Dallas identified a place on the lowest cliff where the top dipped lower, forming a shallow "V." He deduced that it was a ravine at one time that had become filled with regolith and dust over the eons. "I'm shifting our bearing five degrees to our left. We'll camp under that low spot in the cliff for the night. It will be too dark to climb safely, even with our helmet lamps. But the early morning sun should just hit this section of the crater rim. We'll benefit from both the heat and the light for an early climb."

Dallas aimed his visor navigation line at the "V" and said, "Fix." The line and a new bearing flashed red, and he resumed walking in the new direction.

The crew arrived at the cliff base after another two and a half hours' walk. As Dallas suspected, a large fan of debris leaned against the base of the cliff under the "V." He kicked the material in a few places with his booted foot, testing the sediment's composition. It was mostly loose dust and silt, with an occasional cobble mixed in. After a brief rest, he addressed the group, "We're walking up to the top of this debris fan. When we get up high enough, we'll excavate a bench big enough for all of us to sit on. Hopefully, we'll be above the worst of the cold air drainage. We can further conserve heat by covering ourselves with our thermal blankets. We can fix the blankets to the slope above our bench with rocks, then drape it over ourselves for the night. We should be pretty comfortable, maybe even downright toasty."

After a brief rest, everyone followed Dallas to the top of the debris cone, roughly one hundred feet off the crater floor. Luis and Dallas produced small shovels from their packs and started excavating a ledge. Everyone else pitched in using their gloved hands, scooping out dust and cobbles. Ann and LaDonna collected all five thermal blankets and placed their upper edges two feet upslope of their excavation. They overlapped the corners a foot and anchored each overlapped corner in place with a large rock.

Everyone settled in, seated with backs against the vertical wall of their excavation, their feet extended out in front of them. Their view of the central mountain disappeared as the thermal blankets were carefully pulled down over them for the night. Dallas ensured the blankets covered their feet. He was the last to switch off his helmet lamp.

In the ensuing quiet, he thought of Ann. During the past eleven years, whenever he climbed, he still thought of her. Whenever he played a blues song off of her playlist, he thought of her. His mind wandered to their first climb together after she graduated from climbing student to instructor. To celebrate her hiring, she'd invited him to accompany her on a climb of the south face of Grand Teton Peak.

They summited before dawn on the second day, where they sat together and watched the dawn in a cloudless sky. As ultramarine blue gave way to rosy pink, he put his arm around her in congratulations. He intended to let his arm linger just a moment, hoping not to upset her. But before he could pull his arm back, she leaned into him and gently kissed him. When she pulled away, his emotions were a comical mixture of shock and delight. Her eyes flashed the twinkle of calculated mischief.

For the next year, they instructed together. When they weren't instructing, they were climbing together, all to the accompaniment of his playlist of the greatest blues artists in history. But at the end of a year, they parted ways. They had different paths to follow. When their paths crossed at EPSILON, his old feelings for her stirred. He put them aside as best he could, assuming that she had moved on. Now, as he sat silently in the dark, he asked himself, *Will I ask her if I survive?*

Dave jarred Dallas's introspection. "Now that we're settled in, do we finally get our tropical drinks with the little umbrellas?"

Dallas emerged from his thoughts. "Go to sleep, Dave. We have a long day ahead of us tomorrow. Besides, if you had something, you couldn't open your visor to drink it, anyway."

"The service around here sucks. Gonna give this joint only one star when I write my review."

CHAPTER 16

Ann sat at the conference table with Malcom McDowell and Ajay Kumar in the early morning. Their coffee cups rested untouched on the polished mahogany table. She was unable to focus, distracted by the incredible danger to the landing party, and now just this morning, Cliff Sherman had not reported for work. He had not responded to Ann's calls. Before leaving for this meeting, she'd tasked Alice Hatch to call Santa Maria PD for a welfare check.

Ann forced her attention back to the big screen mounted on the wall. John Carpenter detailed the results of his investigation into the Trojan horse introduced into the Prospector Command Module computer and subsequent infection of the Descent/Ascent Vehicle computer. "We triangulated the origin of the transmission that delivered the Trojan horse. Based on the time stamp differential between the number three and number four solar weather sats, we calculated the signal originated from the Moon."

Three pairs of eyebrows rose in unison. John continued before anyone seated could ask a question, "We know based on the Moon's position relative to Earth and Mars that the transmission originated on the far side of the Moon. We've checked with hundreds of celestial receivers orbiting Earth. Not one of them detected that transmission."

China had established a lunar base on the far side of the Moon, near the lunar south pole. They mined ice from perpetually shaded crater floors to electrolyze into hydrogen and oxygen—rocket fuel. The fuel powered their weekly shuttles back to Earth. Many speculated that the same type of fuel would someday power Chinese spacecraft on missions outside of Earth's orbit.

The base possessed a communications transceiver able to send and receive signals from Earth. China leased access to the transceiver to most major players in space: Russia, India, Japan, BMAC, and a host of research institutions. China benefited by offsetting its lunar base's enormous operating costs. The others benefited by minimizing their capital outlays for redundant communications infrastructure. Only EPSILON and NASA maintained communications systems robust enough that they could afford to forgo participating in China's venture.

Ann spoke up, "John, that leaves two questions unanswered. One, how did China encrypt and authenticate the transmission so that the Command Module would have accepted it? And two, how did the Trojan horse get to the Chinese base in the first place?"

"Don't assume that this act was China's doing, Ann. It could have been any one of the entities that lease time on the transceiver," John replied.

Ann turned and spoke to the NASA representative seated beside her. "Ajay, is there any chance that China will open their transmission logs to us? We know the time of transmission. It should be a simple matter to match the billable use with the transmission time we determined."

"It's hard to say, Ann," Ajay responded in his thick Hindi accent. "China has never released its raw communications logs. The CIA has accused China in the past of using the facility to support secret military testing, using the Moon itself to block their activities from our view.

"The State Department has already offered to negotiate with China for just the timeframe of the Trojan horse transmission. However, there are a couple of issues. State's sense is that if China was knowingly involved, we'll never see the log. If it was a client, China may not want to lose the future revenue for ratting them out."

"So we're at an impasse for now?" Ann's tone was exasperated.

John reassured her, "Maybe not, Ann. We can still investigate how our encryption and authentication were leaked. It's the only way such a transmission could have originated from the Chinese lunar base."

The implications of John's assessment left Ann incredulous. "I refuse to accept that someone from our team compromised our mission and our astronauts in such a way."

Malcom interjected, "John, your number-one priority is to find the leak."

John had anticipated his director's order. "I've already marshaled the entire network team and nearly all of IT."

"Good," Malcom affirmed. This level of corporate espionage not only threatens the Prospector 1 mission, it threatens the safety of every AV EPSILON has put on the road. I don't know what the end game is here, but millions of lives could be at risk. There's an FBI field office right here in Santa Maria. I'm personal friends with the director. I'll contact him to see if they'll get involved."

CHAPTER 17

Ann left the meeting and headed down the short hallway leading back to the flight control room. As she reached for the door, it suddenly pulled open from the control room side. A paler-than-usual Alice Hatch nearly bowled her over.

Ann did not have a good relationship with her—or rather Malcom's—Public Affairs Officer. She considered Alice's press interview skills mediocre at best. But Alice was a stunning brunette, statuesque, with a clear alto voice. Ann had originally interviewed Alice with Malcom. They had disagreed on their scoring of Alice after the employment interview, and Malcom had hired Alice over Ann's objections. Ann was convinced Malcom only hired her as a talking head, a pretty face to mouth the company line at news conferences and interviews—someone to distract male reporters from asking probing questions.

Ann reflexively said, "Excuse me," but was cut off before she could utter a sound.

Alice brushed aside Ann on her way to the conference room and Malcom. "Cliff was found dead at his condo this morning! The police are calling it suicide."

Ann froze in place, struggling to process Alice's statement. She turned back toward the conference room just in time to see a six-inch spike heel disappear behind the conference room door. Without hesitation, Ann rushed back to the conference room and burst in as Alice was mid-sentence: "…police found him when we requested a welfare check."

The welfare check Ann had ordered prior to attending her meeting. Cliff's absence was out of character, especially so because he didn't call in.

Alice continued breathlessly, "The police say it was suicide! He left a note."

Malcom's mouth hung partially open in disbelief before he replied, "Did the police say how he died?"

Alice tried dabbing her eyes but only succeeded in smearing her mascara. "He dropped his hair-dryer in the bath. The preliminary cause of death is electrocution."

Malcom offered her a tissue from the tabletop. Ann finally gathered her wits enough to voice the thoughts that were welling up in her mind. "This doesn't make sense. Cliff gave no indication he was depressed. His job performance was top rate. He interacted well with the rest of the team. He loved what he did."

After further reflection, Ann asked Alice, "What did his note say?"

"The police didn't say." Ann dabbed her eyes. "Only that he left one behind."

Malcom turned his attention to Ann. "After this morning's conference with John, we need to know what Cliff wrote. This can't be a coincidence, just as our internal investigation into the Prospector cyberattacks is heating up."

Malcom retook his seat at the conference table. Ann, Ajay, and Alice all stood off to the side. Once seated, Malcom typed on the tabletop keyboard in front of him. The big screen flickered back on. A matronly receptionist appeared onscreen. "Good morning, Chief Wallace's office. Oh, Director McDowell, it's you. I'm so sorry for the loss of your employee." Her voice and face conveyed her genuine sympathy.

Malcom returned her courtesy. "Thank you, Bonnie. We've only just now learned the news. Is the chief in? This horrible news may have some bearing on our investigation into the Prospector 1 crash landing."

The public was closely following the Prospector 1 mission events, and Chief Wallace's executive secretary was no exception. "Yes, he's in. I'll transfer you right away."

The screen went black briefly. Then the image of Police Chief Greg Wallace came into view as he pivoted his office chair toward the camera. "Malcom, I wish we were speaking under better circumstances. You've already had a rough week, and now this."

Malcom McDowell made it a point to frequent all the local civic events, as did the police chief. Their paths crossed often. Their growing friendship extended to the golf course.

"Thank you, Greg. We've really had our hands full. We're just thankful our astronauts are alive and able to work their way toward our Hellas base. But there's only so much we can do for them from here. Right now, they're on their own. All we can do is watch. In the meantime, we've launched an internal investigation to find out exactly what happened, and find a way to assist the crew, if possible."

He paused, then launched in. "Greg, the timing of Cliff Sherman's suicide could be significant to our investigation. Is there any chance that we can see what Mr. Sherman wrote in his suicide note?"

The police chief's face grew even more somber. "Malcom, our policy is to not release the contents of a suicide note until the ME concludes her autopsy and the family is notified. But under these unusual circumstances, I'm willing to share it with you."

There was a brief pause as the chief reached down and pulled a transparent evidence bag off his desktop. A sheet of white paper was visible inside. The chief pulled on his reading glasses and read from the side of the paper facing away from his audience, "I'm sorry."

Malcom exchanged a glance with Ann. "That's it, Greg?"

"That's it, Malcom. It's printed in block caps, apparently for emphasis."

He set the bag down. "As a matter of procedure, I've assigned Detective Henderson to follow up on any leads, including this note. If your findings show Cliff Sherman had any connection to what happened to your Prospector spacecraft, it will aid our investigation. Detective Henderson will be in contact with you to follow up."

The chief sighed. "Malcom, I want to offer my sincerest condolences again for all of your project's misfortunes over the past week, and especially for this loss of your employee."

Malcom appreciated the Chief's consideration. "Thank you, Greg. You've been most helpful."

Malcom touched his keyboard, and the screen went dark. Then he turned to Ajay and Ann, who had remained offscreen during the call. "If Cliff Sherman was involved with sabotaging our mission, he had to have help, and money. Somebody paid the Chinese to lease the airtime on their transceiver. And to my knowledge, Cliff was no hacker. He would have needed help to compose the Trojan horse code. If this extends outside our company, the FBI will have the resources to pursue it. The field office director is unavailable for the rest of the morning. I've left him a text message to set up a call with me in this room this afternoon."

"Thanks, Malcom," said Ajay. "I'd very much like to be in on that call."

Malcom turned to Ann. "Ann, please share all of this with John Carpenter. Get his resources looking at how Cliff did this."

Ann nodded her head, her mind a jumble of disbelief, sorrow, and misgivings. "I just can't believe Cliff would have done this. None of this is like him."

Numbly, she pulled out her smartphone and called John.

CHAPTER 18

Synchronized alarms went off simultaneously in each astronaut's helmet. Dallas woke to Robert Johnson's "Sweet Home Chicago." LaDonna's helmet reverberated with the ring of a mechanical alarm clock. Dave woke to "Oh Canada." Luis preferred the sultry Latin ballad, "Besame Mucho." Allie employed a rotation of the current top-ten pop songs. The combination was pure bedlam.

Dallas silenced his alarm and threw off the thermal blanket. He noted with satisfaction that the upper half of the crater's western wall caught the dawn light. The light imbued a metallic patina on all that it touched, almost like burnished bronze. Dallas's visor indicated an ambient temperature of minus 49° F, a good 10 degrees warmer than what they would have experienced on the crater floor.

Wearing their pressure suits altered their usual morning routine. Dave was most vocal about the change, "What I wouldn't give for a cup of coffee. Oh, wait! I forgot about this tube beside my mouth." He took a long dramatic drag on his reclaimed water tube. "I almost forgot about our endless supply of piss water. So much better than that sludge coffee Flash tried to poison us with during our climbing training in Wyoming. Thank God we can't drink any of that swill here!"

Everyone laughed. Even Dallas cracked a smile behind his visor. He had to agree with Dave's assessment. They had forgotten to bring a coffee pot on that particular trip. Dallas made cowboy coffee in a spare cooking pot, throwing several handfuls of grounds into two quarts of boiling water. Everyone had to spit it out, himself included.

After the laughter settled down, Dallas addressed the group. "We'll be climbing in two teams, just like we practiced in

Wyoming. Luis, LaDonna, and I will climb in a team of three, using two ropes. Dave and Allie will climb in a team of two, using the remaining rope.

"I'll lead the first pitch. LaDonna, you're first on belay. Luis, you belay LaDonna when she follows me up and I pull up the slack rope. Then LaDonna, you'll top belay Luis. Luis, you are not to clean out the protection that I set as you climb— leave it for Dave. Just unclip as you go.

"Allie, you're first up of the second team. I'll do my best to set anchors closely enough, but if you're uncomfortable with any distance between, feel free to set a supplemental anchor. But we're up against the clock. Don't waste time setting extra anchors if you don't absolutely have to. If we can't scale all three cliffs today, we have no hope of reaching Prospector Base before our air runs out.

"Dave, as last up, you'll clean out and save all anchors. Have you got a chock pick and hammer?"

"Got them right here, Flash," Dave responded as he patted his gear rack. "I'm locked and loaded."

Dave had slung a runner made of one-inch-wide webbing over one shoulder and under the opposite armpit. Then he'd clipped the tools to the runner using non-locking carabiners.

"What would you like me to do?" Robbie asked.

Dallas suppressed his consternation at his exposed oversight. "Robbie, you have four arms with opposable digits that don't experience fatigue. You free climb, following behind Dave. Collect any anchors Dave is unable to retrieve. Clip the anchors to the ring on your right side so you always have four hands free."

Then Dallas returned his attention to the group. "We have three cliff faces to scale today. Because of their height, each cliff requires at least two pitches, so we've got six pitches to complete."

Dallas scanned the route he selected yesterday as they approached the crater wall. Debris falling from above over the eons had worn a rough V-shaped indentation into the cliff face, except for the top ten or twenty feet, which remained vertical, if not overhung. The "V" was nearly ten feet wide at the cliff base, where Dallas would start, but it got progressively narrower higher up. It disappeared altogether at the base of the overhang. Dallas noted several ledges scattered up the face of the cliff. They ranged from a few inches to roughly three feet wide. He had plenty of options to choose from to end the first pitch. Dallas looked at a fixed point at the top of the cliff. "Find distance."

A fine black crosshair appeared near the point he was looking at. He oriented the crosshair on his intended target. "Fix distance." The crosshairs flashed red, and the distance appeared in red numerals in the upper left of his visor. "Two hundred and six feet, everybody. Let's gear up."

Everyone stepped into their climbing harnesses. All three coils of rope were carefully laid out on the ground near the base of the cliff. LaDonna scooped out a level place to sit three feet to the side of where Dallas waited to start climbing. She sat facing the cliff wall with feet spread shoulder-width apart against the rock face. This position allowed her to brace herself against the wall when she was pulled upward if Dallas fell. LaDonna tied a fisherman's knot into her end of the rope. The knot served as insurance that the rope would not inadvertently pass through the belay brake if Dallas fell when the rope was fully extended. She clipped the rope into her belay brake, then clipped her belay brake to the belay loop on her harness and nodded to Dallas.

While LaDonna situated herself, Dallas methodically tied himself in to the other end of the rope. He tied a loose figure eight knot an arm's length from his end of the rope. Then he threaded the end of the rope through his harness tie-in loops, first through the one on his waistband, then through the tie-in loop between his leg loops. Finally, he wove the end of the rope back through all the loops of the figure eight knot so that each loop was doubled. As he tightened the knot, he made sure the figure eight knot ended up close to his harness tie-in loops.

He looked beside him at LaDonna, who mentally replayed her training. Her job was to play out rope with her left hand to

Dallas as he climbed. As her right hand allowed the rope to slip through, she remained vigilant to grip the rope tightly and pull the rope to her right hip if Dallas slipped. By adjusting the angle of the rope before it passed into and through the belay brake, she increased the friction from nothing to 100 percent, arresting Dallas's fall.

LaDonna met Dallas's eyes, then spoke. "Belay on."

Dallas called up his blues playlist before responding. John Hooker's "Blues Boogie Jam" reverberated in five helmets. Dallas responded, "Climbing."

"Climb," LaDonna answered back.

Dallas wedged his hands into two cracks, set his booted foot on a one-inch ledge, and lifted himself off the detritus pile the group had camped on overnight. Direct sunlight shone on the crater wall to the west. If he leaned far enough back from the rock wall he clung to, he could see it shone on the top half of the uppermost cliff a thousand feet above him. The multitude of anchors and carabiners clipped to his rack rattled softly, the song of titanium and steel so familiar to Dallas since his youth.

Dallas reached a height of twenty feet and stopped. He unclipped a hexcentric chock and wedged it into the vertical crack, with the chock sling hanging below. Dallas tugged down hard on the chock sling. Then he clipped a carabiner to the chock sling, lifted his rope up to the carabiner, and clipped it in.

He worked his way up the center of the "V," placing protection every ten to twenty vertical feet. In wider cracks he used a cam anchor; in narrower cracks, a simple chock. In general, he alternated sides as he set his protection to maintain the rope as straight as possible. This reduced the risk that a fall might put horizontal or upward stress on any anchors, causing them to fail.

Dallas progressed to a ledge about fifty feet below the top of the cliff. He knew he was down to the final thirty feet of rope; LaDonna had called out the remaining rope length since it had been at fifty feet. The ledge was two feet wide. He pulled himself up onto it and dropped to his knees. He set two anchors four feet apart, clipped two three-foot-long runners to each, and clipped the runners to his harness, creating a double anchor.

Dallas stood, faced into the cliff, and called down, "Off belay!"

LaDonna unclipped the rope from the belay brake, untied the fisherman's knot from the end, and called back, "Belay off!"

Dallas found a waist-high crack three feet to the right of the double anchor. He set a chock, added a runner, and clipped the runner directly to the tie-in loops on his climbing harness. He pulled the rope up through all the protection he had just set, carefully coiling the rope back and forth behind his head as he did so. When the rope was fully retrieved, he set it out of the way so Ladonna would have a clear space to land on the ledge. He turned outward and admired the view of the crater as he waited for the rest of his climbing team to ascend.

The direct sunlight now illuminated half of the crater floor. The bronze cast was much less pronounced, but the dust suspended in the upper atmosphere still unmistakably colored the light. The shadow of the central peak stabbed westward to the base of the western wall like black daggers. Situated on the northeastern section of wall, Dallas was still in shadow. He was thankful for the southern hemisphere summer, giving them roughly fifteen hours of daylight to complete the climb out.

LaDonna stood and tied herself in with a rewoven figure eight knot on the end of the second rope as Luis situated himself on the belay ledge she just vacated. He clipped the rope into his belay brake, clipped his belay brake to his belay loop, tied a fisherman's knot on the end of the rope, and nodded. "On belay!"

"Belay on!" LaDonna placed her hands and feet just as Dallas had done when he started. She clipped into the first anchor and was just beginning to climb higher when Luis spoke.

"You know, 'Donna, the view from down here was so much better when you were wearing climbing shorts."

LaDonna paused, "Luis, have you forgotten about my extensive collection of medical instruments? I can reduce your high testosterone levels to a more acceptable level during your next physical exam."

"Point taken, ma'am. Climb!" Luis played out rope through the belay brake.

About halfway to the ledge, LaDonna grabbed a large flake of rock protruding from the cliff face. As she transferred her weight to it, it peeled away. She cried out, "Fall!"

Luis leaned back and pulled the trailing end of the rope toward his right hip. LaDonna pushed away from the cliff face, her hands and feet ready for impact with the cliff. She dropped eight feet before the rope tensed, swinging her hard into the cliff. The anchor held.

She remained motionless until she remembered to breathe. No longer preoccupied with her survival, she called out, "Rock!"

Luis was so much heavier than LaDonna, he barely left the ground. Undistracted, he watched a rock flake three feet across and an inch thick drop with LaDonna. Careful not to release any tension on the rope, he walked his feet to his right. The rock flake speared into the ground mere inches from where he had previously sat.

"Dammit, Doc, that was close!" Luis's voice betrayed a slight trill. "I'm sorry, I'll keep my testosterone levels in check. I promise!" He paused only briefly. "You okay up there?"

LaDonna responded through her breathlessness, "I'm fine. I'm resting on four points for now. No leaks detected in my suit. I just need to catch my breath. You okay, Luis?"

Luis's voice modulated. "I almost got a three-foot hole in my suit. That would have ruined my day."

LaDonna's composure returned, knowing she had not caused a calamity. "Glad you're alright, Luis, even if you are a sexist pig."

"Just part of my charm."

LaDonna took a few deep breaths. "Climbing!"

"Climb!"

Ladonna made the ledge without further incident. She clipped directly into the double anchor, then stood up. While she climbed, Dallas moved to the opposite side of the double anchor and clipped into a fourth anchor he set there.

Unlike Dallas, LaDonna did not unclip from her rope. Instead, she pulled four feet of slack toward her and clipped the rope into her belay brake. She stood facing the double anchor at a forty-five-degree angle relative to the cliff face and called down to Luis, who had tied-in with a rewoven figure eight knot. "Belay on!"

Luis began to climb. "Climbing!" As he did so, LaDonna carefully coiled the rope with her right hand as she pulled the slack through the belay brake. In twenty minutes, Luis stood anchored in opposite Dallas and Ladonna.

"Allie, when you hear that I'm on belay, start climbing," Dallas called down. "Everyone listen carefully to who is giving which voice commands. I would prefer we all make this ledge before pressing on, but the last thing I want is to get caught out on this crater wall at nightfall.

Dallas redirected himself to Luis. "Luis, I'm leading this next pitch. There are fewer cracks on the overhang, so this will be more technical."

"No complaints from me, Flash." Luis untied the end of his rope from his harness and passed it to Dallas, who tied in.

Dallas checked in with LaDonna. "'Donna, do you need a break before I start?"

"I'm good, Dallas. Luis is such a lightweight, it's no effort to belay him."

"Ouch, Doc," Luis complained. "You're hurting my ego."

LaDonna's sarcastic bedside manner shone through. "Honestly, Luis, you have so much ego, you'll never miss what I cut."

"If you say so—my heart's in your hands."

Dallas rolled his eyes out of habit, even though no one could see them.

LaDonna focused back on Dallas. "On belay!"

"Climbing!"

"Climb!"

Over the next thirty feet, Dallas used smaller anchors, an adjustment to the smaller cracks on this part of the cliff face. He examined the overhang above him, trying to map out a route. His hands were sweating. He wished he could use a chalk bag but knew nothing could be done about the sweating inside his suit. Setting an anchor in what appeared to be the last available crack, he clipped the rope in.

"'Donna," he alerted, "I'm going to have to free climb the last twenty feet. Good belay!"

LaDonna eased the rope back, minimizing the slack. Given the stretch in the dynamic rope they were using, Dallas could impact the ledge she stood on if he fell from the top of the overhang. But she was cognizant not to pull back too much slack. She did not want any tension to pull against Dallas as he climbed.

Dallas set his feet and pushed his body outward from the cliff face. While there were no cracks to give him purchase, there were more knobs than lower down. He turned his wrists and hands palm up in a technique called underclinging. With his feet pushing upward and outward, his hands resisted the downward pull of Martian gravity. He moved deliberately by moving mere inches at times. But after twenty minutes, he reached the top of the overhang. By pushing with his feet, he cleared his head above the precipice.

The sand and scree slope above the cliff looked to be about thirty degrees—walkable once he got on it. He scrutinized the edge of the cliff top. Eventually, he found a sound rock horn that protruded about six inches above the surrounding scree. He placed two runners around it and clipped them together with a carabiner before calling down, "Slack!"

LaDonna carefully played out more rope as Dallas clipped it into the carabiner. He alerted her of his progress: "Protection!"

Everyone gave out a silent sigh of relief. None looked forward to free-climbing the overhang without any top protection.

Dallas worked his feet further up the overhang until his arms were straight and could support his weight. He brought up his left leg and placed his foot on secure rock. Then he leaned into the slope and pushed gently with his left foot. Walking his hands farther away from the cliff face, he brought his right foot up, then crawled ahead on all fours until the cliff edge was three feet behind him. A large boulder rested on the slope in front of him. Dallas created a long runner with some loose webbing and double-wrapped it around the boulder, then clipped two carabiners to the runner. He clipped the carabiner directly to his tie-in loops and called down to his flight surgeon, "On top! Off belay!"

LaDonna unclipped the rope from her belay brake, unclipped it from her harness, and untied the figure eight knot. "Belay off!"

She carefully held the rope in her left hand, allowing it to slip through as Dallas pulled it up. She did not want the rope to swing out and drop off the edge of the ledge if Dallas happened to lose his grip on it. After Dallas pulled the rope over the top of the overhang, LaDonna tied-in to the next rope. Luis took over her belay position beside the double anchors and clipped the rope into his belay brake. After tying a fisherman's knot into the end of the rope, he nodded to LaDonna. "Belay on!"

"Climbing!" LaDonna followed Dallas's route, clipping in as she reached each anchor.

"Belay on!" It was Dave's voice.

Allie responded as she ascended the route taken by the previous three astronauts. "Climbing!"

Two climbers now ascended the cliff at once—LaDonna above and Allie below.

Dallas scanned to his left and his right, taking in the 180-degree panorama. The entire crater floor glowed in the mid-morning sun, as well as the slope he stood on. He saw one dust devil off in the distance near the central peak; otherwise, all was still and desolate.

The base of the next cliff loomed two hundred feet higher up the terrace slope he stood on. He was grateful for every inch his team did not have to climb. It would take them nearly all day as it was, and they still had to traverse sixty kilometers of unknown terrain, all before their oxygen ran out.

LaDonna's right hand appeared on the cliff top. She eventually got both arms up but could not raise her torso higher than the bottom of her sternum. She looked at Dallas. "I can't find any other footholds to push off of."

"Are you stable where you're at?"

"Yes, I can maintain this for several minutes."

Dallas quickly pulled out a three-foot runner and clipped it to the runner on the boulder. He wiggled into the runner, then unclipped from the larger runner on the boulder. He turned to LaDonna and sat down, legs extended, the runner around his waist. Then he pulled fifteen feet of the rope that lay coiled at his feet. He tied a bowline on the end, then holding the rope tightly in his left hand, wrapped the loose end around his back. Using his right hand, he tossed the bowline end down to LaDonna. "Can you get one of your feet to step into the bowline?"

LaDonna fished around until she felt the rope under the instep of her left boot. "I'm in."

Dallas coached her, "I'm going to lean back. Push up with your arms when you feel your boot start to lift, then see if you can get the other boot on top."

He pulled the slack out of the rope, then clamped his left hand hard and leaned back with all of his strength. LaDonna rose another six inches and lifted her right boot on top of the cliff. She flopped forward onto the slope. "God, I hope we don't have to negotiate any more overhangs." She was breathing heavily, half out of exertion, half out of terror.

Dallas waved her over. "Come clip into this boulder and take a breather."

"Gladly." Her relief was palpable. She worked her way to the boulder on all fours. Rather than stand to clip in, she clipped two carabiners to a short runner, then clipped one to the boulder webbing and the other to her harness ring. She turned out to face the crater floor below her and let out an audible sigh of relief. She called down to Luis, "Off belay!"

"Belay off!" Luis called back.

LaDonna breathed heavily for another 30 seconds until she caught her breath. Then she called out to Luis, "Belay on!"

He quickly replied, "On belay!"

Allie reached the ledge just as Luis began to ascend. He was a much stronger climber than LaDonna. He reached the top of the overhang in fifteen minutes, then performed a muscle up and flopped onto the slope.

"Show off," LaDonna growled at Luis's display of strength.

"Doc, I got a reputation as a lightweight to maintain."

It is nearly impossible to see inside the reflectorized visor of a pressure suit from the outside, but LaDonna was sure she saw a toothy grin inside Luis's helmet.

Allie joined them twenty-five minutes later. Dave began his ascent, removing protection as he climbed. It took him twenty-five minutes to reach the overhang. The collection of protection and tools not only weighed him down, they swayed, shifting his center of gravity in unpredictable ways. Dave was two feet below the top when his right hand lost its grip on a knob. His body fell away to his right, compromising the friction that held his left hand in place. "Fall!"

Allie felt the rope tense before she heard Dave's shout. She leaned back against the boulder and pulled the rope in her right hand toward her hip, engaging the belay brake. She arrested Dave's fall, but he dangled upside down below the edge of the overhang, three feet out of reach.

Climbing on Mars was complicated by wearing a pack. The respiration gear and the fuel cell that powered the suit heaters all resided inside the pack with quick connect fittings. Those fittings mated with integral fittings located on the suit proximal to the wearer's right-side kidney. The power cord quick connected to the left side of the suit near the wearer's left kidney. Removing the pack from the suit resulted in unconsciousness within two minutes, brain damage within five minutes, and death within seven.

Clipping his pack to a thrown rope, and then removing his pack to right himself, was not an option for Dave on Mars. However, the EPSILON engineers foresaw the need for climbers to right themselves, and they provided a high-strength loop at the top of the pack, just behind the wearer's head.

Dallas called down to Dave, "How far are you below the top?"

Dave's response was calm, "My feet are about three feet below. No rush. This is almost like being in zero-G. My blood isn't rushing to my head, like back on Earth."

"Dave, quit admiring the view." Concern and irritation mixed in Dallas's voice." The longer we delay, the less oxygen we have to make it to base."

Dallas quickly tied a loop using a figure eight knot in the end of one of the free ropes, then clipped a carabiner into the loop. Then he clipped the rope to the double webbing around the boulder.

"Rope!" Dallas gently tossed the end with the carabiner over the edge.

Dave called back, "Give me another foot of slack."

Dallas played out another foot of rope. Dave grabbed the carabiner, reached behind his helmet and clipped it to the pack loop. "Clipped in!"

Dallas pulled on the rope, using the carabiner like a pulley. The combined weight of Dave's pack and his torso in Martian gravity was less than one hundred pounds. Dallas continued to slowly pull Dave upright until Dave called out, "Stop!"

Dallas secured the rope in place with a double overhand knot. He walked over to the second free rope in case it was needed.

"Now that I'm upright, I can reach the cliff face." Dave gripped two knobs within his reach, pulled himself closer to the rock face, then planted his feet. "I've got purchase."

Allie pulled in slack just as Dave's hand appeared over the top of the edge. He quickly pulled himself up and onto the slope with the rest of the crew.

Dave had not even had time to stand before everyone's attention was directed to a metallic scraping sound emanating from the cliff edge. Two metallic "hands" firmly gripped the exposed rock immediately beside where Dave hauled himself up. Robbie's screen popped into view, revealing a smiley face. The mechanical assistant deftly flipped up and over his hands, landing on his treads. The upper unit then rotated 180 degrees, so the screen was facing everyone again.

Dallas was consternated. "Robbie, were you right under Dave just now?"

"Yes. I was approximately three feet below him. I was monitoring his vital signs. His heart rate and respiration briefly spiked, then quickly returned to the elevated levels comparable to all of yours."

Dallas could feel his blood pressure rise. "Why the hell didn't you assist?"

"You did not ask me to."

Dallas's controlled breathing was audible over everyone's helmet speakers. Presently, he spoke through gritted teeth. "Collect the gear and prepare to stage at the base of that inclined ledge over there."

He pointed to his right up the slope they stood on. There, at the base of the second cliff, about two hundred feet above them and a quarter-mile distant, a fault line ran diagonally upward. It created a jagged, eighteen-inch-wide ledge inclined at about sixty degrees the entire three-hundred-foot height of the cliff.

Gear was quickly sorted and returned to its original owners, who stowed it securely for the angled traverse.

Dallas called out, "Move out."

Five figures clad in dusty pressure suits trudged uphill, closely followed by a penitent dishwasher on tractor treads.

CHAPTER 19

"Chief, have you got a moment?" Detective Tom Henderson poked his head inside Police Chief Greg Wallace's open office door.

The chief looked up from his desk. "What is it, Tom?"

"It's a development in the Sherman suicide case. After going through his financial records, we found $50,000 was deposited into his checking account at the end of the business day yesterday."

The top cop perked up. "Have you traced the source?"

"Yes and no. The transfer originated from a Cayman Islands institution. But the account is completely anonymous. The account manager isn't exactly a font of information. He claims he has no record of ownership. The account was entirely funded by cryptocurrency, so it's untraceable. To my surprise, he sent me a copy of the account records. They confirm his statement. It appears that Sherman was paid to sabotage the Prospector 1 mission and suffered an attack of conscience in the end."

The chief nodded knowingly. "Thanks, Tom. I'll pass this on to EPSILON. In the meantime, get the case file ready to transfer to the FBI when they're brought in."

CHAPTER 20

Dallas read the time display on his visor and frowned. Everyone assembled at the base of the second cliff at 09:30. Scaling the first cliff had taken four hours.

"Stage all of our gear over here." He pointed to an area just left of the base of the inclined ledge. Everyone laid out the ropes, double-checking that no gear was missing.

From the vantage point of the staging area, the ledge looked like a steep ramp, ascending upward to the right at an impossibly steep angle. It was nearly three feet wide at the base, but in places, it narrowed to six inches. There were three locations along its length where the ledge disappeared entirely.

"Find distance." Crosshairs appeared on Dallas's visor.

He centered the top of the ramp on the crosshairs on his visor. "Fix distance." The crosshairs flashed red, and the number 354 appeared in red numerals.

Dallas turned his attention back to the group. "We'll ascend with the same teams and gear as our first ascent. I'll follow the ledge for my route. It's 354 feet long as measured along the incline, so we'll do this in two pitches again. It's a longer climb, but at least we don't have an overhang to contend with. Hopefully we'll make better time."

Just as Dallas concluded organizing for the ascent, an alarm softly chimed in his helmet speaker. "Who's running low on O_2?"

The alarm announced that someone in the group had only fifteen minutes of oxygen remaining. LaDonna had reminded Dallas at the bottom of the slope that they did not have enough oxygen to make it up the next pitch. Dallas waited until they were at the base of the cliff in order to maximize use of the dwindling supply.

"It's mine," Luis spoke up. "Robbie, can you swap out my bottle?"

The team had trained extensively on replacing a depleted oxygen bottle. Yet in spite of all their training, the average time to remove and reconnect the air supply was forty seconds. As anyone who has stuck their head in an inverted goldfish bowl could tell you, forty seconds is a long time to rebreathe the same air. So they let Robbie perform the task, since his four hands could replace a bottle while holding a spare, all in ten seconds or less.

"I can assist you, Luis." Robbie positioned himself beside Luis when the group assembled around the climbing gear.

"Thanks, bud." Luis turned his back toward Robbie and dropped to his knees. Robbie deftly opened his robotics handler's pack and substituted a full red oxygen bottle for the depleted one in less than eight seconds. He discarded the empty bottle on the ground and closed the pack.

LaDonna critiqued Robbie's technique. "Robbie, honey, you swapped the wrong bottle. You're supposed to give Luis a blue bottle."

Everyone laughed. To avoid confusion, oxygen bottles were bright red, nitrogen bottles bright blue. Nitrogen, of course, was not metabolized by the body. Its chief function in a pressure suit was maintaining pressure. A bottle of nitrogen could last a week or longer, barring a leak in the suit.

Robbie protested, "Dr. Pleasant, I replaced Luis's red oxygen bottle with another red oxygen bottle."

LaDonna patted Robbie affectionately. "Don't worry about it, Robbie. I'll swap Luis's bottles next time to make sure the blue bottle gets hooked up. He always says I leave him breathless."

Everyone laughed harder. It was the first real laughter since the group set out that morning. The laughter had just died down when the same low oxygen alarm chimed in Dallas's helmet, accompanied by a yellow flashing symbol on the lower left of his visor.

Everything else being equal, oxygen consumption was proportional to body mass. Luis was the heaviest crew member, followed by Dallas.

"Robbie, replace all of our O$_2$ bottles," Dallas ordered the medical assistant. "Start with me, then proceed based on our body mass in decreasing order."

"Yes, commander. Please lower to your knees so I can reach your pack easily."

Robbie dutifully replaced oxygen bottles, proceeding from Dallas, to Dave, to LaDonna, and finally Allie. Soon, five empty oxygen bottles littered the ground. It reminded Dallas of video he had seen of Camp Four on Mount Everest.

As Robbie closed up Allie's pack, Dallas and LaDonna reached for the rope nearest to the ledge. He tied into his tie-in loops, while she attached her belay brake to her belay loop, then clipped the rope into her belay brake about ten feet from Dallas's end of the rope. She tied another fisherman's knot to the far end of the rope, then faced Dallas. They inspected each other's work and gave each other a nod of assent.

Dallas turned to face the ledge. This climb would be especially tricky. He intended to follow the ledge. But setting the protection required a great deal of care. Here, the line of protection would be set at a sixty-degree angle as he ascended the ledge. If he fell, the nearest anchor would likely be off to the side and below him. So instead of falling straight down, Dallas would swing like a pendulum, putting tremendous lateral pressure on anchors designed and set to be pulled in one direction only: straight down.

Dallas planned to set anchors closer together to mitigate the length of the pendulum swing. Instead of setting anchors every twenty feet apart as he had done on the first cliff, he would set them fifteen feet apart. This would increase the number of anchors he set by a third, plus the additional anchors required to cover the extra length of the two pitches. So many anchors hung from Dallas's racks, it restricted his arm movements on the bottom fifty feet of the ramp.

The call and response announced the climb to all. "Belay on!" … "Climbing!"

Dallas progressed slowly, but steadily. He reached the first gap in the ledge, one hundred feet up its length. The ledge was barely six inches wide on either side of the gap. The gap itself was about six feet wide, too far to step across. Due to the steep incline, the far side was at eye level to him. As the ledge narrowed, Dallas positioned himself face-in to the cliff. As he stood at the bottom lip of the gap, he extended his right arm, easily touching the far side with his fingertips.

Rather than jumping the gap, Dallas opted to climb up the face of the cliff until he was high enough to traverse to his right a few feet and stand on the upper ledge. The rock was nearly featureless on this part of the cliff face. There were no cracks. Projections were barely a quarter inch. It took him several minutes to ascend high enough to begin his traverse, little more than a step three feet to his right. He placed his right boot on the upper ledge and transferred his weight, grateful for the wider purchase.

As he released his left hand, the segment of ledge under his right foot gave way. "Fall!"

The last anchor that Dallas placed was located below him and about six feet to his left. He swung downward and to his left as if he were the bob of a plumb. As the load transferred from right to left, the anchor chock worked its way out of the crack he had placed it in. Dallas went weightless again as he plummeted downward another ten feet and five more to the left. His protection risked unzipping, and he knew it.

As he swung, Dallas "walked" the wall face with his feet, arresting his momentum. As he moved past vertical, the chock wiggled outward. Dallas arrested his swing to about half before his momentum reversed direction. Nearly half out of the crack by the time he stopped his swing at vertical, the chock still held.

Dallas tried to locate his partner. "'Donna, where are you?"

LaDonna was pulled up and rested feet-first against the cliff face about five feet off the ground. The bottom anchor nearly pulled free, but held her weight for now. "I'm about five feet off the ground. The bottom anchor held."

"I'm about fifteen feet below my anchor," said Dallas. "The top anchor popped out. It slid down my rope and is resting against my figure eight knot. As I climb, you will lower back to the ground. Call out when you're back on the deck."

Dallas worked upward, aided by LaDonna's counterweight. He was five feet below the ledge when she called out, "I'm back down. Belay on!"

"Climbing!" Dallas continued up until his weight rested on the ledge again. He examined the chock that held him. Barely half an inch had maintained contact with the sides of the crack. He repositioned it and resumed working his way back to the gap, which was now about eight feet wide.

This time, Dallas climbed twenty feet vertical and traversed about ten feet. The ledge was about a foot wide at that location, and he hoped it would be more stable. He reset the top anchor that pulled loose when he fell, then continued on up the rock face. As he got higher above the ledge, the quality of the rock improved, becoming easier to climb.

After traversing without incident, he finally stood with both feet on the ledge again. He stopped and carefully examined the ledge ahead of him. It widened to three feet over a distance of thirty feet, then abruptly ended in another gap, this one ten feet wide. The ledge beyond was less than a foot wide for at least another hundred feet.

He called down to LaDonna, "How much rope?"

"About thirty feet!" her response came back.

"Climbing!" Dallas resumed his way up the inclined ledge.

LaDonna counted down the remaining distance of rope as she played it out for Dallas. "Twenty feet … ten feet … five feet … four feet … three feet."

Dallas reached the wide part of the ledge, relieved to find places to set a double anchor within arm's reach. Once he was clipped in, he called down to LaDonna, "Off belay!"

"Belay off!"

Dallas carefully coiled up the rope back and forth across the back of his neck as LaDonna prepared to ascend the route he created. She arrived beside him about half an hour later, followed by Luis a half hour after her.

When Luis arrived, Dallas and LaDonna prepared for the second pitch. Dallas led it without incident. Thirty minutes after he started, he stepped off the top of the ledge onto the slope above the cliff. The nearest boulder he could use for an anchor lay about thirty feet upslope. He walked up and anchored to it as he did atop the first cliff. "Off belay!" he notified LaDonna.

"Belay off!" echoed back.

As Dallas coiled his rope, he examined the crater spread out before him, as he had three hours earlier. The shadows had diminished to a remnant clinging to the northernmost crater wall off to the west. He counted three dust devils drifting northwest to southeast across the crater floor on the near side of the central peak. Their movement indicated that the daily prevailing wind had begun. But there was little evidence of wind where he sat. The remaining tier of crater wall behind him shielded him. Even with the sun nearly directly overhead, the light felt pale, as on a winter day in the high northern latitudes on Earth. His visor readout advised him it was a balmy 19° F. He noted the time: 11:32.

Dave arrived just under two hours later, with Robbie right on his heels. The climbing gear reapportioned as before, the group headed upslope toward the final cliff at 14:39. Hunched shoulders and frequent foot scuffs as they walked betrayed their fatigue. From his position up front, Dallas knew they were tired by the lack of banter.

He angled toward his left, more-or-less directly above where they scaled the first cliff, now five hundred feet below them, aiming toward a large gully etched into the upper third of the otherwise monolithic cliff face. A fluvial fan nearly 150 feet high had been deposited at the base of the cliff below the gully. That represented a 150-foot head start on the 400-foot-high cliff confronting him. Dallas reached the top of the fan and noted it was now 15:15.

"Same order as before. I'll make for the bottom of that hanging couloir and end the first pitch there." After a brief pause, Dallas added, "Let's get the hell out of this glory hole by nightfall."

He tied himself in to the end of the rope and approached the cliff face, Led Zeppelin's "Cashmere" playing in everyone's helmets.

CHAPTER 21

Mission Director Malcom McDowell and Flight Operations Director Ann Waters stared across the table video conferencing with Steve Coleman, the field director for the Santa Monica field office of the FBI. Neither Malcom nor Ann had any idea of the man's age. In many ways, he looked the part of a timeless beach bum. He sported a full head of sun-lightened, sandy-blond hair, flawlessly tanned skin without crease or wrinkle, and teeth so straight and white that Ann swore she saw a twinkle when he smiled. She imagined the suit he wore stuffed with bulging muscles. Steve Coleman was the visual opposite of Malcom, who shaved his head to camouflage his premature baldness. Malcom's smile revealed a substantial gap between his front teeth, their white accentuated by his ebony skin. Malcom's open off-the-rack suit coat always fell away from his ample mid-section.

"Thank you for making time in your busy schedule, Director Coleman. Ann Waters, my flight operations director, is seated beside me. Do I assume correctly that Chief Wallace briefed you on the criminal interference with our Mars Prospector 1 mission?"

The perfect smile responded, "Malcom, it's the least I could do given the circumstances. I'm following the updates on the crew as I'm sure the entire country is.

"We received the case files from Santa Maria PD. We're combing through them, and your analysis of the cyberattack transmission that originated from the Moon. I've assigned Field Agent Ted Gilmore to your case. Ted has contacted our Financial Crimes Division to get them backtracking the source of the funds deposited into your late employee's account."

Ann shifted uncomfortably. She wanted nothing to do with this conversation. She just couldn't accept that Cliff could have betrayed the mission, in spite of the evidence against him.

"Over the next week," Steve Coleman continued, "Agent Gilmore will interview many of your staff. I promise you, Malcom, we'll find the people who did this to EPSILON."

"Thank you, Steve." Malcom's attention turned to operations. "I'd appreciate coordinating the interview schedules with Agent Gilmore. With enough advance coordination with him, I can schedule replacements for our critical personnel. It's imperative to keep the disruption to our operation to a minimum. Our astronauts' lives are literally hanging in the balance right now."

"Of course, Malcom. We'll make every effort to minimize any disruption to your operations. Agent Gilmore will contact you sometime in the next few hours."

The screen went blank, even as Ann felt a shiver of a new fear. It wasn't that the "critical personnel" might be disrupted but the thought that Cliff Sherman's INCO position was included in that list. If it was possible someone she trusted as much as Cliff had sabotaged them, could others on staff also be compromised? Suspicion and paranoia threatened to twist her sleep-deprived mind, and she shook it off. They had enough real problems to face; no need to assume new, unfounded ones. But the doubt had wormed into a corner of her mind, waiting patiently to reemerge at its next opportunity.

Malcom and Ann stood silently for a moment, then returned to the flight control room together. There they resumed helplessly watching their astronauts attempt to exit the crater that they had crash-landed into yesterday.

CHAPTER 22

"On belay!" … "Belay on!"

LaDonna gave extra emphasis to her response, as much to raise her own spirits as to raise those of the three crewmates standing behind her.

As Dallas climbed, he noted immediately that the character of this rock differed from what he had climbed earlier. The rock below was obviously igneous in origin, possibly of the original molten floor of Hellas Planitia when it was created by an impact of planetary proportions. This rock he now climbed seemed to be sedimentary in nature. It had distinct horizontal layers. And it was brittle. Just setting a chock sometimes caused the edges of a crack to spall. He was thankful the cracks were deep enough to reset the chocks into. Once reset, they held firm—usually.

Dallas had climbed fifty feet above the fluvial fan when he encountered a layer of rock so soft, he could scuff material off the surface with his gloved hand alone. The soft layer was twelve feet thick. He stood ten feet above his last anchor, examining the crack he had followed up the cliff face. It continued upward through the soft layer and terminated another seventy feet above him at the base of the hanging gully. After considering his options, he called down to the four crew members below, "I'm going to widen this crack enough to provide hand and foot jams. It's too soft to set anchors."

Dallas pulled up his piton hammer, leaving it attached to his rack by its lanyard. Using the pick end, he scraped the two sides of the crack, widening it four inches—enough to fit a gloved hand or a boot into while still providing friction against the sides. He beveled each side of the bottom of what he widened to minimize the risk that it would flake away under the weight of a jammed boot.

When he finished shaping the crack, he jammed his left fist in, reset his feet and repeated the process eighteen inches above the first jam hole. He continued in this manner until he reached the more competent rock above. There he wedged in a chock, clipped his rope into it, and let out a deep breath. The work had cost him an extra half hour. It was now 16:01. The west crater wall was fully in shadow. The darkness nearly reached to the base of the central peak. He called down to LaDonna, "That's the last of the soft rock. Give me rope faster, now."

Twenty minutes later, Dallas stood in the base of the hanging gulley. He ran runners around two rock horns on opposite sides of the couloir and clipped himself in.

"Off belay!" … "Belay off!"

After coiling his rope beside him, Dallas surveyed the couloir. He fixed his gaze on what appeared to be the crest. "Measure distance. Fix distance."

One hundred-twenty-nine feet to freedom. As big as this crater was, it felt more like a tiger trap. He wanted out.

Dallas noted that the back of the couloir climbed at a nearly vertical grade, matching the cliff face it was etched into. The gulley sidewalls and the back were studded with numerous ledges and knobs. At its widest, near the top, it measured five feet wide. Where he stood, it was three feet wide. Placing minimal protection, he could be out in about twenty minutes.

LaDonna joined Dallas at 16:55. What had taken him over an hour to lead climb, she had scaled in twenty-five minutes. When Luis arrived at 17:14, Dallas quickly tied into his end of the rope and immediately started up. The climbing was so easy he only placed anchors every twenty feet. When his head breached the top of the gully, his visor read 17:36.

The slope above the third cliff lay much flatter than the terraces below. The ground sloped away at five degrees by his estimate and crested about a quarter mile distant. Dallas heaved himself up onto the flat ground, stepping five feet back from the cliff edge.

"Off belay!" His voice cracked with emotion.

"Belay off! "LaDonna didn't bother to hide her excitement. The rest joined her with exclamations of their own.

Ten minutes later, LaDonna breached the top. Dallas set runners around a boulder for her to clip into to belay for Luis. She clipped in and shouted down, "Belay off, thank God!"

Luis quickly tied-in to his loops and called up, "Doc, you should be thanking me. I'm the one doing all the work belaying you. Belay on! Get me outta here!"

"On belay! Come on up, doctor's orders."

Luis climbed up in seven minutes. He walked over to LaDonna and Dallas, giving them high fives.

Allie joined the celebration ten minutes later. "Belay off! God, I thought we'd never get out of there!"

"Off belay! Don't leave without me." Dave called out again as quickly as he could tie in, "Belay on!"

"On belay! Don't delay!" Allie called back cheerfully.

Dave shot back, "On belay, don't delay? That's the best you've got? You are such a nerd, Ms. O'Donnell!"

"Zip it until you're up here, mister. I got a base to walk to."

Even with the added duty of cleaning the protection, Dave arrived in nine minutes. A confusing array of hugs, high fives, and back slaps greeted him.

Robbie crested the cliff in time to witness the commotion as it died down. Everyone redistributed their gear. Dallas and Dave re-coiled their ropes to pack away in preparation for the long hike.

Luis walked over toward the cliff edge, then stopped three feet from it to admire their accomplishment. He dropped his rope there in order to coil it for the trek to the base, pausing and looking out over the crater floor a thousand feet below. The sun was low in the sky, 10 degrees above the western crater rim. The shadow from the west wall reached the base of the east wall. As Luis bent over to gather his rope, he noted the time on his helmet visor: 18:14.

Dallas had nearly finishing coiling his rope when he felt a gust of wind push him from behind. A shadow fell across the group. A second gust quickly followed, much stronger than the first. Dallas tasted the tang of fear when he recognized what was happening. "Down! Everybody hit the deck!"

He stood close enough to Allie to grab her by the arm as he dropped down flat. Startled, LaDonna and Dave followed them to the ground.

Luis casually finished coiling his rope, watching the group as they dropped. "Come on, it's just a little wind."

A third gust struck. A dense cloud of dust enveloped Luis. He locked eyes with Dallas just as Dallas called out again, "Dust devil! Get Down!"

The dust closed in. Everyone turned their visors away from the wind. Sand and pebbles up to half an inch in diameter pelted whatever faced into it. The wind increased for what seemed an eternity. It threatened to roll the women over, their packs disproportionately larger on their lighter bodies than the men's. Then, as quickly as it started, the wind died down. The air cleared.

Allie screamed when she recognized what had happened. "Luis!"

Dallas saw the empty space that Luis had occupied prior to the wind. "Everyone stay back!"

Too shocked to stand, he crawled on all fours the ten feet to the spot where Luis had stood, then peered over the cliff edge. Luis lay face-down and motionless near the bottom of the fluvial fan, four hundred feet below them. Judging from the disturbance pattern visible on the cone of soil and rock, Luis had impacted near the base of the cliff some 250 feet below, then slid down the remaining 150 feet to the base of the alluvial fan. LaDonna crawled beside Dallas and looked down at Luis as well. Dallas cast a sideways glance at her to warn her back.

"Sorry, commander. I outrank you in this situation." LaDonna cautiously placed her arms at the cliff edge, placed her weight on them, and leaned out over the edge. She noted

Luis's left arm had an extra bend in it between the elbow and the wrist.

"Luis! Please respond!" LaDonna paused, but no response was forthcoming. "Luis, if you can hear my voice, move your right arm."

The pressure suit remained motionless. She addressed Robbie, "Robbie, are you receiving any of Luis's biometric telemetry?"

"I am, Dr. Pleasant. Respiration 19, pulse rate 59, blood pressure 98 over 46. Based on these parameters and his brain activity, I conclude that Luis is unconscious."

Dallas's gaze remained fixed on the motionless pressure suit of his mechanical engineer and Robbie's handler. He disregarded Dave and Allie as they crept up beside him to see their fallen comrade. Now he queried the digital assistant, "Robbie, how far are we from Prospector Base if we continue on our intended route?"

"Sir, we are 59.997 kilometers from Prospector Base."

"So if we maintain a walking pace of two kilometers per hour, it should take us about thirty hours to get there from here?"

"That is correct, sir."

Dallas eyed the project time display on his visor. It read 18:16. "Robbie, if we extract Luis from the ledge, will you be able to carry him to base if he's unable to walk?"

"Yes, sir. I can configure my arms as needed to safely support Luis in any position, depending on the type and extent of his injuries."

Dallas remained deep in thought for another minute. His eyes remained fixed on Luis's motionless body below. Then he broke the silence. "Everyone step back from the cliff edge. Reconvene at our gear. We have a group decision to make."

The group slowly backed away from the cliff edge and returned to their partially packed gear. Dallas grabbed the rope that Luis had placed on the ground just before the vortex hit. He marveled that it had stayed in place. It lay coiled around a large rock. When the wind had hit, the rock prevented the rope from sliding over the edge with Luis. It was the one piece of good luck in the midst of an otherwise disastrous event. If that rope had gone over with Luis, it would have severely limited Dallas's options.

Dallas reached the group. "Did everyone hear my exchange with Robbie?"

Three helmets nodded.

"Here's our situation, then," he continued. "We have about thirty-six hours of oxygen left. Assuming we can maintain a pace comparable to our pace across the crater floor, we could reach Prospector Base in thirty hours. That's a big if. The resolution of the imagery that we used to plot our route was poor. While the terrain looked gentle from this point forward, we could still run into substantial features that could hinder our progress.

"We have three ropes. While it's not optimal, we can splice two ropes together for a rappel down to the terrace. We have enough daylight for Dr. Pleasant and me to reach Luis before nightfall.

"What is unknown is the extent of Luis's injuries. They may be so severe that we will simply be unable to move him. Assuming that we can move him, we only have six hours to get him stabilized, extract him from the terrace, and resume our trek to base, at full speed.

"Here are our options. One, we salvage Luis's oxygen, leave him in place, and proceed to Prospector Base, with a slightly bolstered oxygen supply."

Allie blurted out, "We can't just leave him here to die! If we do, and I walk into that airlock breathing oxygen from his spare tank, I'll never be able to look myself in the mirror the rest of my life! How can you even say that?"

Dallas continued, "Or two, Dr. Pleasant, Robbie, and I rappel down to the terrace. Dr. Pleasant and Robbie will evaluate Luis's injuries and stabilize him, if possible. In the meantime, Dave and Allie will rig up a zee pulley so you can haul Luis up.

"If Luis can be stabilized, then we'll carry him to the base of the cliff. Dr. Pleasant and Robbie will climb out first. 'Donna, use your ascenders. It will be the safest way up in the dark. I will accompany Luis, using the rope as my fall restraint. It's risky, but our only option is to extract Luis at night. If we wait until morning to lift him out, *none* of us will make it to Prospector Base in time.

"If anything, *anything,* goes wrong with this plan, all able-bodied persons are to abandon Luis, and whoever else has been injured. Salvage what oxygen that you can and make for Prospector Base with all speed.

"How do you vote? Allie?"

She was in tears. "Option two. I'm not going on if we can save Luis."

"Noted. Dave?"

"I vote for option two. Luis still owes me twenty bucks from our last poker game. If we leave him here, I'll never collect."

Allie elbowed Dave in the ribs. Hard.

Dave flinched but maintained his balance. "Okay, okay! If he makes it, I'll write off the twenty bucks!"

Allie reared back to deliver Dave another blow when Dallas grabbed her arm. "Enough, you two. We have a long walk to base, no matter how this turns out. Dr. Pleasant, how do you vote?"

"I vote for option two, provided this evacuation doesn't go beyond midnight. While I, too, could not forgive myself if we just left Luis here, I could not bear losing you all trying to bring him with us."

Dallas voted last, "And I also vote option two. That makes it unanimous—"

Robbie interjected before Dallas could finish, "Sir, I also vote for option two. Luis is my friend."

Dallas's throat tightened ever so slightly as he looked over to the digital assistant. "Robbie, accompany and assist Dr. Pleasant and me. You're too heavy for the rappel. You'll have to free climb both down and back up."

Dallas turned back to the group. "Dave and Allie, get one end of Luis's rope anchored for the rappel. Dr. Pleasant, put on your harness and attach your belay brake."

Dallas retrieved his own climbing harness and belay brake. After securing himself in, he retrieved the second rope and tied it to the end of Luis's rope with a double fisherman's knot. Then he coiled the newly spliced rope into a single coil. He picked up the coil, walked to the edge of the cliff, and flung the rope out into empty space. The rope reached the terrace at the base of the cliff with several large loops of slack.

Dallas walked back to inspect the anchor Dave and Allie had installed at the end of the rope. He tugged hard on the rope to ensure the anchor was sound. Then he walked to the edge of the cliff, where he clipped a loop of rope into his belay brake. Facing the anchored end of the rope, he leaned back, holding the rope below the brake in his right hand. He tested the braking friction a few times. When he was satisfied, he backed up to the edge of the cliff, still facing the anchor end. Then, in one fluid motion, he leaned back, flexed his knees, and pushed out and away from the cliff. As his body disappeared over the edge, the sun set behind the west crater rim.

CHAPTER 23

Dallas spotted LaDonna as she completed the final ten feet of her rappel. Once on the ground, he helped her unclip from the rope. Then he called up to Dave and Allie at the top of the cliff, "Dr. Pleasant is off rope. Prepare the zee pulley and await further instructions."

"You got it, Flash," Allie's voice responded through his helmet speakers.

Dallas and LaDonna proceeded down the alluvial fan toward Luis in total darkness. The beams from their headlamps cast about until they fell on Luis's still form. Robbie reached the bottom of the cliff, rotated his treads down to the ground, and rolled toward Luis behind Dallas and LaDonna. Dallas allowed the flight surgeon first access to Luis, who had not moved since he had fallen.

The doctor queried her medical assistant, "Robbie, what are Luis's vitals?"

"Respiration 19, pulse rate 57, blood pressure 95 over 44. His brain activity is unchanged. Luis is still unconscious."

LaDonna kneeled beside Luis, observing his face as best she could through the sides of his visor. "It's difficult to see much detail. There's quite a bit of blood pooled on his visor. His nose and lips look swollen, but the blood source seems to be his nose. I don't see any scratching on the back of his helmet, so it appears that he landed face-down. It wouldn't surprise me if his nose is broken. Lack of swelling or bruising around his eyes contraindicates any fracturing of the orbits or zygomatic processes. I can't evaluate the rest of his cranium, but his persistent unconscious state indicates he may have a concussion."

Next, LaDonna pressed her fingers simultaneously on both sides of his neck. After working her fingers up and down its length several times, she reported, "Swelling on his neck. I don't feel any bone displacement or movement, but I can't rule it out. Pretty hard to palpate through his pressure suit and my gloves. I can't rule out a sprained neck."

She examined his spine and pelvis, and both legs, finding no fractures.

Rocking back on her heels, she explained, "I won't examine his thorax until he regains consciousness. I don't want to risk puncturing a lung if he's broken any ribs."

Next, she turned her attention to Luis's arms. Starting with his right hand, she worked her way up to the man's right shoulder. "Right arm and shoulder appear uninjured."

Then she began with his left hand. "Left hand is okay."

Noting the extra "joint" in his left forearm, she stopped and pulled out a moldable foam sheet splint from Robbie's medical supplies. "I'm going to attempt to reset his left forearm before I evaluate the rest of his left arm and shoulder. Robbie, can you perform this procedure on someone in a pressure suit?"

"Yes, Doctor. I can sense the movement of bone better than you, because my hand is not gloved like yours. Please hold his upper arm immobile while I perform the reset."

LaDonna held Luis's upper arm with both hands. Robbie placed one "hand" over the fracture site and grasped Luis' left wrist with another. He pulled evenly on the wrist until he sensed the radius and ulna bones pop back into place. "His forearm is reset, Doctor. You may apply your splint."

LaDonna molded the splint around Luis's forearm and secured it in place with duct tape. Then she evaluated his upper arm and left shoulder. "Left collarbone is broken, too." She rocked back on her knees, deep in thought. "Can't reset it with his suit on. The best we can do is immobilize his left arm to minimize any movement. While we're at it, we need to immobilize his head as a precaution."

She turned to Robbie. "Robbie, get me a roll of duct tape. Pull off four three-foot-long segments and have them ready for me.

"Dallas, I'm immobilizing his head with a cross pattern of tape. I'll fasten one end of a three-foot segment to his back, over the top of his helmet, then fasten the other end to his chest. I'll fix the first two segments to each side of his back and cross them at the top of his helmet. What I need you to do is roll Luis onto his back while Robbie holds Luis's head, so his neck doesn't twist or bend. I'll hold the two ends of tape off the ground and fasten them to his chest after Luis is on his back. Any questions?"

"No questions," Dallas and Robbie answered in unison.

They spent ten minutes taping up Luis, adjusting his position several times until the tape was in place. Luis ended up in a seated position. LaDonna gently applied pressure to the sides, front and back of Luis's helmet. It stayed in place relative to his body. Then she placed his left forearm across his stomach and duct taped it in place by wrapping two loops of tape around his arm and chest. "How's he doing, Robbie?"

"Respiration 25, pulse rate 62, blood pressure 98 over 56. His brain activity resembles REM sleep. Luis may be regaining consciousness."

LaDonna was encouraged. "That's good to hear. Robbie, carry Luis in a reclining position to the bottom of the rope. Dallas and I will meet you there."

Dallas watched as the AI Assistant lifted the patient with such care that he had to question his earlier disbelief that Luis was, in fact, this RBI's friend. Then Dallas and LaDonna followed Robbie up the slope of the alluvial fan. Their head lamps cast ovals of light on the ground in front of them.

When they reached the rope at the top of the fan, Robbie seated Luis on the ground, his back propped against the base of the cliff. Dallas helped LaDonna attach her ascenders. She scaled the 250 feet to the top of the cliff in less than ten minutes as Robbie free climbed beside her. Once they cleared the top,

Robbie positioned himself so he could observe his stricken handler's progress from above.

Dallas quickly tied a figure eight knot ten feet from the end of the rope. He clipped it into Luis's belay loop, thankful that Luis had not removed his climbing harness before he fell. Then he created a cross tie between Luis's shoulder straps using more duct tape. He tugged on the cross tie to make sure it was secure, clipping it to the rope above the figure eight knot. This would ensure that Luis remained upright even though his pack made him top heavy.

Dallas tied a second figure eight knot in the end of the rope ten feet below Luis and clipped it to his belay loop. He would free climb beside Luis, where he could monitor him, and free him should his suit get snagged on a projection of rock. The tie-in served as his emergency fall protection. Normally, he would have his own independent rope, but there was no more rope to use. The fate of the two men was literally tied together. Dallas looked up into the darkness and called out, "Pull Luis up!"

The rope tensed, and Luis hovered above the ground. He swung gently from side to side as he was pulled upward in six-inch increments.

Dallas followed along beside him, working his way up the same crack as the first time. He recalled his unease with the flaky rock. Relying on his head lamp made him even less confident. About fifty feet up, he ordered the others to stop pulling Luis so he could catch up. He paused at the soft rock layer. The passage of the climbers following him up the first time had eroded the hand and footholds he had previously dug out. He carefully reshaped the holes to improve his grip.

By the time he reached the midpoint of the cliff where the rock became more competent, Dallas sweated profusely from the added exertion and stress. He called for another stop so he could rest and catch his breath. Sweating in a pressure suit was not good. If it got in his eyes, he would not be able to wipe them to clear his vision or get the sting out. Worse still, if his visor fogged up, he had no idea how long it would take for his internal climate control to evaporate it. He could be blind for hours, for all he knew.

But after a few minutes, he regained his breath and his composure. The suit climate control prevented his visor from fogging. He silently thanked the engineers who had designed the suit, then took a deep breath and resumed climbing.

Fifteen minutes later, Dallas and Luis were even with the hanging couloir, their final route out of the crater. But this time, they remained out on the cliff face, about twelve feet to the right. Dave and Allie anchored the rope to the side of the gulley to avoid friction on the rope where the gulley met the cliff face. Dallas called another halt and considered the remaining 130 feet of cliff, scanning carefully on both sides of the rope to determine which offered the best hand and footholds. He settled on the left side, noting that as the gulley widened at the top, the edge came close enough to the rope to allow him to work into the gulley, with its superior rock projections.

Twenty minutes later, Dallas rested on his hands and knees as Allie and Dave unclipped Luis from the rope. Dallas unclipped himself. He noted the time on his project clock: 23:53. He estimated they had 36.5 hours of oxygen left. "Untie all of the knots, collect all of your anchors and pulley hardware, and coil both ropes. Leave Luis in his climbing harness. We leave in five minutes."

Dallas stowed his gear, ensuring that he left nothing behind. Once again, he pulled his smartphone out of his sleeve pocket and tapped his visor app. The thin vertical line reappeared in the center of his field of view. He tapped in N 58° 00' 00" W and then 45, the bearing and distance in kilometers to reach the saddle above the valley that contained their destination, Prospector Base. The bearing the vertical line represented once again appeared in his upper right field of view. He turned his head back and forth in the general direction they needed to go. Whenever the line crossed over their intended direction of travel, the line and the bearing flashed a bright red on his visor. He tapped his app one more time for the low-visibility setting.

Martian nights were much darker than on Earth. There was no moon to reflect the light from the sun. The dust in the atmosphere filtered out most starlight. Only the brightest stars were visible in the Martian night sky.

The low-visibility setting caused the red line on Dallas's visor display to flash every time his visor crossed the bearing whenever his head turned. He found the setting annoying, but since he was unable to make out any landmarks in the gloom of night, it allowed him to maintain a straight line of travel. He walked in the direction of the new bearing and exclaimed, "No rest for the wicked. Move out!"

The party of four walked in a northwesterly direction, once again followed by Robbie, who this time bore their wounded crewmate. The crater wall dropped off precipitously on their left. Gradually, the cliff edge receded from the range of their headlamps as the crater wall arced away from their direction of travel. Within half an hour, they crested the crater rim and began the slow descent down the gentle slope of the impact ejecta. They couldn't see it in the dark, but below them and beyond the impact ejecta field stretched the Hellas Planitia floor. It was mile after mile of undulating terrain, a complex mixture of lava flows, regolith and dust. As they walked, their headlamps cast tiny ovals of light on the dusty ground, islands in the inky vastness.

CHAPTER 24

"Ann, can you meet me in the conference room?" Obvious to Ann through her headphone, Malcom's voice bespoke his discomfort. He had left the mission director's flight control console to take a phone call in the conference room a few minutes earlier.

All was quiet in SaMMCon as the staff poured over updated satellite imagery. They continued following the progress of the missing Prospector 1 landing party. Ann slipped off her headset and headed for the hallway leading to the conference room.

When she opened the door, she caught Malcom rubbing his temples. He looked up, worry creasing his forehead. "The FBI just shared their initial blood toxicology results. They found chloroform in Cliff's blood. The concentration was high enough to render him unconscious."

Ann felt rummy from viewing satellite imagery for the past several hours. "He knocked himself out with chloroform? Malcom, that doesn't make any sense."

Malcom closed his eyes and resumed rubbing his temples. "He didn't knock himself out. No chloroform was found in the bathroom, let alone anywhere else in his house."

Ann understood. "If someone else knocked him out, Cliff didn't kill himself, did he?"

"It appears that he was rendered unconscious, then set in the bathtub, and electrocuted with his own hair dryer. Between this and the untraceable $50,000 deposit to his bank account, it looks like someone staged his suicide."

"Meaning he was murdered." Ann's eyes widened with the realization. Conflicting emotions crowded each other for her attention—elation at the news that Cliff did not commit suicide, and an even deeper sense of loss that someone would have wanted to kill him.

Malcom dropped his hands to the tabletop and sat slightly more erect. "What isn't clear is why. Outside of that $50,000 deposit, his life was uncomplicated. He was squeaky clean in his employment background check. He remained squeaky clean in each annual security update. Cliff's life revolved around his work here."

Ann cocked her head to one side. "Do you think this still may have had something to do with the cyberattacks on Prospector 1?"

Malcom looked squarely at Ann. "I had the same thought. The FBI hasn't yet discerned a clear motive for his killing. They warned me not to jump to conclusions, but …" Malcom shook his head. "So many things keep going through my mind. If he had helped with the cyberattacks, maybe whoever paid him to do that feared he'd say something."

"Yes, but why pay him off, in that case?"

Malcom shrugged. "Maybe that was only a down payment? Maybe Cliff demanded more money after the fact?"

Ann recalled her own doubts and shook her head. "It makes no sense. We all knew Cliff as dedicated to this mission. I don't believe any of that. I won't believe that."

"But someone killed him," Malcom said. "And if Cliff's death is somehow tied to the sabotage, we may all be in danger.

Malcom paused to consider his course of action, an expression of resolve replacing his earlier weariness, "Ann, I'm ordering all SaMMCon staff restricted to the property. That includes all night shift and backup flight control staff. I'll have HR pull in everyone currently off site and convert our office building across the parking lot into living quarters. Once here, no one is to leave our campus without an escort by the police or our security staff."

His eyes refocused on Ann. "Ann, please inform the day shift. I hate to add a distraction like this when we're trying to focus on locating the landing party, but I can't take the chance of losing anyone else."

Ann objected, "Malcom, what if it turns out to be someone else here at SaMMCon? This restriction to campus could put us all at risk."

Malcom explained his rationale to his flight director. "There's another piece of info the FBI shared with me, but it's not to be repeated. There were absolutely no prints in Cliff's apartment but his. Whoever did this was both thorough and methodical—someone who's done this before, a professional. If it was someone here at EPSILON, I'm convinced that degree of pathological cunning would have shown up on our annual psych evaluations."

Ann considered Malcom's logic. "I have to agree, Malcom. But why kill Cliff—to cover their tracks? Tracks to where, or what?"

"Or who. I wish I knew, Ann. But until we know the answers to those questions, I think it's prudent to keep everyone close, where we can better control their security."

Ann nodded her head in agreement, then spun around and returned to the flight control room. As she reentered the control room, she found everyone gathered around the INCO's workstation. Courtney Plumm had come in two hours ago at Ann's request. She normally replaced Cliff on weekends, and now filled in for him full time. An excited buzz emanated from the group.

Ann hurried to Courtney's console. The crowd of flight controllers parted, giving her access to the screen.

CHAPTER 25

The landing party traveled four hours before they reached the base of the ejecta field slope. Instead of a gentle northerly downhill slope, the terrain now seemed flat. Difficult for them to discern, the terrain in fact sloped to the southwest at a modest 2-percent grade. The new surface was a mixture of sand dunes and dust, intermixed with areas where jagged rocks protruded above the soil.

Dave scanned his headlamp beam in all directions as far as it would reach. "Lava flows. See how the areas with exposed rocks are higher than the surrounding terrain?"

As lava cooled, the surface became a jumble of boulders. If the material underneath was still viscous, it would carry the boulders for miles, like chocolate chips on melting ice cream. When it finally cooled, a boulder field could stretch for dozens of miles. Big basalt flows like the Grand Ronde flood basalts in eastern Washington and Oregon flowed as far as the Pacific Ocean from the Grand Ronde dikes near the Idaho border, a distance of some three hundred miles. The total depth of the flows in eastern Washington reached over a mile in places.

Dave continued, "I see the voids between the boulders filled in with dust and regolith. We should be able to maintain our heading with minimal detours, unless we encounter pressure ridges."

On really large lava fields, if a lower portion of the flow cooled and hardened a bit faster, the hydraulic pressure created on the upstream side could push up ridges of boulders or semi-solid lava over a hundred feet high.

Dave pontificated, "Pressure ridges can get quite long, sometimes several miles. But they're usually not very wide. Even so, I wouldn't want to cross one. The rock can be quite jagged and sharp. Pretty hard on a pressure suit. But from the looks of the side slope, we're more likely to encounter a pressure ridge edgewise, so our detour should be minimal."

Everyone noted how Dave became uncharacteristically chatty once the group reached the Hellas Planitia floor. Allie interrupted him to bring up the topic that likely motivated it. "Dave, do you think we'll reach Prospector Base before we run out of oxygen?"

Dave remained silent.

After a longer than brief pause, LaDonna spoke up as she walked between Allie and Robbie. "Of course we will. Remember that time when we were training in the Wind River Mountains in Wyoming? We had to reach our pick-up point by noon on a Thursday or we'd forfeit the case of beer waiting for us in an ice chest?"

"I remember," Allie replied. "It was 17:00 on Wednesday. We had twenty miles to go, over two mountain ranges. We crossed both ranges by moonlight, then drank beer for breakfast on Thursday!"

"Yeah, I remember," Dave affirmed as well. "It was a mixed case. I took all the cream ale. Flash, you had the stouts. LaDonna, you took the pilsners. Allie had the Belgians. And Luis had the IPAs …" His voice trailed off.

Everyone walked on in silence for another five minutes. Dallas suddenly stopped. His headlamp beam illuminated what looked like a wall of rock. He stepped back a few paces, scanning up and then side to side. Soon, the outlines of a large boulder emerged. It was fifteen feet high and thirty feet wide. On either side lay more boulders of various sizes. Some were stacked atop each other; some were separated by gaps large enough two people could walk through side by side.

"Flash," Dave said, "we've encountered a lava flow. Once we get up on top, the walking should be level again."

Dallas walked to his left. After he had traveled ten feet, his visor flashed a warning that he was off the programmed route. He continued to the edge of the boulder, turning to walk around it, but the way was blocked by another boulder. He walked another thirty feet and found a gap wide enough to walk into.

The soil within the gap was loose and inclined at nearly forty-five degrees. Being careful not to snag his pressure suit on any ragged edges, he half walked, half pulled himself up a thirty-foot incline. At that point, the gap opened up to a plateau littered with half-buried rocks. He called back down to the group, "I'm up. Follow my tracks. Be careful of the sharp edges on the sides."

Presently Dallas saw light down by the base of the gap he had just scrambled up. LaDonna, Allie, and then Dave soon joined him.

"Sir, I can't get through without risk of injury to Luis." It was Robbie. He had paused at the bottom of the lava flow. "I am concerned that if I slip to either side, I will be unable to shield Luis from impact. All of my arms are engaged carrying him."

Dallas turned to his geologist. "Dave, help me carry Luis up this incline."

Dave and Dallas half-walked, half-slid down the path to Robbie. After a brief deliberation, Dallas laid Luis on his back to drag him up the short hill. He grasped Luis under his right shoulder, with Dave grasping under the left. Together, they pulled him head-first, using their free hands to grab hand holds to aid their climb. Robbie followed close behind.

Dallas and Dave left Luis lying on his back on the flat ground. Robbie gently picked him up and cradled him in his four arms again. LaDonna drew close to reexamine Luis. Dried blood covering the center of his visor restricted her view, so she looked in from the side. An eye fluttered open.

"Luis! Can you hear me?"

The eye blinked a few times. Then Luis began struggling. Robbie gently restrained him. Luis settled down after half a minute. "I can'd move my head! I can'd see." Luis's badly swollen nasal passages affected his voice.

LaDonna and Allie each placed a hand on opposite shoulders, keeping him from falling to the ground. LaDonna attempted her best bedside manner, "Luis, this is Dr. Pleasant. You're with us, now. You were blown off the cliff at the crater rim. Please, don't struggle. You might have a sprained neck. It might even be broken. We have immobilized your head as a precaution."

Luis struggled again. "I can'd move!"

"Please lie calmly, Luis. You also have a broken nose, a broken arm, and a broken collarbone. You ended up face-down, so your nose bled onto your visor. You just can't see through the dried blood, that's all. Look straight forward. Can you see my headlamp to your right?"

"Yeth. I can thee it! Doc, are we thdill in the crader?" Luis visibly relaxed.

The flight surgeon continued, "No. We've traveled about four hours since we pulled you out. You've been unconscious for about ten hours. Robbie has carried you the whole time."

"Ten hourth?" Luis coughed and visibly winced.

LaDonna crossed her arms, concern in her voice. "Yes, ten hours. Luis, are you having any trouble breathing?"

"Hurdth to cough. Hurdth to breathe in."

She persisted with her patient, "Do you have any shortness of breath?"

"No, juthd hurth."

LaDonna gently pressed on Luis's chest. No reaction. Then she examined his back as best she could around Robbie's arms and Luis's pack. Still no reaction. She pressed on his left side near his immobilized left elbow. Robbie's grip restrained Luis again, as he jerked and called out, "Thid! Thad hurdth!"

"Sorry, Tiger. But I have to know what's going on."

LaDonna then pressed Luis's right side but got no reaction. "Luis, you may have cracked ribs on your left side. We should wrap you up a little better to help with the discomfort. How does your head feel?"

"My fathe is killing me."

"It's killing me, too!"

LaDonna flashed an angry stare. "Dave!"

She turned back to her patient. "Do you have a headache?"

Luis pondered a bit before he responded, "No, I don'd think tho."

The flight surgeon continued her examination. "Luis, I want you to turn your eyes toward me. I want to check your pupil response."

Luis looked as best he could to his right. LaDonna moved the beam of her headlamp back and forth across his right eye. His pupil contracted and dilated normally. Then she moved to his left side and repeated her exercise. "Pupil response normal. You have one hard head, mister! You did a swan dive from 250 feet, and the worst you have to show for it is a broken nose and a few broken bones."

She patted him on his right shoulder, being careful to avoid the broken collarbone on his left side.

"Doc, you've trained with him for three years, and you just now figured out he's hard-headed?" Dave had drawn close to Luis as the flight surgeon examined him.

Luis responded quickly, "Shud ub! Wherth my foam ballth?"

"Sorry buddy," Dave offered in mock condolence. "Unlike you, they didn't survive the fall."

LaDonna intervened, "Technically, Dave, Luis broke their fall. Luis sacrificed himself to save them."

Luis folded his good right arm over his left arm, a smile visible on his swollen lips behind the blood-caked visor.

"Just so I'm clear, Doc. You're saying that Luis did a face plant from 250 feet to save his balls?"

Now everyone smiled, except Luis. LaDonna struggled but maintained her professional demeanor. "That's enough, mister! Back off from my patient, or you'll deal with me."

Dave backed up a few paces, hands positioned palms forward in mock deference.

LaDonna turned her attention back to Luis. "Luis, we have to get going again. I'm going to monitor how well you can tolerate travel now that you're conscious."

She turned to Dallas. "We're ready to go."

Dallas returned his attention to his visor navigation's direction of travel. He walked back in the general direction of the imaginary line of their route. After he walked forty feet, he stopped and faced their direction of bearing. Nothing. He turned another fifteen degrees. Still nothing. He felt his mouth go dry, and his pulse in his ears. Dallas turned back, facing the gap they just climbed, thinking he had missed the flashing indication on his visor's direction-of-travel line. Nothing. His heart pounded in his chest.

He took a deep breath and slowly rotated to his right, intending to continue until he scanned a full 180-degree arc. To his great relief, his direction-of-travel line flashed red just past where he stopped on his first attempt. He scanned past until the flashing stopped, then scanned back until he reacquired the flashing indicator.

"Thank God for MGPS. I would have had us so off course in this darkness ..." Dallas did not finish his sentence. Instead, he resumed walking, with Dave close behind.

Dave scanned around as far as his headlamp beam would allow, remarking as he walked, "This looks like a big flow. It originates somewhere northeast of us and flows southwesterly across our direction of travel. The gentle uphill grade to the northwest indicates it gets progressively deeper as we follow our route."

After thirty paces, Dallas stopped, and Dave almost collided with him.

"Dallas, was it something I said?"

But Dallas ignored Dave and addressed Allie. "Allie, what frequency do our helmet comms use?"

Allie, Robbie, and LaDonna came to a stop immediately behind Dave. Allie pondered a moment before answering. "Our helmet-to-helmet comm system is UHF frequency 399.4 MHz. The phone-to-helmet data link is 401.3 MHz."

"What about direct phone to phone? What frequencies do they use?"

"Phone to phone is 399.9 MHz.

"And what frequency does Prospector Base and the DV use for uplinks to the orbital communications satellites for relay to Earth?"

"UHF, but the frequency is 400.1 MHz."

"Why can't we just uplink directly from our phones to the comm satellites?"

"The signal is too weak to reach a satellite in high Mars orbit."

Dallas paused before he resumed his line of questioning, "What about a satellite in low Mars orbit? Could our phones reach that far?"

"In theory, yes. But there are no communications satellites at that altitude."

"Don't MGP satellites occupy low Mars orbit?"

Allie's voice raised a pitch in excitement. "Yes they do!"

"And on what frequency does MGPS downlink for our navigation?"

"UHF, 402.5 MHz."

"And all MGPS satellites can double as communication relays to Earth?" Dallas asked.

"Correct. They all have S-band capabilities to and from Earth. But I don't know what UHF frequency reaches them from the surface. No one uses MGPS for communications because they have such limited bandwidth." Allie pulled the stylus from her phone and started a data search. She pumped a fist when she found what she was searching for. "Yes! If we tune our phones to 400.7, we can uplink to MGPS!"

Dallas continued pressing his communications officer, "So we can phone home?"

Allie turned her excitement down a notch. "I don't think so. The atmosphere attenuates the signal strength too much to carry voice communications to the satellites. But"—she looked up at Dallas—"a text message should get through. That might work, Flash."

Dallas checked the time on his helmet visor. It was 05:41. They had traveled about ten kilometers in a little over four and a half hours, most of it an easy downhill. They had roughly fifty kilometers to go, with about thirty hours' worth of oxygen. At their latest rate of progress, they could walk to the base in only a little over twenty-two. But that would be without sleep, and avoiding difficult terrain or any other impediment. A faint, bronzy light glowed above the east horizon now visible in silhouette.

Even though he planned to walk without sleeping, he was concerned they might not cover all fifty kilometers before their oxygen gave out. "Allie, can you tune my smartphone transmitter to 400.7 MHz?"

"I can. It will take me about twenty minutes. But you'll lose communication between your phone and your helmet."

Dallas thought for a moment. "But my helmet navigation will still work, and I'll still have helmet-to-helmet communication with the rest of the team?"

"Yes. But your helmet navigation relies heavily on your phone for processing power. The navigation readout on your visor will be noticeably slower. The accuracy will be the same, though."

Dallas had everything he needed to know. "Do it, and tune Dr. Pleasant's phone to 400.1, also. We need a backup in case something happens to me or my phone."

Allie collected phones from Dallas and LaDonna. She pulled out a stylus, accessed the connectivity programming, and entered code. Finally, she created a transmission header commanding MGPS to relay any attached text message to Earth. Twice, she carefully read through the code she had created. Then she reopened Dallas's phone to navigation. His phone no longer communicated with his helmet, but he could still see the navigation app on-screen, giving him a backup in case his helmet got balky. He could also read his phone screen if SaMMCon sent a reply. She returned both phones to their respective owners. The entire process took less than fifteen minutes.

Dallas took out his stylus and typed into his messaging app.

> Prosp 1 crew to SaMMCon. DV at 36.2425S
> 57.5011E. 5 evac to Prosp Base on ft 12:23 Day
> 1. 15 km at N00.00.00E, 45 km at N58.00.00W,
> 15 km at N00.00.00E. crrnt pos 36.0512S
> 57.3340E. Est Oxy dpltn 12:23 Day 4. Luis
> injured. RBI effctng his evac. We prcd to base
> on route gvn.

He reread his message, hit SEND, then pocketed his phone. "Let's keep moving," he addressed the other four. "We've got at least forty minutes until we get a response, if any, and I'm freezing my ass off just standing here."

Instinctively, all cast a glance at their temperature readouts: minus 39° F. No one objected.

Dallas scanned in their intended direction of travel until he acquired the route bearing on his visor, then he took off. He walked at a brisk pace, in part warding off the cold seeping through his pressure suit, in part buoyed by hope that SaMMCon might somehow aid them. He buried his dread that they would run out of oxygen before reaching base.

CHAPTER 26

Dallas walked for another forty-five minutes before pulling his smartphone out, looking for a text notification. He hoped the time they had taken to reconfigure the two phone transmitters was worth the oxygen lost.

As he viewed the lit screen in his hand, the albedo of the soil suddenly changed. The reflection of the early sunrise off the ground gave way to black. He froze mid-stride, his left foot held aloft. He lowered his phone, revealing his booted foot hovering over a black abyss. Carefully, he retracted his left foot and planted it beside his right.

Dave, who had been trailing Dallas, joined him. "You found a fissure! Cool! Big volcanic lava fields like this one sometimes develop fissures when the underlying rock subsides from the weight above. There's probably a fault below that reflected up, creating this fissure."

Dallas didn't bother hiding his anger. "It would have been nice to get an advance warning, Dave."

"You were closer. I figured you could see it."

Dallas took a breath and lowered his voice. "Sorry, Dave. You're right. I should have stopped walking to read my phone. I was hoping SaMMCon would have responded by now."

The two men scanned the length of the feature to either side with their headlamps. The edge they stood on receded into the distance in either direction. Looking forward, they clearly saw the opposite side of the fissure, twenty-five feet in front of them. The sun was still so low the fissure lay entirely in shadow. They both looked down. As his eyes adjusted to the shade, Dallas was surprised to see a smooth, rusty brown surface twenty feet below where they stood. It almost looked glassy.

"What do you make of that, Dave?"

Dave picked up a large rock with both hands, raised it over his head, then threw it down onto the surface. Small shards of material skittered away from the impact in all directions. The rock left behind a small divot that matched its diameter, and came to rest against the far wall of the fissure.

Dave became even more animated. "Ice! It's full of ice! It's just colored from all of the dust that's settled on it over time."

Dallas understood Dave's excitement. One mineral the mission absolutely required for success was water. It would provide for the needs of a growing population. Not just for drinking and irrigating crops, but as a source of rocket propellant when hydrolyzed. Rare earth elements, once refined, would have to be boosted into orbit before being nudged Earthward. The sun's gravity would take it from there, the shipments spiraling down toward Earth's orbit in what amounted to a controlled fall.

Dallas turned to Dave. "Is it strong enough to support us walking across it?"

Dave examined his handiwork more carefully. "No spider cracks radiating away from the impact site. I threw that rock down pretty hard. All it did was gouge a hole in the surface. Yes, it will support our weight, no problem."

Dallas examined the ice surface carefully. He leaned forward, bent his knees, and dropped off the edge.

"Dallas!" LaDonna watched the two men as they conversed. She deduced what Dallas would do as soon as he leaned forward. Allie was looking attentively at Luis and did not see him drop. Dallas was airborne before Dave could react.

After 1.8 seconds elapsed, Dallas deftly landed on the surface below. His knees absorbed the shock, and he remained standing. He stood up tall and thrust both of his arms into the air, like a gymnast who had just stuck a difficult landing during a meet.

"And the crowd goes wild!" He made a hissing sound at the back of his mouth to imitate crowd noise.

"Flash! How did you do that?" Dave took half a step back from the edge.

Dallas responded matter-of-factly, "Do the math. A twenty-foot drop here is equal to seven and a half feet back on Earth. The trick is to land on balance so your knees can absorb the force."

"Mister, you nearly gave me a heart attack!" LaDonna did not share Dallas's frivolity. "As your physician, I demand that next time you explain *before* you take a flying leap!"

Allie, whose attention had been directed at Luis, finally realized that Dallas stood on the "floor" of the fissure. She looked back and forth between him, and LaDonna, who stood beside her. "How did he get down there?"

"He took an unauthorized shortcut." LaDonna was still fuming. "A mistake I'm confident that the commander will not repeat!"

Dallas controlled his laughter to calm down his flight surgeon. "'Donna, I'm sorry. It's just a waste of time walking around searching for a way down. The shortest distance between two points is a straight line."

Then he addressed the group, "If anyone doesn't feel confident jumping the entire distance, there are a few hand-holds over here that will get you over halfway down. It looks scary, but it's really like jumping just a few feet. I'll spot anyone who's not comfortable."

He walked closer to the rock face to his left, directly below LaDonna and Allie. Allie turned her back to him, working her way down. She got halfway down and prepared to jump backward.

Dallas stood to the side and watched her drop. She tried to compensate for her pack but leaned forward a little too much. When she landed, she pitched forward toward the rock wall. Dallas caught her around the waist and helped her stand straight. "Allie, spot LaDonna from the opposite side."

LaDonna lowered herself to the same spot that Allie jumped from. She landed straight, but Dallas and Allie still caught her under her arms, reducing the strain on her knees.

Dave stood where Dallas jumped off. "Don't spot me. It's a one-point deduction if you touch me."

Dave leaned forward as he crouched down, much as Dallas had. But he left the cliff edge with a little more forward momentum. He landed on his feet, but took a step forward to maintain his balance. Dallas reacted instantly, "Yes! Half-a-point deduction!"

Dave held his head high and responded with false stoicism, "It's alright. I'll beat you next time." Then he added with a bit more gravity, "There may be many more opportunities. This lava flow has gotten deeper as we've walked. We could run across more fissures like this. But there's no guarantee the next one will be full of ice like this one is."

Dallas grasped the significance of Dave's deduction. If they encountered one or more empty fissures, it could compromise their chances of reaching Prospector Base while they still had oxygen. He scanned the far wall and found a route to climb up and out. "Let's get going. Gotta give Dave his chance to even the score."

"Hey, whad aboud Robbie add me?"

LaDonna held her hand to her mouth in horror. "Luis, I'm so sorry! I got so focused on this fissure I forgot all about you."

Dallas felt his face flush red. Luis had been so silent as he was carried by the RBI unit that Dallas had also forgotten about his disabled crew member. "Robbie," he called across to the AI, "if we throw up a few coils of rope, can you carefully lower Luis over the edge? Dave and I can spot him from below."

"Yes, commander. I have sufficient mass to serve as a counterweight for that maneuver."

Dallas quickly pulled the hank of rope attached to Dave's pack. He laid it on the ground and pulled on the free end until he had five coils in his hand. In the meantime, Robbie carefully off-loaded his passenger. Luis stood weakly with two of Robbie's four arms supporting him. Robbie signaled. "I'm ready, commander."

Dallas slung the coils upward to the Assistant, who grabbed the end of the rope with one of his free arms. He deftly tied a figure eight knot and clipped it into Luis's climbing harness using one of the man's carabiners. Then he gently walked Luis to the cliff edge and turned him backward before addressing his handler. "Luis, grasp the rope with your right hand. I can provide friction so you can walk your way down. Dallas and Dave will assist you at the bottom."

Luis emitted several grunts. His pain was obvious. "Thdop. Let me rethd a thec." His breathing was ragged and labored.

LaDonna assessed her patient from below. "Luis, are your ribs bothering you?"

Luis took a few more breaths. "Yeth, Ma'am. Hurdth having my arm thdredched out—maketh it hard to breathe."

"Take your time, Luis."

When she was certain Luis was stable, she turned to the men beside her. "Dallas and Dave, when you spot Luis, grab him around his thighs to lower him to the ground."

Luis resumed his slow walk, and after four more steps, Dallas and Dave each grasped a thigh. They lowered Luis to a standing position on the ice. Robbie followed closely and touched down beside the three men.

Dallas resumed instructing Robbie as they crossed to the far side of the fissure. "Robbie, as you climb to the top, hold the rope in a hand, letting it play as you go. Once you're on top, let me know when you're ready to pull Luis up."

Robbie skittered up the rock face. Dallas marveled at the climbing skills he had developed while training with the landing team.

"I am up, Commander. Luis, just use your feet for balance. Let me pull you up."

"Roger, liddle buddy. Pull me up." Luis's grimace was evident to Dallas even through the blood-crusted visor. Several more grunts confirmed his discomfort.

Dallas shouldered the remaining rope coils and then quickly climbed out of the fissure. He recoiled the rope as the others climbed up. After everyone was out, he fastened the rope to

Dave's pack. Before he resumed walking, he checked his phone once again. "Oh my God! It worked. SaMMCon responded!"

Allie, LaDonna, and Dave quickly crowded around him as he read the message.

CHAPTER 27

Ann's heart pounded so hard, she had difficulty rereading the text message on Courtney's screen. She noted the timestamp from the MGPS satellite that had relayed the message—twenty-three minutes old. After she re-read the contents, she regained her composure and directed her flight control team, "Courtney, forward this text file to all flight control stations."

Courtney's fingers danced on her keyboard.

"Monica," Ann addressed her FDO, "overlay the route described in this message onto our most recent satellite imagery. The rest of you, get back to your stations"

Monica stepped back out of the thinning crowd around Courtney's workstation and quickly covered the twelve feet to her console. The text appeared on her screen just as she sat down. She input coordinates, bearings, and distances, her keyboard clicking furiously. Lines quickly appeared over the imagery displayed on the monitors mounted on the front wall.

The crowd around the INCO station quickly dissolved. The last chair squeaked under the weight of its owner just as the third line appeared onscreen in the front of the room. The route connected the crash site to Prospector Base in three distinct segments. The first and last segments were fifteen kilometers long, oriented due north, but offset. A diagonal segment forty-five kilometers long connected them. In all, they defined a cross-country route seventy-five kilometers long.

Ann noted that the first segment originated at the Descent/Ascent Vehicle crash site, then crossed the crater floor. The second crossed the Hellas Planitia plain to the small ridge east of the base. The final segment traversed the ridge slope down to the valley floor and ended at Prospector Base.

Ann returned her attention to Monica. "Zoom in on their given current position and mark it."

A small "X" appeared a quarter of the way into the diagonal segment. "They're out of the crater."

Ann let out what felt like a long overdue breath. "Okay, Monica. How far have they come as of the transmission of the text file?"

"Fifteen kilometers across the crater floor, plus another twelve on the diagonal segment, Miss Ann."

"Alan, pull up a chair. You're sharing my station."

Alan Scripps served as the Prospector program planetary geologist. He had remotely scoured thousands of square kilometers of terrain and overseen half a dozen robotic prospecting missions within Hellas Planitia. He had selected the location of Prospector Base.

After he arrived, Ann resumed. "What's your assessment of the flight crew's remaining route?"

Alan grabbed Ann's mouse. Starting with the "X" in the middle segment, he scrolled along the route between the crew's last known location and the base. As the on-screen terrain scrolled northwesterly, he furrowed his brow. Halfway to the end of the segment, it bisected the distance between two smaller impact craters.

The crater to the north was seven kilometers across, obviously old, with badly eroded crater walls. The crater floor was buried under fluvial deposits, dust, and regolith. Its features appeared soft and rounded in the satellite imagery. The crater to the south was newer, with walls vertical and distinct. The crater floor was flat, except for the central mountain. The mountain cast a sharp shadow to the east, like a sundial.

The terrain between the two craters extended west to the ridge that separated the landing party from Prospector Base. Even as zoomed out as the image was, Alan discerned that the flat terrain was a lobe of a larger lava flow. He zoomed back in, examining the lava flow along the crew's proposed route.

As he did, Ann noted irregular black lines, cutting across jagged pressure ridges.

Alan narrated for her, "These black lines are fissures that opened up when the underlying rock subsided. Some fissures are filled with ice. Others extend downward to the full depth of this lava field, probably over three hundred feet in places. Ann, I eliminated this area from consideration as a base site because the terrain is so rugged and dangerous."

Ann quickly checked the mission clock on her second monitor: D2 06:06 Hr. She raised her voice to be heard at the front row of the flight control stations. "Dr. Knox, the flight crew must travel forty-eight kilometers to reach Prospector Base before their oxygen supply runs out. Can they reasonably cover that distance in thirty hours?"

Portia Knox rotated her seat to face Ann. "The suits and oxygen supply will allow a crew member to travel at two kilometers per hour. That's a moderate pace under ideal conditions. I'm concerned that they've only covered twenty-even kilometers in the first thirty-six hours. Their net pace is less than one kilometer per hour so far. If they can't increase their pace to one and a third kilometers per hour, they'll run out of oxygen before they reach base."

Ann continued to project her voice, "But that estimate includes the time it's taken them to climb out of the crater."

"But we don't know the extent or severity of Luis's injuries," Portia responded. "It may not be much of a factor on gentle terrain, but the worse it gets, the more difficult it may be to transport Luis, even being carried by an RBI unit."

Ann quickly transferred her display image onto the big screens at the front of the room. Then she zoomed out, so the final two route segments were visible. She spoke loudly enough to be heard throughout the entire flight control room. "Alan, outline the extent of the area with the pressure ridges and fissures."

She handed her mouse back to Alan, who outlined in bright orange an irregular shape. He outlined an area roughly twenty kilometers by twenty kilometers. The route ran through the northeastern third of the outlined area.

Ann zoomed in on the flight crew's route to Prospector Base, starting at their last given coordinates. As she passed over the lava field, the route crossed pressure ridges and fissures in quick succession. When she reached the ridge on the far side of the lava field, she paused. "Dr. Knox, what is your assessment of the delay these features will create?"

"Ann," Portia responded immediately, "it will take the flight crew days to navigate this terrain— days that they don't have."

Ann redirected her attention to Monica Gonzales. "Monica, map the quickest route from a point two kilometers west of the crew's last known location to Prospector Base."

Monica grabbed her mouse and snapped a straight line from just west of the "X" to Prospector Base at the north end of the third segment. The line crossed less of the terrain outlined by the planetary geologist. It grazed the southwest limits of the old crater's ejecta field, crossed over a high summit on the ridgeline above Prospector Base, then downslope on a steeper angle of descent than did the original route's third segment.

Monica's Spanish accent became more pronounced in tension. "There you go, Miss Ann. The distance to base is 42.88 kilometers. This reduced the distance they have to travel by over five kilometers."

Ann zoomed in on the origin of the shortcut Monica had just mapped. She briefly stopped whenever the new line crossed a fissure or a pressure ridge, counting four fissures and three ridges. She continued past the edge of the ejecta field and up the slope of the ridge, pausing again just east of the summit, noting a cliff with a substantial scree field below it. The west slope was steep but appeared free of major obstacles. "If the landing party maintains one and a half kilometers per hour, they can reach Prospector Base in around twenty-nine hours. But this new route crosses difficult terrain. What's your assessment, Dr. Knox?"

Portia Knox closely followed Ann's "flyover" of the proposed reroute. She, too, noted the fissures, pressure ridges, talus slope, and cliff. She mentally estimated the delay each feature would cause before she responded. "Ann, if we assume it takes an extra hour to cross a pressure ridge, and two hours to cross an ice-free fissure, that adds up to five and a half hours. Add another two hours to climb up to and cross that talus slope, and another four hours to climb to the summit. The crew runs out of oxygen just as they summit the ridge."

"I agree. Monica, lay out the quickest route that gets them out of Alan's orange outline, then gets them to Prospector Base."

"Let me try a mirrored alignment, Miss Ann." Monica quickly laid out a line fifteen kilometers long bearing due north from the previous origin of her shortcut route. From the end of that line, she laid out another thirty-three-kilometer segment at bearing N58° 00' 00" W. The north end of the new segment touched the original route terminus at Prospector Base. The team's current route and Monica's proposed route created a perfect four-sided parallelogram.

Once again, Ann zoomed in on the new route. She passed outside of Alan's orange line without encountering any fissures or pressure ridges and continued over gently undulating terrain to the angle point. The new bearing intersected the gently sloped ejecta field of the old crater, traversing up the southeast face to the crater's rim then down to the base of the ridge above Prospector Base. The line then led straight upslope to a saddle, minus the talus field and cliff of the previous shortcut. Prospector Base lay directly downslope of the saddle, shining in the pale Martian sunlight. It was beautiful.

Portia Knox quickly gave her assessment: "This route is the same length as the route the flight crew is currently on but has no terrain obstacles to slow them and their RBI unit down. One feature worries me, though. Based on the shadows cast on the terrain to the east, the ridgeline saddle that this route crosses is higher than the original route. The slope they must climb is steeper, too."

She turned. "Ann, there's something else. I'm not convinced Commander Gordon's assessment of their oxygen supply is accurate. He's based his estimated time on twenty-four hours per bottle. But given their level of exertion, the bottles won't last that long. During training, they ran as low as twenty hours per bottle. It's almost certain that they'll run out of oxygen hours before 12:23 tomorrow." She held her voice steady as she finished. "In my opinion, the odds are against them ever reaching Prospector Base before they run out of oxygen, even on this easiest route."

The room was silent, save for the soft hum of electronics.

Ann resisted the urge to scream in frustration. She had suspected as much even as she worked with the different route options. She sat motionless, staring at Prospector Base on her monitor, paralyzed by the hopeless situation the flight crew—*her* flight crew—faced.

Memories unbidden flashed before her mind's eye: her first kiss with Dallas at the summit of Grand Teton, the first awkward and clumsy down payment of a deeper love to come; making love beneath the Milky Way in Patagonia after sneaking away from their OLS students, the celestial canopy wheeling overhead as she lay below him; Dallas's supreme confidence in any climb he attempted, a classic blues tune echoing off the mountain sides; the tearful goodbye after their last night together before he flew to Naval Air Station Pensacola and she left for Stanford to pursue her PhD. It all came back.

She loved Dallas those many years ago. And here, as all eyes in SaMMCon were locked on her, sharing her despair, she admitted to herself that she still had feelings for him. She wiped tears from her eyes with her shirtsleeve before they spilled out onto her cheeks.

Resolve displaced frustration. It started in her chest as a vague warmth, quickly spreading outward to her head and torso, gaining momentum and heat as it went. When it reached her eyes, the tears vanished like raindrops flashing to steam on molten rock.

Resolve led to action. Ann would not watch Dallas and the flight crew collapse in the Martian dust, drawing their final breaths. Her attention snapped to her keyboard and she typed furiously.

> SaMMCon to Prosp 1 crw. Proceed immed on new heading N00.00.00E for 15 km, then heading N58.00.00W approx 33 km. Update SaMMCon with crrnt pos every hr on the hr. Advise re oxy status. Advise re cond and location of Luis and RBI. ANMHE.

"Courtney, transmit this message to the MGPS fleet. Have all satellites relay it to the Martian surface."

The text file appeared on the INCO's monitor. She quickly composed a file header implementing the flight director's instructions, appended it to the text file, and sent it on its way across twenty light minutes' worth of vacuum to the fourth rock from the sun.

Ann focused on the Autotronics representative for the first time. "Roger, is there any way for us to transmit instructions to the landing party's RBI unit?"

"The landing party's unit is strictly dual frequency UHF to enable communication with project smartphones and pressure suit helmets only. A separate MGPS receiver only communicates with its internal MGPS navigation module. I'm sorry, Ann, but there's no way for us to communicate directly with Robbie."

"But the two units assembling and monitoring the base itself," she pressed him. "We can communicate directly with them via our S-band frequencies, correct?"

"Correct. It's how all commands and troubleshooting are transmitted to and from those units."

Ann contemplated her next move. "Roger, prepare instructions to the base RBI units to override whatever instructions they're currently operating on. I'll provide you with the replacement instructions."

She refocused her attention to her keyboard. Her fingers flashed furiously for two minutes. Then she stopped, read what she had composed, and forwarded the text file. "Roger, forward the completed communications package to Courtney. Courtney, wait for my signal to uplink the package to Prospector Base."

Ann sat at her flight control station, hands folded and pressed against her lips, as if she were praying. Then she turned to the NASA representative. "Ajay, can we get eyes over our landing party and their RBI at first light? I want to assess their progress and ascertain their exact route."

"I'll pass on your request to our Mars sat flight controller."

Ann addressed the entire room again. "We expect the landing party to travel at less than two kilometers per hour. Get me eyes on them."

CHAPTER 28

SaMMCon
MSD: 57481
MTC: 06:47:52
FROM: CAPCOM

Proceed immed on new heading N00.00.00E for 15 km, then heading N58.00.00W approx 33 km. Update SaMMCon with crrnt pos every hr on the hr. Advise re oxy status. Advise re cond and location of Luis and RBI. ANMHE.

According to the timestamp, the message had arrived two minutes earlier, at 06:47.

"Why do you suppose they want us to proceed north from here?" LaDonna wondered aloud. "Won't that take us over a higher section of the ridge above the base?"

Neither Dallas nor Dave responded as they scrambled up a nearby rock outcrop. Once up, they looked northwest along their intended route. What had looked like scattered outcroppings in the earlier morning sunlight took on more clarity now that the sunlight passed through less atmospheric dust. Pressure ridges and rock outcrops were visible everywhere, rank on rank disappearing into the distance. The mountain ridge above Prospector Base was dimly visible on the far horizon. They turned northward. Dusty, rolling terrain seemed to go on forever, the sameness interrupted by an occasional small outcropping.

"Wow," Dave remarked. "None of that rugged terrain to the northwest was visible on Robbie's low-res sat imagery. I'll wager that there are plenty of fissures toward the center of this lava flow, with no guarantee that they're filled with glacial ice. What we crossed was just a cheap down payment on nastiness to come."

Dallas nodded his helmet toward the northwest. "Looks like SaMMCon wants us to skirt the worst of it to the east and north. Climbing higher on the ridge will burn more oxygen, but probably a lot less than crossing through that."

Both men descended the outcrop and rejoined the women and Luis. Dallas gave the update. "LaDonna, the terrain in our intended direction of travel is incredibly rugged. We saw dozens and dozens of pressure ridges up ahead. Although I'm not entirely comfortable with the idea of crossing the ridgeline farther north of where we had planned, I know that SaMMCon has access to high-res satellite imagery. I have to believe they've given us our best chance at making it back to base before we turn blue."

Three helmets nodded their agreement.

Robbie moved Luis into the conference. "Thorry I can'd nod my head Flath. I thay yeth."

"Then it's settled," Dallas said. "We head due north for fifteen kilometers, then head northwest at fifty-eight degrees."

He quickly typed a response message to SaMMCon.

> Props 1 crw to SaMMCon Crossed first fissure on route. Procding on new heading N00.00.00E for 15km, then heading N58.00.00W approx 33km. Started 1st oxy res bottles 09:30 Day 2. Luis has brkn nose, sprained neck, broken collarbone, broken left arm and poss cracked ribs. Neck immobilized with duct tp. Ribs splinted with duct tp. Unable to walk. Transport by RBI. ANMHE.

Dallas checked his work and pressed send.

Ladonna had peered over his shoulder as he composed. "What's 'ann mee'?"

"It's code for "'There's a case of beer on ice at the base'," he responded.

"That doesn't make any sense."

"Of course not. It's a code."

LaDonna knew better than to probe too deeply when Dallas got cryptic like this. She turned and walked back to Luis.

Dallas quickly reprogrammed both his helmet and smartphone nav apps, turned his head until he acquired the new bearing on his visor display, and started walking north.

As the women started, Allie turned to LaDonna. "A case of beer at the base?"

LaDonna shrugged. "Don't know. But I'd rather drink a beer than run out of oxygen."

"Me doo. Full thpeed ahead, Robbie!" Luis grimaced as the AI bounced over a small stone. "Juthd wadth the bumpth."

LaDonna tapped Allie's helmet, signing for a private helmet-to-helmet transmission. Allie adjusted her helmet comm setting.

LaDonna kept her voice low even though it wasn't necessary, "Allie, did you really mean what you said when you voted to rescue Luis?"

"What do you mean, Doc?"

"You said that you couldn't live with yourself if you reached base using his oxygen."

The two women walked on in silence for a minute before Allie answered. "To tell you the truth, Doc, the thought of running out of oxygen scares the hell out of me. But I also know I couldn't live with myself if it meant leaving him behind to die. Doc, why did you vote to rescue him? You had to know our best chance to make it to base alive was to leave Luis behind."

Now it was LaDonna's turn to consider her thoughts. "To be honest, I considered it. You know, the needs of the many … blah, blah, blah. But we've been a team under Dallas's leadership for so long, I just had to trust him that he'd figure some way to get us all out of this together."

Allie nodded. "I have to agree with you, Doc. Live or die, we do it together."

The older flight surgeon put her arm around the younger engineer. They walked together several paces before they separated and switched their helmet settings back to group communications.

The landing party traveled for fifty minutes. The fissure they crossed slowly receded to the east and was now no longer visible. Dallas detoured around two small outcrops. In each case, he detoured only fifty feet off route before returning to their original line of travel. Everyone breathed noticeably harder now that they were walking uphill instead of traversing across slope, even though the slope was barely perceptible.

Dallas's oxygen sensor flashed yellow. Since all four of Robbie's hands were full carrying Luis, Dave swapped out the now-empty bottle for Dallas's final replacement bottle. Dave tossed the bottle and they resumed walking.

Dallas looked to his geologist. "You're next, Dave."

"Yeah. Thanks for being my canary in the coal mine."

Everyone in the landing party understood the relationship between oxygen consumption and body mass. Assuming a common level of exertion, the higher the body mass, the faster the rate of oxygen consumption. Normally, Luis emptied a bottle first, since he was the heaviest crew member. But he had been at rest since falling off the cliff.

Dallas swapped out Dave's bottle seven minutes later. In another twenty minutes, LaDonna's alarm went off. Allie fitted her with her last bottle. Luis's and Allie's alarms both went off within thirty seconds of each other, eight minutes later. LaDonna helped Allie while Dave assisted Luis. Meanwhile, Dallas updated SaMMCon.

> Prosp1 crw to SaMMCon. Replaced final oxy bottles 07:30 – 08:00. Location geotag attached. ANMHE

When he closed up Luis's pack, Dave took a deep, exaggerated breath. "I love the smell of oxygen in the morning. It smells like a case of beer!"

Dallas glanced again at his time display. 08:01. They still had forty-five kilometers to go. He had gotten only twenty-two hours out of his second bottle, and only twenty-one hours out of the first. If they maintained that rate of consumption, they would run out of oxygen three hours before they reached Prospector Base.

Dallas replayed in his head the same argument he had waged since rescuing Luis. *Damn, I regret sleeping that first night at the base of the cliff.* Dallas shuddered. *But if we risked climbing that first night, we might all be busted up as badly as Luis. How the hell was I supposed to know he would be blown back into the crater by one of those damned dust devils? I ought to kick his ass into the next fissure and leave him there. Fact is, it was just bad luck, plain and simple. In spite of our bad luck, we have a fighting chance. And I'm not going down without a fight. Plus, we've got an eye in the sky sending us the best routes. If we just pick up our speed ...* He quickened his pace.

The morning wore on. Rock outcrops became more widely scattered. Dust devils formed by 11:00. From a distance, they appeared sedate, slowly traveling from northwest to southeast, coaxed by the gentle prevailing wind. None approached any closer than two kilometers.

The travelers took no breaks. Dallas felt blisters forming on his heels. Pressure suits were engineered for the conditions that the astronauts were expected to encounter, including extensive rock climbing. But no amount of engineering prepared a pair of feet for seventy-two hours of nonstop travel without the option of removing one's boots.

They reached the fifteen-kilometer point, changing their direction of travel at 14:56. He could tell everyone was exhausted. The idle chatter had ended hours ago.

Dallas called out, "Take five, everyone."

Four pressure-suited figures dropped to the ground where they stood.

Allie massaged her calves. "What I wouldn't give for a steak and a baked potato right now. I'm so hungry, and my legs keep cramping."

Dave shot back at her in mock contempt, "You should have packed a lunch before we left the DV."

Allie deadpanned back, "Kinda hard to get it past my visor, Dave."

"It's a problem. Gonna give those engineers a piece of my mind when we get to base. How the hell are we supposed eat when there's no door in our visors?"

"Give it a rest, you two," Dallas broke into the conversation. "I'll assign our mechanical engineer to work on it after we get to base. Luis, make it your highest priority."

"On it, Flath!"

After another minute, Dallas stood. His helmet echoed with groans as Dave, LaDonna, and Allie stood as well. He quickly acquired their final bearing on his visor display and set out. Once again, they traversed the lava flow, their breathing slightly easier.

It was difficult staring ahead into the sun. Dallas made out what looked like a gently sloping hill ten kilometers ahead. He surmised it was the ejecta field around the eroded crater, but was unable to make out the ridge between the crater and the valley—just too much light scatter from all the atmospheric dust. He took comfort that the slope of the ejecta field was only about a 5-percent grade. Their path would traverse the slope from the southeast, taking them just across the southwest edge of the rim.

Dallas faithfully updated SaMMCon hourly as requested. Often, it was no more than a geotag of their current location, ending with the acronym ANMHE. He looked forward to the responses. They contained an average speed for the distance covered between the previous two update locations. They averaged just under two kilometers per hour while they were northbound. He hoped they would do better traveling northwest, at least until they encountered the ejecta slope ahead. The messages from SaMMCon also contained statements of encouragement, or goofy platitudes. But they were always appended with ANMHE.

During the monotony between messages, Dallas thought back to the first time he had seen Ann at EPSILON. She was the flight director for the new mission control center that oversaw his mission. He was so surprised to see her, he was literally speechless. Looking back on it now, it made perfect sense that they ran into each other. EPSILON leased one of NASA's nuclear ion propulsion boosters to power the Prospector missions. When they parted, she had been heading to Stanford to get a PhD in nuclear ion propulsion. As smart as she was, it was no surprise EPSILON had pursued her.

He recalled how he had awkwardly thrust out a hand to shake hers during the introduction.

"Nice to see you again."

He couldn't even look her in the eye at the time.

They met numerous times over the course of mission development and training. At first, whenever he did look her in her eyes, a sense of dread came over him. He was certain she had moved on, found someone new, though she never wore a ring to work. But what he saw in her eyes was not the steely demeanor of a jilted ex-lover in a new setting. He saw professionalism and self-confidence, but also something softer. He couldn't quite put what he saw into words. But it felt quiet—and accepting. Eventually, he grew more comfortable around her. They did the work that they had left each other to do, and they did it well.

But now, he wished he had said more, done more. She was his only real love. He had to admit that his happiest days were the days that they shared together. The silence of the dusty desolation that surrounded him only deepened is regret.

They marched on in silence. The sun lowered in the Western sky, growing dimmer and more orange as it went. At 19:01, the sun disappeared just above the silhouette of the crater ejecta slope. It had settled behind the still-not-visible ridge separating them from Prospector Base.

Dallas estimated they would reach the ejecta field in about an hour, putting the mountain ridge about twenty-five kilometers ahead. He activated his headlamps in the quickly gathering gloaming. Soon, five ovals of light once again passed over the terrain. Luis turned his headlamp on, though Robbie did not need light to "see" at night. It just helped Luis better anticipate a bump before Robbie went over it, so he could shield his ribs.

At 20:10, Dallas noted the ground sloping up toward the northwest. They had reached the crater ejecta field.

"Take five."

Once again, four pressure suits plopped down, raising small clouds of dust. The still Martian air settled the dust quickly. Helmets hung down, their lights cast onto exhausted laps.

Allie broke the silence. "Flash, how are we doing?"

"We've come fifty kilometers, so we have twenty-five to go."

"And you figure we have enough oxygen to reach base by 07:30 tomorrow?" Allie was fully aware they were not getting a full twenty-four hours out of each canister.

Dallas did a quick mental calculation. If they maintained their two-kilometer-per-hour pace, they should cover the twenty-five kilometers in 12.5 hours. That meant they would arrive at 08:40. They would only have to hold their breath for an hour and ten minutes. "Yeah, we'll arrive with time to spare."

"Liar."

"It won't be the first time I made you do the impossible."

Dave interjected, "All I can say is, that case of beer better be ice cold."

"Dave, ithe cold on Marth thould nod be a problem."

Dallas admired Luis's fortitude. Even as busted up as he was, he still maintained his sense of humor.

Dallas stood. Everyone took his cue and rose alongside. As he ascended the slope toward the crater rim, his thighs burned and his breathing became labored.

"Pace yourselves. I want us to make up the lost time on the downslope on the far side." He slowed to one and a half kilometers per hour by his estimate. After seven hours, the slope flattened out. Dallas paused long enough to turn around. He strained to make out where the black of the sky met the black of the horizon.

The lava field at the base of the crater ejecta field lay featureless in the black shadows of night. Another dark expanse to the north hinted at the crater they stood beside. Unlike the one that they crashed into, the rim around this crater was rounded. The walls had fallen in, succumbing to the forces of wind, water, and ice over the eons. If any of the original cliff remained, the deep shadow that filled the basin cloaked it from view.

Dallas quickly typed their position and time, ANMHE, and sent the file. He reestablished their direction of travel, noting that the line would take them ever so slightly down inside the crater rim before climbing back out. Normally, he would just follow the rim around until they intersected their intended line of travel. In the grand scheme of things, the additional distance was insignificant, and it would save them from slowing their pace on the uphill grade, no matter how short it might be. But he feared getting off SaMMCon's recommended course, even if it meant slower progress. Dallas stuck to the bearing, gradually dropping down the gentle slope inside the crater rim. He walked quickly, hoping to make up for some of the time they would lose climbing back out. The rest of the landing crew followed him, mute, grit and gravel crunching softly underfoot.

At 05:00, they stopped descending. Following the direction-of-travel line on his visor, Dallas saw the terrain gently rising ahead to the crater rim. The rim, dimly visible, reflected the predawn light coming from the east. He saw the western rim sweeping away from them to the north, the crater basin below still hiding in a remnant pool of black night.

At 06:59, Dallas crested the crater rim. Ahead, the mountain ridge that lay between them and Prospector Base shone in the dim morning light. Their direction of travel ran directly through a high saddle nestled between two higher peaks. He estimated the saddle lay a thousand feet higher than where he now stood. They still had to descend about a thousand feet before they reached the base of the ridge. In all, they would have to climb two thousand feet before they stood in the gap, where he hoped they could see the base below.

Just as Dallas stepped forward to begin the descent down the ejecta field, his oxygen sensor began to flash yellow. *Damn it, I really hoped to see the base before running out of oxygen.* Dallas had understood it was a fool's errand from the start. They all had. They were the first humans to land on Mars, albeit not exactly where and how they intended to land. They knew the risks. Statistically, 60 percent of all previous unmanned missions to Mars had ended in disaster. Even EPSILON's early reconnaissance and supply missions had not been completely immune.

Dallas continued walking, though slower now. Once he and the crew had understood where they landed, they had understood the odds of getting to Prospector Base were against them. But the opportunity to walk on the surface of Mars— well, it beat sitting around in a battered tin can waiting to die. So they struck out to see the neighborhood, so to speak, even if it was unlikely that they would make it home. And to their credit, he and his crew had traveled over fifty kilometers— across the surface of Mars! They were the first in human history to do so. How many billions of people had come before them, and only now, they were the first?

The oxygen alarm flashed red. Dallas knew he had only a minute left before the effects of hypoxia set in. As a weight-saving measure, the EPSILON engineers had designed the CO_2 filtration system to vent to the atmosphere. As a result, his blood CO_2 levels would not rise, giving him an uncomfortable "out of breath" sensation. He would merely slip into unconsciousness, like an airline passenger experiences when the cabin suddenly depressurizes. It almost pained him to consider that those soulless bastards had done him a mercy.

It was an amazing phenomenon, how many memories the brain could recall in a minute's time, passing before the conscious mind like colorful entries in a parade, marching past his mental review stand. Dallas thought of his parents. It was their love and support that had encouraged him to take up and excel at climbing. Their financial support that got him through college. When he brought Ann home to visit before leaving for Patagonia, they had absolutely adored her. He had not dared to tell them in person when he and Ann broke up. They flew cross country from Seattle to Pensacola, their pride in him fully on display when he graduated from Naval Aviation Officer Candidate School. They constantly communicated with him when he was stationed in the Middle East during the Iranian War. They were the first to greet him after his release from POW prison, weeping profusely as they embraced him. And they absolutely gushed when he announced to them his selection to the Prospector 1 flight crew on the first manned mission to Mars.

Dave walked up to Dallas's side, slipped an arm under his, and gently eased him to a sitting position. Allie dropped down beside him, holding his gloved hand in hers. *I am so proud of this team.* In the three years that they had trained together, they had developed a profound love and respect for each other. It was difficult at first, throwing five alpha personalities together. The clashes in those early days had been epic. But they eventually united around a common objective—to be the first humans on Mars. It was out of their recognition that they needed each other to accomplish that goal that they learned to tolerate each other's quirks, and to rely on each other's strengths, to trust one another. In the end, their bond was unbreakable, even as they faced imminent death.

Dallas became light-headed. He noted with curiosity two dust devils down-slope on the ejecta field. *How odd—dust devils at this early hour of the morning.* His conscious mind flickered and guttered, like a candle whose wick had burned to the end. As his eye lids drooped shut, his final thoughts were of Ann. Then the candle burned out.

CHAPTER 29

"What do you mean you won't authorize sending the base RBIs to intercept the landing party?" Ann was incredulous. According to Monica's calculations, the RBI units could intercept the landing party, delivering extra oxygen and ensuring that they reached Prospector Base. Ann had never known Malcom to countermand her like this.

"Ann, understand my position here. My hands are tied. I'm responsible to the owner for the investment in the entire Prospector program, with thirteen missions in the pipeline. Those RBI units are responsible for base construction and maintenance for all of those missions, and maybe more. EPSILON has invested billions—*billions*—in the Prospector program. The loss of those RBIs would be catastrophic to EPSILON's presence on Mars, far more catastrophic than the loss of a single manned crew. Without those RBIs, the crews we send will be too overworked to mine, refine, and ship product back to Earth, which I remind you is the reason we are there in the first place. I've been forbidden to send those units unaccompanied across dozens of kilometers in the hope we can reach the crew in time. I'm sorry Ann, but that's the way it has to be."

Malcom's voice softened as he made his final point. He had dreaded this possibility ever since he realized that his flight operations director and his Mission 1 commander had had a relationship at one time. He had been reviewing personnel files during the annual performance evaluations two years ago when he noted the intersection of their work histories. Ann, of course, assured him that there was nothing between her and Dallas. It had been over ten years since they had been a couple. Malcom had observed their interaction at EPSILON. They were always professional and detached. He had even hired a private detective to observe them after-hours. After a month of negative reports, he dropped the matter.

Malcom was a master at understanding human behavior, keeping what he knew tucked away in a back corner of his mind, in case he needed it for future reference. It was, after all, his understanding of politics as a NASA administrator that had attracted EPSILON's owner to him for his current position. But right now, Malcom was counting on his flight operations director to do the right thing, even though he could not tell her so.

Ann had spent the past four hours working with Monica, calculating the range of time and location of intercept based on various speed of travel assumptions—both for the landing party and for the base RBIs. She also coaxed the RBI v 3.4 navigation software module, along with a software patch, out of Roger. He, in turn, had persuaded the RBI v 3.4 engineering team to provide a copy of Robbie's navigation module. When they learned he wanted it installed in the 3.0 RBIs used for base construction and maintenance, they provided the patch. They were already considering the software upgrade in the older machines based on their own contingency planning.

From what Roger could tell, Robbie performed flawlessly on his cross-country trek. He was still with the landing party based on the most recent satellite imagery. He assured Ann that download plus launch time would be less than fifteen minutes for the two older RBIs.

Everything had been prepped and ready for transmission when Ann approached Malcom. Now he had shut off their one chance of saving the crew, evaporating all her efforts and hopes.

He turned away from her distraught expression. "Ann, I absolutely need some shuteye. I have a news conference scheduled for tomorrow morning that I still haven't prepared for."

With that, he excused himself. Malcom let himself out the back door of the SaMMCon building, walking around it and then across the parking lot to his office and waiting cot. Regret weighed him down like sandbags, burdening his every step.

After Malcom left the conference room, Ann took a moment to compose herself. Her encounter with Malcom made her so angry she found herself fighting back tears. She took a few deep breaths, daubed her eyes, then returned to the mission control room. She detoured over to Courtney's INCO flight control station.

Without breaking stride, she looked Courtney in the eye and uttered two words, "Do it."

Ann continued to her station, sat down, and took another swallow from the cold cup of dark roast coffee beside her keyboard to steady her shaking hands. The next eleven hours were going to be pure hell for everyone, waiting to see if her gambit worked. It was the landing party's only hope, their only chance to survive. Ann resigned herself. Whether she saved the landing party or not, she was out of a job once Malcom found out tomorrow. Either way, she knew she would never regret her decision. She settled in for the wait.

CHAPTER 30

Massive waves pounded, crushing blows in steady succession, each more massive than the previous one. The interlude between waves was a relief, even peaceful. The incessant pounding continued. It felt as if he would die, the pain nearly unbearable. Seconds became minutes, minutes became hours, hours became an eternity. *Dammit, leave me alone!*

Dallas's eyes fluttered open. LaDonna leaned over his chest, both hands together, fingers interlocked, arms straight. She dropped her full weight onto his chest in the same steady rhythm as the waves. "Come on, Dallas! Come back to us."

Dallas tried to breath, but he was out of sync with the rhythmic pressure on his chest. He started to cough. LaDonna immediately stopped administering CPR. "Roll him on his side. Quickly!"

Dallas retched. His newly conscious body was determined to rid itself of his stomach contents. But after nearly seventy-two hours of fasting, his stomach was as empty as the wasteland he lay in. After twenty seconds, the retching stopped. He lay there on his side, too exhausted to speak through his ragged breathing.

Once his breathing eased, he spoke to LaDonna, his voice a mixture of confusion and incredulity. "I'm alive? 'Donna, how is this possible?"

She patted him on his shoulder. "The cavalry arrived just after you passed out."

Dallas was too confused to respond. LaDonna rolled him so he was facing the opposite direction. He saw Robbie inserting a red oxygen canister into Dave's backpack. About thirty feet beyond, Luis sat on Robbie, facing in Dallas's general direction. A third Robbie was partially visible behind the second Robbie, evidently replacing Luis's oxygen canister.

LaDonna spoke to Dallas again. "For redundancy, they each brought enough oxygen canisters for all of us to safely reach base, in case one of them didn't make the full trip."

Dave joined the conversation once his new canister was secured and his pack closed up. "I can't believe SaMMCon sent them all this way. Their normal programming forbids them from traveling more than ten kilometers from base unaccompanied. Every Prospector mission on the books is dependent on these RBIs for their success. Not that I'm complaining, mind you."

Dave's RBI unit next rolled toward Allie, who was assisting LaDonna with Dallas. The second RBI unit moved to LaDonna after closing Luis's pack.

The cobwebs rapidly receded from Dallas's mind. He slowly pulled his legs under himself and sat up. His chest hurt like hell. It felt like LaDonna might have cracked the cartilage in his sternum, a common outcome of CPR. But he was alive. He deduced that he had been the first to have his oxygen canister replaced, but by then he had quit breathing. LaDonna began CPR as soon as his pack was closed.

Dallas's voice was hoarse. "Donna, I can't thank you enough."

"That's right, you can't."

Dallas smiled to himself. Her steely demeanor was forged by years of practice on test pilots during her air force career. But underneath, her heart beat in time to the Hippocratic oath. She cared deeply for her patients. "And while you're at it, you can spend the rest of your existence thanking SaMMCon for delivering the oxygen that made your resuscitation possible in the first place."

"It's my next priority, doctor." Dallas retrieved his smartphone from his sleeve pocket and pulled the stylus out of the phone. He composed a message and sent it to SaMMCon.

DELIVERY RECEIVED! THANK YOU!!!
ANMHE.

Dallas replaced the stylus and tucked the phone back into his sleeve pocket. He got to his knees, then slowly stood up. A few stars danced about in his field of view, but they quickly faded.

The RBI units finished up their work with Allie and LaDonna, then stood motionless, awaiting new orders—which Dallas provided. "Fall in behind us for the return trip to base."

Dallas scanned the ground to the west. He located the tracks the RBI units had made as they traveled up the ejecta field toward the stricken ground party. Finding Prospector Base now was simply a matter of following the tracks. He set out, LaDonna hovering nearby like a mother hen. Dave followed close behind. Allie walked beside Luis, who reclined once more on Robbie. The two base RBI units followed Robbie in single file.

Dallas strode forward. "Let's get to base. I'm starving!"

CHAPTER 31

The walk down the ejecta field was uneventful. Dallas found that if he walked bow-legged, with his feet splayed outward, he could better bend his knees to absorb the shock of stepping down. He winced in pain whenever he stumbled. But being in pain beat being dead.

With a redundant supply of oxygen, there was less urgency to travel as quickly as possible to reach Prospector Base. Dallas was grateful. His pace uphill to reach the pass two thousand feet above was glacially slow. His cracked sternum precluded heavy breathing while ascending.

Dallas paused at the base of the ridge. He sat down on a boulder and surveyed the hillside that they were about to climb.

After checking Dallas's vitals, LaDonna walked back to Luis to check on him. His face was pale, his eyes listless. It was obvious he was in pain. She worried about internal bleeding. But he did not have a fever and was not thirsty. She forced herself to relax. "Are you ready for the final climb?"

Luis half smiled. "Don'd mind the climb, jusd the fall ad the end." He intended to chuckle at his own humor but winced instead. His cracked ribs made laughing impossible.

"No cliff at the end of this hill, Luis. Nothing that Robbie can't handle." She gave him a reassuring pat on his leg and walked back to Dallas. He, too, was pale, but his eyes were clear and focused.

"On your feet, sailor. I'm dying for lunch and a hot shower."

Dallas slowly rose to his feet and saluted her. "Aye aye, Doctor."

Dallas immediately set out, following the RBI tracks uphill. He stopped to rest every half hour, checking the group's progress. He opted to skirt around a scree field that extended across their path from the base of the peak on their left. It added an extra half hour. But neither he nor Luis could travel through the uneven and uncertain footing crossing the scree field. And for the first time since they had started out on this journey, he didn't need to worry about oxygen depletion by taking a little extra time.

At noon, they crested the ridge. Higher peaks loomed above them on both their left and their right. But ahead lay a broad valley, the opposite ridge about twenty-five kilometers distant. The valley floor was gently rolling terrain, much like they had crossed before climbing the crater that lay behind them. The ridge sloped down from their position at the same angle they had just climbed. The valley floor was five hundred feet lower than the point where they had started uphill.

Dallas scanned his helmet from side to side until his direction-of-travel line flashed red. His eyes followed the red line past the base of the ridge out onto the valley floor. About a mile out, he saw it—a cluster of white domes and equipment. He estimated that Prospector Base was only about eight kilometers away, as the pressure-suited crow flies. He pointed. "Prospector Base! Have you ever seen anything more beautiful?"

Everyone responded in unison, "Where?"

"Follow your direction-of-travel lines about eight klicks out onto the valley floor. It's partially obscured by a small rise, but you can see it."

Four helmets turned from side to side. Each stopped when their direction of travel locked in. The helmet comm airwaves quickly clogged with exclamations of joy, accompanied by all manner of fist-pumping, high-jumping exuberance. The two women hugged each other. Dallas high fived Dave, even though he winced in pain.

"How aboud a liddle love over here?" Dave and the two women crowded around Luis and high fived his free hand. He, like Dallas, winced with every slap, but his smile never dimmed.

Dallas waited until the celebration expended itself before redirecting everyone to the remaining task at hand. "Standing here won't get us any closer. Move out!"

Dallas set off, following the RBI tracks downhill. In spite of his painful sternum, it was all he could do not to break into a run. But he held his pace, determined that the team would arrive as a group. They came this far by working together. He had no desire to allow their hard-won *esprit de corps* to devolve into an everyone-for-themselves mad dash to the airlock.

When they reached to valley floor, their walking pace slowed, but the chatter remained unabated. They all felt a sense of elation to be so near their goal. As the tops of the domes and the communications antennae rose into view, the lighthearted chatter intensified.

Prospector Base was a cluster of five ten-meter-diameter inflatable domes, arranged in a tight pentagonal formation. Each dome touched two others on either side for mutual support against the fierce spring winds of the southern hemisphere. The void in the center of the pentagon was filled with a smaller dome, seven-and-a-half meters in diameter. The only equipment the central dome contained was the base water recycler unit. The recycler received wastewater from the galley, and from the shower and sink. Dubbed "the hall" by the EPSILON engineers, hatches connected the smaller central dome with each of the larger five domes that surrounded it. Each large dome was accessible to the others only via the hall.

The larger dome closest to the landing party's direction of travel possessed an airlock to the outside atmosphere. Known as the common room, it housed the main base computer, the communications equipment, the primary electrical supply panels, the CO^2 scrubber, the oxygen generator and the backup oxygen supply tanks. The oxygen generator electrolyzed water collected from dehumidifiers located in all domes except the greenhouse and from the CO^2 scrubber. It released molecular oxygen directly back into the air supply. The hydrogen it generated was directed to the carbon dioxide scrubber. By combining the Sabatier Reaction with the pyrolysis of waste product methane, the only reaction products were water—which was sent back to the oxygen generator—and graphite. The graphite was removed from a small steel reactor vessel once a week and stored in the shop where Dave and Luis intended to test the feasibility of carbon fiber manufacture. Excess heat generated by the water recycler, the oxygen generator, and the CO^2 scrubber supplemented the heat output from the base heating system.

The dome to the immediate left contained the crew sleeping quarters and a well-provisioned sick bay. The next dome housed the galley, food storage, and exercise equipment. The table in the galley doubled as the base conference table. The fourth large dome served as the greenhouse. It also housed the composting toilet and a shower. The final dome contained the shop, an assay bench, and a small smelter. The smelter was intended to develop proof-of-concept smelting processes for the various rare earth elements collected from the surrounding region. Subsequent Prospector missions would construct and operate a commercial smelter. A second manual airlock was attached to the shop dome to allow direct unloading of ore and loading of ingots for shipment to Earth.

After walking another two hours, Dave pointed to his right. "Hey, a DV! Why didn't SaMMCon send this to pick us up instead of the RBI? Could have saved us some walking!"

The landing party passed by a Descent/Ascent Vehicle two hundred yards to their left. It was identical to the now-wrecked vehicle they had left behind over three days ago—except it still possessed its Lander Module and it was outfitted for shuttling cargo, not crew. Fully deployed, the legs held the Descent/Ascent Vehicle vertical. It was one of several vehicles that delivered the various base components, plus the two RBI units that assembled the base in preparation for its human occupants. The ten-meter-tall white cylinder stood out starkly against the sere landscape and butterscotch sky. The word EPSILON was printed down its side in bold block letters.

Dallas surmised that with the loss of their original DV, this cargo DV would need to be somehow refitted to maintain the proper vehicle rotation. A portable fuel generator was partially visible behind the Descent/Ascent Vehicle to electrolyze water mined by the RBI units into hydrogen and oxygen, the fuel needed to power their ride back into orbit to dock with the Prospector 2 Command Module when it arrived. The Prospector 1 and 2 flight crews would have about six hours together at Prospector Base to debrief before his team would lift off for their return to Earth in the Prospector 2 Command Module.

The crew walked another five hundred yards. Then Dallas spoke. "Here's the power cable supplying the DV fuel generator. Watch your step, everyone."

They all stepped over a two-inch-thick black power cable lying on the ground. The cable ran from the nuclear Kilopower reactor array to the landing/launch pad.

The landing party knew they were four hundred yards away from the base when they passed by the Kilopower reactor array nestled in the bottom of a crater off to their left. The five ten-kilowatt units were arranged in a semi-circle around, and connected to, a primary bus splitter. Two cables emanated from the main bus, one which the landing party had just recently stepped over that served the landing/launch pad, and the other paralleling the party's direction of travel to serve the base.

The reactor units looked like beach umbrellas on steroids. Each reactor generated up to 10 kW. Since the base and vehicle pad utilized a maximum of 40 kW, one reactor unit was maintained on standby, essentially serving as a spare. Each 1500-kilogram main reactor unit housed a forty five-kilogram core of highly enriched uranium 235 and operated between 1,000 and 1,200° F. Twin neutron absorbing boron carbide rods controlled the rate of fission. In the event of an electrical fault, the boron carbide rods passively drop into the HEU core, dampening the nuclear reaction.

Heat passively transferred to a Stirling engine via liquid sodium housed in stainless steel tubes. A shaft from the piston turned an in-line 240-volt electrical generator. The conversion of heat to electricity was an efficient 30 percent. The remaining 70 percent of the heat dissipated to the atmosphere via a radial metal array, "the umbrella shade," atop the ten-foot-high reactor.

"The RBIs constructed an access road down into the crater," Dallas noted. "Allie, that should come in handy when you service the reactors."

"The radiators look pretty clean. I bet I don't have to dust them off for months."

Though the reactors were the primary source of energy, the base itself was equipped with enough fuel cell capacity to keep the greenhouse warm and lit for a week, the assumed maximum down-time for routine reactor maintenance or repairs. What was unspoken was that in the event of a complete loss of electrical generation, the base occupants would last no longer than two weeks before they froze to death. Once the backup fuel cells ran out of fuel, the greenhouse would go dark, the food growing within it would freeze and die, the water supply would quickly freeze, and atmospheric CO_2 would begin to build up. The chance was miniscule, but it was part of the risk that one accepted when signing on to Prospector missions.

Dallas was one hundred yards away when he finally saw the ground the base rested on without obstruction. He continued walking toward the airlock outer door that faced them directly. Placed on the lee side of the building, it minimized ingress and egress complications during the spring wind storms.

Dallas stopped short. "What the …?"

Debris lay scattered about on the ground outside the door. It was a curious assortment of flotsam. Dallas stepped over a clipboard. He passed a fabric dome patch kit. RBI tracks radiated away from the doorway in all directions, including the set of tracks that Dallas had followed since the RBIs intercepted the landing party earlier this morning.

He stopped again. As he looked at the open outer door, he realized he could see directly into the common room through the air lock. Everyone else stopped as they drew even with Dallas. The chatter hushed, and they all stood in silence.

Dave was the first to break the silence, "Well, at least the beer will be cold."

Dallas was incredulous. "The goddam RBI units forgot to close the inner airlock door." He distrusted the machines, but this sort of incompetence exceeded anything he had ever imagined.

Dallas stepped around an office-style chair and quietly walked forward toward the air lock. He inspected the outer door. In many regards, it resembled a submarine hatch, only shaped like an upright oval. It swung out away from the frame. The handle was a large wheel that was spun to lock and unlock the door. Gauges on the interior and exterior indicated the internal airlock pressure, useful information to prevent inadvertent explosive decompression events.

Dallas walked into the airlock. Something small crunched underfoot. He paused at the inner door, identical to the outer door, except it swung inward into the crew common room. But otherwise, the hardware was identical to the outer door. Both doors possessed a failsafe to prevent one from opening when the other was open. Both could be operated electronically from the console in the common room, or manually.

Dallas stepped through the inner door into the common room. Various lightweight items lay scattered about the floor. Cabinet doors were flung open by explosive decompression. He set an overturned chair upright and rolled it toward the console.

Sitting down, he typed on the keyboard, calling up environmental information. "The other compartments are still pressurized."

He typed some more. "Temperature in the other compartments is nominal."

Dave and Allie entered the common room. Dallas continued typing. "Reserve air tanks are fully pressurized."

He turned around and faced the open airlock door. "Dave, help Dr. Pleasant assist Luis inside. Allie, come in behind them and close and seal the outer door after Robbie gets in. Then close and seal the inner door. Keep those damned base RBIs outside!"

After everyone was inside, Dallas turned back around to the console and resumed typing. A hissing sound pervaded the room. As the pressure increased, everyone opened and closed their jaws to equalize the pressure on their eardrums. After a few minutes, the hissing subsided.

Dallas announced, "Cabin pressure nine hundred millibars. It's safe to remove your helmets."

Everyone cautiously unsealed their helmets and slowly removed them. LaDonna helped Luis, since his left arm was still restrained. He had two black eyes, both nearly swollen shut. The blood had begun to drain downward into his cheeks, turning them green. Blood crusted the lower half of his face. Luis smiled broadly. His teeth shone white behind his swollen lips. But Dave, LaDonna, and Allie cast anxious glances to one another.

When Dallas spoke, his voice sounded odd to himself, having spent the past three days inside a small echo chamber. "Dave, go to the galley and break out provisions for everyone. Allie, you're on the second console keyboard. Research the activities log. I want a copy of the record showing how the RBIs depressurized the base. I want to transmit what they did back to SaMMCon ASAP. 'Donna, take raccoon-face back to sick bay and get him patched up." He nodded and winked at Luis.

For his part, Luis only smiled. He was too happy at being alive to acknowledge his commander's good-natured jab. He held out his good arm, which was accepted by the flight surgeon. She assisted him out the door to the hall.

Once they cleared the doorway, Dave reentered with an armload of rations. "Couldn't find any beer. Must be hidden behind this giant cache of energy bars." He tossed half a dozen bars each at Dallas and Allie. Then he handed out sip-cups of water. Once done, he stood another chair upright, sat down, and tore the wrapper off an energy bar. Dallas stared at Dave, one eyebrow raised, posing his unspoken question.

Dave quickly responded, "Gave Doc and Luis their share in the hall." Then he attacked his hapless energy bar like a wolf eating a fresh kill.

Dallas unwrapped a bar and handed it to Allie.

She had already opened the files with the base activity logs, scrolling through the entries to find when the RBIs left the base. "Flash, the RBIs didn't leave the airlock open. Here's the log, showing when they left yesterday afternoon."

Dallas rolled his chair beside her to view her monitor. The log clearly showed that the inner door was opened, then closed and sealed. The airlock was depressurized, then the outer door opened and closed. He was completely perplexed. "How the hell were the doors opened?"

Allie scanned forward through the entries. They contained typical environmental operations. Heaters for air and water systems turning on and off. Lighting levels in the greenhouse synchronized with the Martian diurnal cycle.

Halfway through an entry, she stopped. "Dallas, the doors opened two hours ago."

"Allie, how is that possible? Nobody was here."

"The commands came from the base computer. See here?" She pointed out a line of text to Dallas.

The confusion on his face was obvious. "Why would SaMMCon send a command to open the airlock?"

Allie opened the base communications log. Starting with the time shown on the activity log time stamp, she scrolled backward through the communication log entries. Then she expanded an entry in the communications log. As she read the entry, she set her half-eaten bar down. "Dallas, you're not gonna believe this."

Dallas rolled his chair closer to hers to read the text on her screen.

CHAPTER 32

The CEO handed the software engineer an external hard drive. It bore the same bright yellow label with bold black lettering on both sides.

CONFIDENTIAL

PROPERTY OF AUTOTRONICS CORP

DO NOT OPEN UNDER PENALTY OF LAW

IF FOUND CONTACT:

LOSTNFOUND@AUTORONICSCO.COM

Randy Porter's eyes brightened like a child opening a Christmas present. "How did you get your hands on this?"

"That's need to know, and you don't need to know." The CEO paused just long enough to reestablish his well-practiced smile. "This hard drive contains the operating system code for RBI v3.0 units. I know that our arrangement is nearly expired, but would you be willing to extend your services? I'll make it worth your while. I've deposited another million in your account. An additional four million dollars will be deposited upon completion."

Randy hated working for this guy. With his Ermenegildo Zegna suits, Salvatore Ferragamo shoes, Stefano Ricci silk shirts, gold Audemars Piguet watch, and matching gold Leve cufflinks, the CEO was the epitome of the stuffy corporate culture he so despised. Hell, the CEO probably farted hundred-dollar bills. But for what the guy paid him, Randy was willing to overlook a few character flaws.

Even though no details of the "assignment" were provided, Randy deduced what the work entailed. "Throw in that yacht that I partied on last week, and you've got a deal."

Behind his smile, the CEO gritted his teeth. But the company's new black hole facility that they occupied was operational. Going forward, covert operations like Randy's would take place here. Even with the anticipated staff of ten, it would be less expensive to operate than what the CEO paid this cretin, and it would be more secure. He felt his blood pressure drop just thinking about the prospect. He nodded. "Deal."

Randy fondled the hard drive like it was one of his Ukrainian brides. "So, what could you possibly want me to do with the operating system for the same model of RBI units used at Prospector Base?"

CHAPTER 33

"Ann, they made it! They made it to Prospector Base!" Courtney Plumm could not contain her excitement.

"Forward a copy to my station!" Ann's shout toward the front of the mission control room was barely audible above the rising cheers.

She immediately opened the file when it arrived on her screen. She took a deep breath to calm herself, then read:

> PROSPECTOR BASE
> MSD: 57482
> MTC: 14:44:28
> ATTACHMENT: COMM LOG - MSD
> 57482, MTC 12:01:46
> FROM: Commander Dallas Gordon
>
> Landing party arrived at PB with assigned RBI unit and both base RBI units. Found airlock to crew common room unsecured prior to arrival. Base safety and environmental control files appear to have been compromised. See attached communication log file. Base activity log indicates override of failsafe and remote opening command executed 2 hours and 14 minutes prior to crew arrival. Interior doors remained secured. Atmosphere in remainder of base unaffected.
>
> The following actions have been taken. Inner and outer airlock doors have been closed and secured. Crew Common Room repressurized. Safety and environmental

control files are being restored from backup. All communication channels remain open.

Electrical/Software Engineer O'Donnell believes the attached comm log contains a Trojan horse that failed to self-erase due to a coding error on line 17. If true, transmit a firewall patch to block future hacks.

Dr. Pleasant is treating Luis's injuries. Medical evaluations of all landing party personnel forthcoming after we get some sleep.

Thanks for the help. We made it!

ANMHE

A jumble of emotions hit Ann. She felt elation that the landing party had actually made it to Prospector Base after the unprecedented seventy-five-kilometer trek over the surface of Mars. She felt pride being a member of the team that put the first human boot prints on another planet. And she felt apprehension that the cyberattacks were not just limited to the Prospector Command Module and Descent/Ascent Vehicle.

Ann drank cold coffee from the mug on her desk. The bitter liquid helped to ground her disorganized thoughts. She strolled to the front of the mission control room, high fiving any men and hugging any women she encountered all along the way. The flight control staff, to a person, made sure that she encountered them along the way. After she reached the front of the room, she allowed the reverie to continue for a few minutes.

She motioned for silence, pausing until all eyes were on her. "We made it! In spite of the daunting technological challenges, humankind finally stepped outside the gravity well of our home planet. And I'm proud to say that this EPSILON team made it happen! Nice work, everyone."

The room erupted in cheers and applause again. Bottles of Dom Perignon circulated through the flight control room. Hollow pops resonated, and corks bounced off the ceiling and the observation windows.

Ann glanced at the back of the room, where Malcom had apparently just walked it. He stood silent, staring at her, as others around him celebrated. She motioned again for silence. "As most of you are aware, many of the challenges that the Prospector 1 mission has encountered were deliberate sabotage. The Command Module flight systems were hacked. The DV navigation system was hacked. And now it appears that the base environmental and safety systems were hacked. Someone does not want this mission to succeed. But it also appears that whoever that person is, they made a mistake that may lead us and the FBI to them. We finally have a sample of the virus code that they used to embed these damaging commands into our systems." The cheers resumed.

Ann looked over at Malcom, then walked over to her network officer, John Carpenter. She still had to shout over the din, "John, please forward a copy of that comm log attachment to IT. Get them to work right away on a patch for the base computer firewall. If they glean useful insights, share them with the FBI. I'll forward a file copy to Director Coleman to pass on to the FBI cyber unit."

Ann walked apprehensively to the back row of flight stations. When she reached Malcom, she stood tall, chin raised, ready—even willing—to be fired on the spot for what she'd done. But she grew confused as he stood before her, his head hung in contrition.

"Ann, I've never been as ashamed of myself as I am right now. Instead of having the moral courage to stand up to the owner, I let you take the full weight of the decision to deploy the RBIs to save the crew. Thank God, you did exactly as I expected you would." Tears welled in his puffy eyes. "Can you ever forgive me?"

Ann forgot the reverie that surrounded them. "You knew all along I'd disobey your directive?"

Malcom nodded weakly. "I was counting on it."

Ann eyed him cynically. "But I'm still fired, right?"

His face brightened. "Oh, no! In fact, the owner will be paying you a bonus! After we left last night, I couldn't sleep.

I called him back and told him if we lost the landing party, I'd resign immediately. He backed down and told me to deploy the RBIs. When I checked in with the night flight control shift, I learned that you had already implemented the rescue. I spoke with the owner again this morning and told him that you had deployed the RBIs on your own initiative. Thanks to you, he's a national hero in the media's eyes." Malcom weakly tossed his head in the direction of the glass lobby wall above and behind him. A cluster of reporters gathered around EPSILON's owner and Ajay Kumar.

Malcom continued to stand there, head hung, eyes puffy, arms drooping listlessly at his sides. He had been Ann's mentor and champion ever since he had hired her. She owed so much to him. This admission of betrayal stung deeply. "Malcom, how could you do this to me?"

His voice quavered. "Ann, I promise you I'll never place you in a position like this again."

With all of their history together, Ann wanted to believe him. *But what if the crew hadn't made it? And the RBIs were lost in the process? Who would have been the owner's sacrificial lamb? It would be my ass on the line, my call that cost EPSILON everything.* They continued to stand face to face.

Malcom towered a full foot over his FOD but felt as if he were the smaller of the two. "Whatever I can do to make this up to you, Ann, just say the word."

Ann looked past the taller man's shoulders. She nodded at the mob of reporters. "For starters, you can keep me away from that pack of wolves."

Suddenly Malcom reached out and gave Ann a bear hug around her shoulders. "Of course I will!" Her first reaction was shock, but she found herself returning his hug in spite of herself. Maybe Malcom had been too gutless to take charge and too willing to throw her under the bus. But he had found the courage last night to face up to his sins and make amends and was willing now to accept his failure.

Malcom pulled away as quickly as he entered her personal space, his expression half one of relief, half that of a chastened puppy.

Ann looked him straight in the eye. "Malcom, don't ever do anything like that to me again." But this time, they were smiling at each other.

Ann stood back and composed herself. "Malcom, we have a landing party that needs our help. Can I meet with you and Ajay in the conference room?"

Malcom spun and called back over his shoulder as he headed for the lobby stairwell door, "We'll meet you in five minutes."

Ann turned to her desk, still unable to fully join in the reverie. *I just wish Cliff could have been here to see this.*

CHAPTER 34

"Ajay, we now have a definitive time stamp for a malware transmission." Ann highlighted the header above a communications log from Prospector Base displayed on the conference room wall monitor. "Please query your solar weather satellites for any record of this transmission. Triangulate the transmission origin and compare it to the source found for the Command Module hack."

The diminutive NASA Representative's eyes sparkled with anticipation. "Ann, send me a copy of your comm log file. I'll let you know what NASA finds."

"Thanks, Ajay."

Then she turned her attention to Malcom. "Malcom, will you speak with Director Coleman and send the comm log file to him?"

"Of course, I will. It's been a while since the FBI gave us an update. This gives me a good excuse to speak with him about that, too. Let's get the FBI on the trail of whoever is hacking our equipment."

The wall-mounted screen flickered to life as Malcom initiated a video chat with the local field director.

CHAPTER 35

Ann opened her eyes. She couldn't remember the last time she had slept so deeply. Her smartphone continued vibrating on the cardboard box beside her cot that served as a nightstand.

Like her colleagues in the mission control room, Ann slept in the office building across the parking lot from SaMMCon. Landing on Mars should have been a triumph of the human spirit and EPSILON technology. But it felt more like a cloak-and-dagger spy mission where you had to stay one step ahead of an unseen enemy or be killed. She wanted to scream at the top of her lungs "This is *bullshit*!", but she respected the soft—and at times not-so-soft—sounds of her staff sleeping around her. She quietly sat up and grabbed her phone. The call was from Malcom. She whispered as she answered. "What is it?"

"Ann, NASA determined the origin of the transmission. How soon can you meet me in the conference room?"

"Five minutes!" Ann ended the call and stood up. She was still wearing yesterday's clothes. It was one of the "perks" of sleeping in a glass-lined office. She grabbed a clean blouse, grabbed her bag of toiletries and headed down the hall to a restroom.

She quickly changed in a stall, then confronted the large mirror above the bank of sinks. The bags under her eyes revealed the strain of the past two weeks, but at least her eyes were clear. She applied deodorant under her blouse, hurriedly brushed her teeth, and ran her fingers through her hair until it looked presentable. She tossed the toiletries bag into her office as she walked past, then headed for the main door.

Malcom was already seated at the conference table when Ann entered the room. His bloodshot eyes also showed the signs of strain. But his tasteful wool suit was wrinkle-free.

Even the pocket handkerchief looked freshly pressed. The smell of morning cologne was evident without being overpowering. Ann looked down to confirm the spit shine on his patent leather shoes and suppressed a laugh. Even in the semi-darkness beneath the table, it was obvious Malcom sported one light gray and one navy-blue sock.

"Malcom, you really need to give your personal receptionist that raise. I see she laid out mismatched socks again."

Malcom crossed one foot over the other, looking mildly uncomfortable. "Janice protests color blindness. But I'm dubious. Everything else she lays out for me is so well coordinated." He proudly patted the breast of his off-the-rack suit.

It was true. Ann suspected the socks were a ruse for Janice to visit SaMMCon. Malcom inevitably had her bring a matching sock, and Ann had observed that Janice always managed to stop and talk with Drew Usher at his GNC station in the front row after completing her delivery to her boss.

Ann sat down across from Malcom.

He quickly started, "I received this information from Ajay less than half an hour ago. At the time of the malware transmission to Mars, Mars was framed between two NASA solar weather satellites. An encrypted transmission was intercepted by both satellites. Based on the time and position of the satellites at intercept, the origin of this transmission was also triangulated to the Moon. Once again, based on the orbital position of the Moon, the back side of the Moon would have been facing Mars at that time."

"So the Chinese *are* behind this?"

Malcom tempered his FOD. "NASA still can't say with certainty the Chinese are behind the attack, just that the transmission originated from their communications array."

"So, we still don't know who is trying to sabotage us."

"Correct. But the FBI is sifting through laser optical communications records for clues. Sooner or later, they'll track down the perpetrator."

Ann sat back and pondered. Between Cliff's murder, and the cyberattacks against the Prospector 1 mission, she felt so disheartened. She allowed herself to hope that maybe, just maybe, they could put an end to the sabotage and avenge Cliff's murder. But until then, she and the rest of the SaMMCon staff remained confined to the EPSILON campus. For the foreseeable future, she would sleep in her office. But the chances the Prospector 1 mission would succeed were brighter.

Ann excused herself and returned to the mission control room. Members of the day shift trickled in, replacing the night staff. "Day" shift was a misnomer. Shifts at SaMMCon synched to the Martian clock. Because the Martian day was forty minutes longer than an Earth day, there were periods when the "day" shift reported for duty at night on Earth. It was a bit disorienting at first, but she and the flight control staff had adjusted to it over the past nine-plus months since the Prospector 1 Command Module first left Earth orbit.

As Ann stepped through the hallway door into the flight control room, John Carpenter waved to get her attention. She walked over to the network officer's station.

"Good morning, Ann." She smelled coffee on his breath. John, like Ann, was an unapologetic coffee addict. Between the two of them, they consumed as much of the beloved brew as the rest of the flight staff combined. The aroma reminded her to detour to the coffee bar on her way to her flight control station.

"What's up?" Ann replied.

"IT got back to me about that Trojan horse the landing party sent to us."

Malcom, who had followed Ann into the flight control room, now walked up behind her. The network officer briefly redirected his attention to the mission director, "Good morning, sir. I was just telling the Flight Director that IT finished analyzing the Trojan horse the landing party sent to us."

John paused just long enough to equally divide his attention between his superiors. "They don't think that they can code a patch to stop another attack."

He grew nervous when he saw the glare of disbelief in Malcom's eyes and Ann's pursed lips. He quickly cleared his throat and resumed, "The thing is, the code used for the Trojan horse—it came from us."

CHAPTER 36

Dallas woke to the soft pulse of his alarm. After sleeping on the ground—or not sleeping at all—for three nights, waking up on an air mattress on a cot felt like the time he woke up in the Venezia Tower in Las Vegas.

Dallas and five other China Lake test pilots were in Las Vegas on three day's leave. While gambling in the casino at the Venetian Hotel, three of them were recognized by the casino security's facial recognition software. All six of them had been featured at one time or another in TV news segments aired during the Iranian War. The casino manager and her entourage surrounded the embarrassed flyers, and after a very public recognition, comped the pilots three suites in the Venezia Tower.

In spite of the hellacious hangover the next morning, Dallas felt like he had slept on a cloud. He had never slept on a more comfortable bed, or in such luxury—until he woke up on Mars. He attributed his good night's sleep to the planet's low gravity. The pressure points felt on a mattress on Earth simply did not occur on Mars.

Dallas sat up, slipped on his shoes and a jump suit, and wandered into the galley. Luis already sat at the table, drinking coffee from a mug with his good right hand. The puffiness of his face was mostly gone. The lingering discoloration of his face, plus the cast and sling on his left forearm, were the only visible evidence of his fall.

Luis flashed a smile at Dallas. "Good morning, Flash! Can you believe how good the coffee is at this cantina?"

EPSILON had spared no expense when it came to provisioning Prospector Base. The instant coffee tasted like it was brewed in a coffee shop back home. The difference was in the container. Here on the surface of Mars, the rich brown liquid rested in an open-topped mug. Dallas smelled the aroma even before he walked into the galley. In the Command Module, all liquids were provided in a sealed squeeze pouch, which prevented any aromas from escaping. Since much of what one tastes is really what one smells, most foods consumed in space tasted bland. Coffee, even the best that money can buy, had no taste when drunk from a squeeze pouch.

"Luis, you're one helluva salesman. I'll have a cup, too." Dallas turned toward the cabinets to retrieve a coffee packet and finally noticed Allie. She busied herself making breakfast in a microwave. Ann and Luis had been inseparable since the landing party arrived three days ago. They had been attracted to each other since before leaving Earth. But their recent near-death experiences brought their emotions to the surface. They had no intention of waiting for a tomorrow that might not come.

Dallas had counseled them together yesterday, "As long as your relationship doesn't compromise base efficiency or safety, I'm neutral—provided your 'activities' don't keep me up at night." He had also checked with Dr. Pleasant, who assured him that Allie's birth control was bomb-proof until it was reversed after she returned to Earth. The mission planners had accounted for the potential of a mixed-gender crew. They didn't want to see any three-eyed children resulting from the high levels of cosmic radiation experienced on the surface of Mars.

Dallas walked over beside Allie. He reached into the cabinet for a clean mug and a coffee packet. "Good morning. I can't help but notice how chipper you and Luis are this morning."

Allie, who normally radiated her tough-girl aura, blushed. "Flash, can I nuke a breakfast packet for you when I pull ours out?"

"Sure, Allie. What's on the menu?"

Allie rummaged in the cabinet. "Looks like waffles with maple syrup or scrambled eggs. At least that's what I can see up front."

"The scrambled eggs were pretty good during our habitat training. I'll have the eggs." Dallas poured himself a cup of hot water, stirred in a packet of coffee and a pinch of salt, then returned to the table.

Allie wrinkled her nose. "Flash, I'll never understand how you can ruin a perfectly good cup of coffee with salt!"

Dallas cast her a crooked smile. "Blame it on the Navy. It's a habit I picked up when I was stationed in the Middle East on the Gerald R. Ford."

Dallas changed the subject as he sat down across from Luis. "Are you able to set up the assay bench equipment for Dave today?"

"Yep. Dave said he could assist. The setup only requires three hands. Between Dave and me, we've got three!" Luis held up his good right arm. "Besides, Robbie can help me if Dave's not available."

Dallas looked surprised. "I thought Robbie was spending most of the day assisting Dr. Pleasant in the greenhouse. She thinks she can improve on the arrangement of the hydroponic beds the base RBIs set up."

"He is. But she said I could borrow him if Dave and I can't get the shop equipment set up ourselves."

Allie set a plate of waffles in front of Luis, and a plate of eggs in front of Dallas.

"Allie, what are you going to have?"

"Go ahead and eat those, Flash. I'll just throw in another packet of eggs for me. It only takes a minute."

Dallas had just finished his scrambled eggs as Allie sat down beside Luis. He was getting up from the table when he heard a pulsing tone coming from the Hall. He and Luis quickly exchanged glances, then rose to investigate.

The noise grew louder when they walked into the hall. The only equipment there was the water recycler. It rested against the wall to their left between the galley and greenhouse doorways. The alarm came from their right.

Dave popped his head out of the sleeping quarters door, and LaDonna Pleasant emerged from the greenhouse. Dave and Luis both looked at each other, then spoke simultaneously, "The Common Room."

The four crewmates walked toward the Common Room. Allie trailed behind, holding a plate of scrambled eggs in one hand and a fork in the other. Dallas noted that the pressure gauge on the common room door read 900 millibars, then opened the hatch. The noise became louder.

Luis seated himself at the computer console and examined the monitor. A notification flashed in time with the alarm.

Dallas noted that the alarm related to the water recycler. The water recycler operated in two stages. First, it filtered out any macro contaminants, stuff like food particles from the kitchen or Martian dust from the shower. Then, the filtered water was distilled to remove bacterial contaminants or dissolved compounds. The capacity of the water recycler was 100 liters per day, just over five gallons per person. While that volume of water paled in comparison to the millions of metric tons available beneath the surface of Hellas Planitia, none of the native water was drinkable. In fact, it was highly toxic.

All the water on Mars is contaminated with perchlorate, a simple molecule composed of one chlorine atom and four atoms of oxygen. By recycling water, the mission engineers minimized the amount of native water needed to maintain Prospector Base and the resultant perchlorate that had to be periodically removed from the distillation boiler.

Using a mouse in his good right hand, Luis drilled into the water recycler control software. "The isolation valve between the boiler and the cooling coils is closed. The backflow prevention valve on the inlet side is trapping the pressure in the boiler. The boiler pressure is two and a half times higher than the operating pressure and climbing."

Concern registered in Dallas's voice. "Luis, can you open the isolation valve?"

"It's not responding. Dallas, if the pressure vessel blows, it'll take out the hall with it. It could even take out the entire base."

"Come with me." Luis quickly rose and followed Dallas out into the hall. Dallas stopped in front of the water recycling unit. "Where's the isolation valve?"

Luis located the boiler. The condensation coils emerged from a small, box-shaped device at the top. Luis pointed up at it. "There it is. It's operated by an electrical solenoid. I can just see the power wires on the back side."

"What happens if we cut the wires?"

Luis stroked his chin. "Solenoids like this one are spring-loaded in the open position. Electromagnets pull it closed when power is run to the unit. If we cut the wires, the valve will open."

Dallas looked over his shoulder at Dave, who had joined them in the Hall. "Dave, go get me a pair of wire cutters out of the shop."

As Dave headed for the shop, Dallas walked into the galley and grabbed a chair from beside the table. He stood on it in front of the recycler boiler. Dave returned and handed Dallas the wire cutters. Dallas reached around the back side of the isolation valve, the heat of the boiler burning his chest through his jump suit.

"Here goes nothing." Dallas snipped the wire. A loud hissing emanated from the cooling coils. Shortly after, more shrill noises sounded as the pressure relief valve on the storage tank vented steam. The sound level dropped as the recycler returned to its normal operating pressure.

Dallas stepped off the chair and located Allie. "Allie, go through the operations log. Find out what caused this."

"On it, Flash," she responded from the common room, seated at the computer console with her half-eaten plate of scrambled eggs.

Dallas walked over to her, gingerly holding his shirt off his chest until it cooled down. He grabbed another office chair and sat beside her as she scrolled through the log entries.

"Here. The main computer commanded the isolation valve to close at 0600." She tapped the monitor where the entry was located. "This looks a lot like what happened with the airlock. I'm checking the comm log now."

She scrolled through the communications log for ten minutes but found nothing. "Dallas, SaMMCon said that the only reason that we found an entry in the comm log for the airlock hack was due to a coding error. What if whoever sent that virus fixed that error this time around?"

Dallas felt the hair on the back of his neck begin to rise. To his horror, he realized that in all the confusion around the water recycler malfunction, all five of the hatches between the Hall and the large domes were left standing open. A repeat of the decompression event that had preceded their arrival would decompress the entire base. The crops in the greenhouse would be lost. Water anywhere in the delivery system would freeze. Even worse, the oxygen used to repressurize the common room was not fully replenished. There was too little in reserve to repressurize the entire base. Not to mention that if any crew member didn't happen to be wearing their pressure suit and oxygen tank at that moment, they'd be asphyxiated in seconds.

The soft thrum of compressors evacuating the common room airlock filled the air. The hatches were about to open. "Shut it down!"

Allie looked at Dallas quizzically. "Shut what down?"

"The main computer! Shut it down. Take it offline."

She protested, "But what about all of our automatic environmental controls?"

"Shut it down! We can monitor everything manually until SaMMCon figures out how to stop this." Allie closed the open programs, then shut down the computer. The airlock compressors fell silent.

Everyone eyed their surroundings nervously, but the environmental equipment continued to operate as before. After thirty seconds, everyone exhaled audibly. The oxygen generator hummed softly, still making oxygen. The CO_2

scrubber continued removing CO_2. The water recycler purified water. The heaters radiated warmth.

Dallas listened for any further decompression of the airlock, or the characteristic hiss of a breaking airlock seal. He heard nothing. Dallas folded his arms and leaned back against the console beside Allie as he addressed the landing party. "Looks like we're on our own again."

CHAPTER 37

PROSPECTOR BASE
MSD: 57485
MTC: 07:18:36
ATTACHMENT: OPS LOGS - MSD 57485,
MTC 06:36:21 – 06:51:19
FROM: Commander Dallas Gordon

Prospector Base experienced another cyberattack. Base safety and environmental control files were compromised again. See attached ops log entries. Water recycler was sabotaged as a diversion for another unscheduled airlock breach. Water recycler remains operational minus electrical control of boiler isolation valve. Commands to depressurize airlock and breach both hatches were defeated prior to implementation. Interior base atmospheric pressure nominal.

Ann sat back in her chair. *God, not again!* She leaned back in to continue reading.

The following actions were implemented. Airlock manually cycled back to base atmospheric pressure. Inner and outer airlock doors manual operation only. Main computer taken offline. All safety and environmental equipment and controls monitored and operated manually per SOP 46.521. Base Electrical/Software Engineer O'Donnell found no communications log transmitting the malicious commands. She believes the coding error previously found was corrected, resulting in deletion of the comm log entry and the Trojan horse related to this event.

I told IT that Prospector Base had to have a firewall patch! Ann felt her pulse in her temples. IT had declined to develop a patch on the fear that it would preclude remote software updates. Their arguments were persuasive at the time. High cosmic radiation levels on the surface of Mars meant an increased frequency of random coding errors as the high energy particles slammed into the base computer's hard drives.

Hard drive scans were frequent and automatic. Results were included in the telemetry monitored by SaMMCon. When irregularities were detected, a patch was uploaded back to Mars to correct the error. The procedure was so automatic and so routine that only IT paid any attention to it. Until now.

Base computer and S-Band communications and telemetry uplink will remain offline until the origin of the cyberattacks is neutralized. Base MGPS communication channels remain operational through laptops and smartphones. Please direct all communications to Prospector Base via MGPS downlink.

Sorry to make communications difficult. We nearly had a very bad day.

Next base status report forthcoming at MTC 12:00:00.

ANMHE

Ah, that explains why this came through the MGPS channel. Ann reread the base dispatch with the same mixture of incredulity and helpless frustration.

In the meantime, Malcom had forwarded the message and comm log attachments to the FBI. Ajay had NASA searching for suspect communications intercepts in the hopes of confirming the earlier lunar transmissions triangulations.

The knots Ann had felt in the pit of her stomach during the landing party's trek across the Martian surface returned. The Prospector 1 mission teetered on the brink of failure. The five lives of the crew, and the financial stability of EPSILON, depended on what she did next. If only she could figure out what that was.

CHΛPTΞR 38

Ann hung up her phone. Malcom had just summoned her to a meeting in the conference room with SaMMCon IT manager Juaquin Garcia, head of EPSILON corporate security Susan Steinman, Prospector Program Chief Software Engineer Jason Smith, and SaMMCon Human Resources Manager Rebekah Gradwahl.

She groaned inwardly, contemplating yet another meeting as Juaquin explained how IT could do nothing about the cyberattacks the Prospector mission was experiencing. But Rebekah's presence was a new wrinkle to her. Perhaps Juaquin feared her resistance to his intransigence and had called in HR to keep Ann in line. The faintest of smiles crossed her lips at the thought.

Ann entered the conference room and noted everyone's position at the table. Malcom had seated himself at the head. Juaquin and Susan sat to his right, Jason and Rebekah to his left. Malcom motioned for Ann to take a seat beside Rebekah. Ann outwardly maintained a neutral expression, but the seating arrangement confirmed her suspicions about Rebekah's purpose at the meeting.

"Thanks for coming, Ann. Juaquin and Susan were just discussing with Jason, Rebekah, and me something IT discovered late yesterday. Juaquin, would you please re-summarize what you just presented in order to bring Ann up to speed?"

"Certainly, Director." The IT manager directed his attention to Ann. "It's standard company practice to review the contents of any hard drive after an employee leaves SaMMCon."

Ann perked up. This was not the topic she had expected to hear.

"As you are probably aware, we maintain a log of keystrokes for each hard drive. This is then compared to actual data files stored on the hard drive and the backup servers. We do the same for digital communications, voice, text, and email. Software performs the necessary scans, then reports any discrepancies.

"We try to run the scans within two weeks of the departure of an employee, but lately, we've gotten behind due to the increased workload. Anyway, we just yesterday completed the security scans on the last two employees to leave SaMMCon."

Ann was puzzled.

It must have shown on her face, as Juaquin quickly answered the question that was on her mind. "They were Cliff Sherman and Randy Porter."

Ann's heart sank. IT must have found something damning on Cliff's hard drive after all. She just couldn't accept that he had done anything to betray the company.

Juaquin continued, "Cliff Sherman's security scan came back clean. No indication of questionable activity on his hard drive."

Ann wanted to shout, *I told you so!*, but she maintained her composure.

"But we found a number of discrepancies on Randy's hard drive." Ann caught Juaquin casting a furtive glance Rebekah's way, obviously sheepish for the delay in investigating it. Randy had left EPSILON over three months ago. Rebekah remained stony-faced.

"We found a total of five incidents where keystroke entries were deleted from the keystroke log. But the activity log showed no activity at all during corresponding times. Some of the non-activity lasted twenty minutes. We also found gaps in the comm logs before and after most of these time periods. We can't tell if the deleted messages were incoming or outgoing, only that they were deleted from the logs."

Ann tried to recall everything she knew about Randy Porter. Randy had been attached to the Prospector Software Development Group, which explained Jason's presence. She had sat in on meetings with Randy a few times, mostly related to development of the Prospector computer operating systems. The goal of the Prospector Program Administration had been to have all mission-related computers operating on a common software platform. The Command Module, Descent/Ascent Vehicles, base safety and environmental controls—they all operated on the same operating system and utilized a common operator interface.

Randy was a total geek. He lived, ate, and drank software coding. He was renowned within EPSILON for generating the bulk of the code used by the common software platform. Ann did not know him at all outside of work, but she imagined he spent his personal time the same way he spent his work time: in front of a computer monitor.

Malcom spoke next. "Rebekah, please recount for us your interactions with Randy the final three weeks of his employment."

Rebekah cleared her throat and shifted in her seat, obviously uncomfortable sharing company personnel matters. "Mr. Porter approached me about three weeks prior to the date he severed employment at EPSILON. He was adamant that he was underpaid and demanded a salary nearly triple what he was making at the time. I explained to him that the appropriate time to request a salary increase was during the annual review period. He demanded an application for a non-review salary adjustment. He said he would go straight to corporate HR if I didn't give him the form. So, I gave him a blank form. He submitted to me the completed form that same day. It had been signed by Jason."

Rebekah glanced at Jason, who filled in where she left off. "He forged my signature. I was completely unaware of what Randy was doing."

Rebekah resumed her narrative. "I forwarded Randy's salary request on to corporate HR. As I expected, the denial came back three weeks later. I forwarded the denial to Jason per company policy."

Jason picked up the story from Rebekah again. "When I received Randy's salary request denial, I was confused. At first, I thought it was for someone else. After I read through it carefully, I became certain it was in fact Randy's request. Then I got angry. I knew I hadn't signed off on it, so I figured he had somehow gone around my back. I had always tolerated Randy's eccentricities because he was so prolific, but this time he got my blood boiling.

"I called him in to a private meeting, where I laid a copy of the denial down on the table and asked him what the hell he thought he was up to. What happened next was weird, even for Randy. He didn't say a word. He just stood up, went back to his desk, shut down his PC, grabbed a few personal items out of his desk drawer, and walked out. When I got back to my office, there was a resignation letter in my email inbox. That's the last I've seen of him."

Just as Jason finished speaking, a soft knock sounded on the closed conference room door. The door opened halfway. Ann recognized one of Juaquin's technicians.

"Juaquin, here's the results of the scan that you asked for."

The technician handed a sheet of paper to Juaquin, then left the room. Juaquin scrutinized the paper for a few moments, then set it down.

"After finding the irregularities on Randy's PC, I asked for a review of activity on our backup servers within the timeframe of the irregularities. This summary indicates that directories containing the Prospector program's common software platform were accessed and copied. Not just the operating system folders, but folders containing the administrative commands SaMMCon uses to remotely control the Prospector hardware—the Command Module, the Descent/Ascent Vehicles, base environmental and security applications."

The room hushed. Malcom broke the silence. "Thank you, Juaquin. This information clarifies the scope of our vulnerability and realizes my worst fears. Please package the evidence that your team has collected to forward to the FBI.

"Rebekah, create a copy of Randy's personnel file to retain for our records. I'll forward the original to the FBI. Ann, is there some way that we can share what we now know with the Prospector 1 landing party without tipping off Randy or anyone else he may be working with?"

Ann thought for a moment, looking across the table at Juaquin. "Have you got any ideas? Right now, our only means of communication is through the MGPS system."

Juaquin stroked his goatee thoughtfully. "So far, all of our transmissions to and from Mars have utilized our primary carrier frequencies—2.295 GHz for the Command Module and 2.287 GHz for the orbital communications satellites. The MGPS satellites use 3.001 GHz.

"To this point, cyberattacks have been transmitted across the first two, but not the MGPS frequency. None of our equipment operates at that frequency. We're lucky the Flight Operations Center happens to monitor and can transmit at 3.001 GHz."

Ann expressed reservations. "But every time we thwart a cyberattack, a follow-up attempt is made. Doesn't that indicate that Randy has been monitoring our communications through MGPS as well?"

"Not necessarily. He can learn about the landing party's successful countermeasures the same way as everyone else—through the media. Remember, 3.001 GHZ is not an EPSILON frequency. It belongs to NASA. I'll concede that Randy is frighteningly smart, but his familiarity is with EPSILON's systems and processes, not NASA's. I think that our use of NASA's carrier frequency might be a blind spot to him.

"Besides, with the base computer shut down, he can't attack any more of our assets on the surface. The worst that could happen is that maybe he could disable the two smartphones that weren't adjusted to uplink to MGPS during the trek from the disabled DV to Prospector Base."

Ann agreed with Juaquin's logic. But she worried about the prospect that Randy might evade any attempt to locate him if he learned that he had been found out. On the other hand, maintaining communication with Dallas and the landing party was more critical than ever, now that the primary base computer was shut down. She looked at Malcom. "What do you think? I'd like to risk informing the landing party we've figured out who is behind the sabotage. If Randy does know about MGPS communication, it might prevent them from inadvertently communicating with him, thinking that he still works for EPSILON."

Malcom nodded his head as Ann spoke. "Ann, given the common history between you and Commander Gordon, can you frame the message in such a way that an eavesdropper wouldn't understand what you communicated? If you can't, as much as it pains me to say it, we'll have to keep the landing party in the dark. There's no way I want to tip off Randy Porter."

"How about I run the message by you for your approval before I send it?"

"Perfect." Malcom stood up, adjourning the meeting. "Alright everyone, you all have your assignments. Get those packets on my desk ASAP. We've got a hacker to catch."

CHΛPT€R 39

SaMMCon
MSD: 57485
MTC: 11:32:25
FROM: CAPCOM

SaMMCon to Prosp Base.. Received notice of manual operation of base systems. Actions taken approved. No objections to use of SOP 46.521. Disuse of 2.287 GHz and 2.295 GHz approved. You are directed to provide hourly updates for duration of comm blackout. Please continue use of 402.5 MHz uplink frequency for ongoing comm. Oxygen replenishment is your highest priority. RBI-assisted prospecting approved. Transfer of seeds to hydroponic beds approved. EPSILON Prospector 1 Lander Module salvage plan in development. Refurbishment of cargo ascent vehicle for crew evacuation approved. ANMHE.

Dallas puzzled over the response from SaMMCon on his smartphone. While each sentence individually made sense, the organization seemed random. And use of "please" and "no objections" were not normal in these technical messages. It was as if Ann had brainstormed a message but had sent it before doing any editing. Then the double period at the end of the first sentence caught his eye.

When Dallas and Ann worked as climbing instructors, they had devised a way to send each other brief messages embedded within climbing school emails that they sent to each other. The messages were short, and typical of a young couple in love. Mundane notes arranging for supplies or listing needed climbing gear often carried embedded messages like "I love you," "meet me for dinner," or "I want you now."

Dallas smiled recalling the many messages that they sent back and forth. He reexamined the message on his phone, mentally extracting the first letter of each sentence that followed the double period. RANDYPORTER. He frowned. A name? But not one he was familiar with.

Dallas rose from the galley table and walked into the common room. Allie O'Donnell was the only occupant. She looked up from the laptop that she was working on when he entered. "Hello, Flash."

"Hi, Allie." Dallas pulled up a chair and sat beside her. "Are you familiar with the name Randy Porter?"

Allie turned her chair toward Dallas, her eyebrows knit together in an expression that he could not quite decipher. "Why do you ask?"

"Ann Waters and I worked together as climbing instructors for a year after we graduated."

A knowing smile grew on Allie's face.

Dallas ignored her and continued, "We used to send each other secret messages encoded in our climbing school emails to each other."

Allie's smile broadened.

Dallas felt his cheeks beginning to flush. "Ann just sent me a coded message."

He gave his phone to Allie. She read the message, then looked back at Dallas, puzzled.

He explained, "Just read the first letter of each sentence that follows the double period."

Allie looked back down at the phone screen. Her lips moved as she silently read each letter as instructed. She looked back at Dallas after she finished. "Dallas, Randy Porter was an EPSILON software engineer. He basically wrote the operating system used by all Prospector program computers. I never met him, but I would go out for drinks with some of the other engineers that worked with him. They regarded him like a rock star—unapproachable, and a little bit crazy."

"Do you think Ann is trying to get us to communicate with him?"

Allie hesitated briefly. "I don't think so. One of my friends in IT sent me an email while we were in our sleep pods. He said he had just watched Randy leave the company. Randy came out of a meeting with his supervisor, emptied his desk, hung his ID card on the corner of his computer monitor, and left. His supervisor just stood there like he was in shock. My friend asked him if he just fired Randy, but he said 'No, I think he just quit.'"

Dallas contemplated this new piece of information. "Allie, remind me which computers use the Prospector operating system."

"Well, for starters, our base computers." She patted her laptop monitor.

"What else?"

"There's also the Command Module mainframe, and the DV computers." Dallas sat in silence, nodding his head ever so slightly. "Allie, every system that you just mentioned has been sabotaged."

"I'm not so sure about the DV, Flash."

"I am, now." Dallas continued, "The DV navigation system has never failed. Not during Earth trials. Not during any of the base supply missions. Not once, until our mission. When it comes to Mars landings, EPSILON's DV record is the envy of every country and company with missions to Mars.

"Ann just identified the person behind the sabotage. She wants us to know that they have figured it out, even though they haven't caught him yet. That's why she sent the coded message."

"So, what do we do now?"

"Just like she indicates in the body of her message. We get this base fully operational, then we do what we came here to do. We start prospecting."

CHAPTER 40

Ann fidgeted in her seat. Malcom had reconvened the same employees to the conference room that attended yesterday's meeting: Juaquin Garcia, Susan Steinman, Jason Smith, and Rebekah Gradwahl. She noted the expression of human territoriality. Everyone took the exact same seat that they had occupied the day before.

The conference room door opened, and Malcom walked in. Ann marveled that he managed to wear a different suit every day despite the lockdown. The time display on the otherwise-blank wall monitor indicated the mission director was five minutes late. To her bemusement, he too took the same chair he had occupied yesterday.

"Sorry I'm late. I had to reschedule another meeting being bumped by this one." Malcom dialed the tabletop phone pad. The wall monitor flickered to life bearing the image of Steve Coleman, the local FBI field director. "Good morning, Steve. I apologize for being late. On my way out of my office, my receptionist reminded me I needed to reschedule a meeting that conflicted with this conference call."

"Malcom, the apology is mine," the field director demurred, "for pulling you and your staff together on such short notice. I know how busy you all are, so let me get straight to the point."

The field director organized a few sheets of paper lying on his desk. "Our analysts immediately got to work on the information that you provided yesterday. What we learned supports your suspicions about Randy Porter's involvement in the cyberattacks on the Prospector 1 mission. He's our primary suspect.

"Porter has been a busy man—busy, and a bit arrogant. In cases like this, it's common practice to cover one's tracks by reformatting the hard drives of any devices being used. However, after speaking with Mr. Garcia, our analysts learned that EPSILON monitors for such events as part of its security protocols. Mr. Porter simply erased pertinent files and log entries to avoid immediate detection. As most of you are probably aware, erasure simply removes headers without deleting data. He was buying himself some time, knowing his actions would eventually be discovered.

"Here's a summary of what we know so far. The day Mr. Porter left EPSILON, he closed his financial accounts. We've determined that all of his funds were converted to cryptocurrency. We also learned that he keeps all his encryption keys in a dark web e-wallet. We have retrieved the keys and are currently examining the various currency block chains of these now-frozen assets.

"Curiously, the earliest block chain represents a payment three weeks prior to his departure. The payment was made forty-eight hours after a failed external attempt to examine and possibly download your Prospector operating system and files. Because he had unrestricted access as a system administrator, it appears that Mr. Porter was able to detect the breach and trace the source. The source is incredibly sophisticated. So far, its location has eluded us.

"Mr. Porter owns a gaming console and plays several online games in his spare time. He played one game in particular the same day after the cyberattack. That game site has recently come to the Bureau's attention as a place used by drug cartels and munitions dealers for clandestine communications. Mr. Porter was involved in several message exchanges with the source of the cyberattack, followed by that first cryptocurrency deposit. Based on the content of the messages, we believe that first payment on the order of $100,000 was blackmail buying Mr. Porter's silence.

"Two weeks later, Mr. Porter had a change of heart. There was another exchange of messages. The following day Mr.

Porter himself downloaded the Prospector operating system and administrative files to a dark web file sharing site. One message to the source followed that night, and the files were uploaded and erased from the site. What started out as a blackmail attempt ended as an offer of goods and services. A cryptocurrency deposit on the order of ten million dollars was made to Mr. Porter within thirty seconds of those file transfers."

Ann blinked at the mention of ten million dollars and saw the others reacting with raised eyebrows or other looks of surprise.

"The day that Mr. Porter walked out of EPSILON, he also walked off the grid. His house in Santa Barbara has remained empty since that day. We have detected no financial or cell phone activity. We can't even locate an image of the man. No hard copy photos in his house, no digital images anywhere online. He's simply disappeared. While we believe that Randy Porter is behind the cyberattacks experienced by the Prospector 1 mission, so far, we have no idea of his whereabouts. If he is using the same facilities as the source of his payments, he will be hard to track down.

"Until we apprehend him, continue to take every precaution to protect your assets and your people. When we get him, you'll be the first to know."

The conference room was silent until Malcom spoke. "Steve, have you made any progress tracking the source of the transmissions to Mars?"

"We're looking into the working theory that you've offered. We've examined the transmissions NASA intercepted outside of Earth's orbit, and we concur that the origin was the Chinese relay near the lunar south pole. Your idea of a laser optical transmission from Earth to the Moon has some merit. While such a transmission is undetectable by satellites or America's Moon base, the NSA operates a lunar listening post near the lunar south pole with laser optical capabilities. I've called in a favor with a friend of mine there. They're looking at their data as we speak. I'm confident they'll find the transmission, but they're sifting through terabytes of data. It may take some time."

"Ten million dollars," Malcom replied, "that's a lot of money. But what's the end game here? We've received no ransom demands. It's as if someone's paying him to destroy billions of dollars of investment, for what—spite?"

Steve quickly responded, "Ten million is a powerful motive. For us, the larger question is who paid Randy? When we figure that out, we may have a better understanding of motive. In the meantime, keep your SaMMCon staff confined to your campus. This is much larger than a hacker trying to score points. I'm certain this isn't over yet. Someone does not want EPSILON on Mars."

CHAPTER 41

Ann walked out of the SaMMCon Flight Control Center. Late September insects orbited erratically around the parking lot lights in the gathering gloaming. Ann hunched forward, uninspired by the soft serenade of katydids. She had spent the day absorbed with the return flight of the Prospector Command Module for the Prospector 2 mission, and with the Prospector 1 activity reports coming from the Martian surface. Notably, Dave Caraway had taken his first EVA in search of ore samples. An RBI had accompanied him, towing a small two-wheel trailer to stow his samples. When he returned, he would spend a few days in the shop smelting his samples.

She had heard nothing further regarding Randy Porter since the conference call with Steve Coleman in the morning.

Across the pavement lay her destination, the main office building of the SaMMCon campus. It was a two-story edifice of glass and insulated metal panels. In the daylight, the black solar film-treated windows contrasted with the uniformly silver exterior. But at this time of the evening, roughly half of the windows were dimly illuminated from within, like a toothy grin missing half its teeth. Ann turned her attention to the darkened second-floor window that demarcated her office, where she planned to spend the night as mandated by the campus lockdown.

Ann looked above the building to the Santa Maria twilight sky. A handful of the brightest stars shone feebly through the light pollution and the humid coastal air. She turned to the south, locating Mars within the ecliptic plane.

Ann resumed walking when an indistinct figure stepped away from a dark sedan parked just below her office window. The figure was male, above average height and weight. It was too dark for her to assess if he was athletic or not in his suit and tie. The hair on the back of her neck rose as he adjusted his path to intercept hers.

"Ms. Waters?"

Ann slowed her pace when she heard her name. "I'm Ann Waters. How can I help you, Mr. …"

Ann could see the stranger smile broadly in the dark. His teeth were perfectly arranged and as white as pearls. Ann immediately thought that someone's parents had spent a great deal on orthodontia.

"I'm so sorry. I didn't mean to startle you." The stranger quickly reached into a breast pocket inside his suit and removed a wallet. He deftly flipped it open to display a badge. It showed a brass shield with blue lettering and FBI insignia topped by a brass eagle with spread wings. The opposite wallet fold displayed a laminated ID card with a photo of the stranger beside the FBI insignia. Ann was just able to make out the words FIELD AGENT, SANTA MARIA FIELD OFFICE. The stranger continued to hold the items up as he resumed speaking, "I'm Field Agent Ted Gilmore. Director Coleman assigned me as lead agent investigating the cyberattacks on your Prospector 1 mission."

"Yes," Ann responded warily, "I was on the conference call when Director Coleman identified you as the agent assigned to our case."

The man continued, "For the past several days, I've been working with your human resources and IT people collecting evidence related to Randy Porter's activities. I was in our field office this afternoon reviewing evidence when I learned that Mr. Porter has been located. As you're aware, Mr. Porter removed all his images from the web. In cases like this, it's Bureau practice to enlist an eyewitness—someone who can identify Mr. Porter definitively. It greatly speeds up processing him into custody, as well as ensures that he doesn't somehow evade capture if we happen to confuse him with someone else who may be on his team.

"I immediately called Malcom McDowell asking for help. He offered your name. I called your number to confirm, but got no answer. I left you a text message."

Ann looked back down at her phone. There was a text message there. Ann quickly checked her ringer volume. "I'm so sorry, Agent …"

"Gilmore."

"I turned my ringer off for a meeting and completely forgot to turn it back on. Is there any way this could wait until the morning? I'm dog-tired. Besides, I'm certain someone from IT would be available then. They interacted with Randy a lot more than I ever have."

Agent Gilmore was undeterred. "Ms. Waters, the FBI has agents en route to the raid as we speak. We need an eyewitness tonight to properly process everyone we take into custody."

Ann sighed heavily. *Malcom, is this your idea of 'making it up' to me?* "Agent Gilmore, I need to contact Director McDowell first."

Ted Gilmore smiled. "Of course. I understand."

Ann dialed Malcom.

"Hullo, this is Director McDowell." It was obvious she had caught him asleep.

"Malcom, this is Ann. I'm so sorry to wake you. But I'm standing here with Agent Gilmore from the FBI and—"

His voice brightened up. "Oh, good! I was hoping that you'd jump at the chance to be the one to take Randy Porter down. They need an eyewitness."

Ann's irritation with Malcom faded quickly. Frankly, the thought of putting Randy Porter behind bars *was* appealing. How many times had she thought to herself, *I'd do anything to make this craziness stop*?

Ann looked squarely at Agent Gilmore as she answered Malcom. "Okay, I'll do it. Can you have someone cover for me in case this makes me late for tomorrow's shift?"

"I'm one step ahead of you. I spoke with Henry White just after I heard from the FBI. Ann, everything's covered at this end." Henry White was Ann's counterpart for the night shift.

"Thanks, Malcom. I'm sure I'll be back tomorrow morning." She raised her eyebrows as she looked at Gilmore. He nodded.

Ann signed off and hung up her phone. "Well, Agent Gilmore, it looks like I'm yours until tomorrow morning." Ann paused. "By the way, where exactly is the raid, anyway?"

Gilmore maintained his deadpan expression. "Seattle."

"Seattle?"

"Yes. Mr. Porter's working out of a building just north of downtown. Our flight is booked and waiting for us at the airport."

Ann ran her fingers through her hair self-consciously. "Ugh, I must look an absolute mess right now."

"Miss Waters, what you're wearing is fine. It's a charter flight. You won't have to interact with the public at all." He looked at his watch. "If we leave right now, I can have you back before your shift starts tomorrow."

"Agent Gilmore, you've got a deal. Even if I don't sleep a wink tonight, it'll be worth it to put Randy Porter behind bars."

Agent Gilmore reached out and gently grasped Ann's elbow. As he steered her toward the front passenger door of his car, she concluded that he was certainly FBI material: quite strong—strong, but with a well-practiced restraint. He opened the door for her, and she slid into the seat.

The vehicle was one of the latest-model ride share AVs. It had no steering wheel on the driver side. The touch screen in the front console was enormous.

Ted walked around the back of the car and took his place in the driver seat. "On. Airport."

The touch screen and the headlamps woke up. Then the car silently backed out of its parking stall and headed for the security gate. Agent Gilmore coached Ann as the AV drove out of the parking lot. "Ms. Water, I want to assure you that you'll be in no danger at any time. My instructions are to hold you safely out of harm's way until all the suspects have been subdued and secured. Then all you have to do is walk past them and point out which one is Mr. Porter." As they approached the gate, Ted pulled out his wallet, opened it, and pressed it against the driver-side window glass. The guard recognized him and waved him through.

Ann let herself sink into the soft leather seat as the AV glided along the long SaMMCon campus driveway around the south end of the Santa Maria Municipal Airport primary runway. They turned left onto Skyway Drive. Her fatigue evaporated like the damp of a summer rain exposed to the burning California sun.

CHΛPTΞR 42

Agent Gilmore's AV drove north on Skyway Drive, gliding past a dense assortment of aerospace manufacturing firms, suppliers, and hotels. For most of the twentieth century, Santa Maria had been a sleepy agricultural hub. Over time, it had accumulated wealthy refugees from Los Angeles, which was two hours to the south on US 101. In the past fifteen years, Santa Maria had become a boom town commensurate with the expansion of aerospace programs at Vandenberg Air Force Base. As the drive along Skyway Drive attested, Santa Maria had developed into a major center for aerospace companies and their suppliers. In the constellation of companies wanting to cash in on the "space rush," EPSILON was by far the biggest and brightest star.

They turned left at Industrial Parkway and headed toward a hangar abutting the main taxiway, stopping beside a gleaming white Beechcraft Hawker 1000 series corporate jet. Agent Gilmore guided Ann up the rolling steps onto the aircraft wing and toward the cabin door. Ann had flown first class many times in conjunction with her work. But nothing she had previously experienced prepared her for this cabin.

She stepped onto plush wool carpet. The color reminded her of the golden beach sand of Half Moon Bay, where she spent so much time as a teenager. On her left, to the rear, four leather captain's swivel chairs surrounded a mahogany conference table. On her right and toward the front, two reclining leather chairs were strategically placed for unobstructed window viewing. Retractable trays serving each chair were positioned discretely out of the way against the cabin wall. The wall separating the galley was occupied by two large-screen TVs, one on either side of the center doorway.

The cabin was paneled floor to ceiling with cherry. Recessed, indirect lighting illuminated the interior in a warm cherry wood glow.

"Welcome aboard. May I offer any refreshments before we take off?"

Ann flinched. She was so enamored with the cabin interior she had not noticed the statuesque flight attendant to her left as she entered. The flight attendant's merino wool blazer perfectly matched the color of the carpet beneath her feet. Her white jumpsuit exposed just a hint of cleavage and was accented with a blue silk scarf around her neck and a matching sash around her waist. Her leather shoes were a tasteful matte white, with the wide three-inch heels typical of her profession.

Agent Gilmore responded before Ann could answer, "No thank you, Jessica. We need to depart immediately. But we'd appreciate dinner once we reach cruising altitude."

"As you wish, sir."

Jessica closed and latched the exterior cabin door, then walked forward and disappeared into the galley. Agent Gilmore steered Ann to the reclining chair to her right. Once seated, she turned to him as he was seating himself in the recliner opposite hers.

He responded to Ann's question before she could ask. "The jet is a drug forfeiture. FBI partnered with the DEA on a big seizure two months ago. There were actually two jets. DEA took the bigger one. FBI got the leftovers." He waved his hand dismissively in the air. "The jets each came complete with a one-year prepaid contract for a pilot and stewardess."

Ann felt her lower jaw sag open. Upon seeing her reaction, Agent Gilmore's countenance sobered. "I keep it all in perspective by reminding myself how many American kids must have OD'd paying the Mexican cartel enough money to buy this plane."

Then he turned forward and fastened his seatbelt. "Please strap in, Ms. Waters. We'll be taking off immediately. The sooner we take off, the sooner I can get you home." After a brief pause, he added, "I hate to inconvenience you, but all unsecured phones must be shut off during the flight. It's FBI policy."

Ann pulled out her phone and turned it off. "I've got no use for it at this point, anyway." She dropped it into Gilmore's outstretched hand.

By the time Ann fastened her seatbelt, the twin Pratt & Whitney PW305 engines were already spooling up. Within seconds, they were on the taxiway, headed for the south end of the main runway. The aircraft U-turned onto the runway, then paused while the engines spun up to full throttle. When the pilot released the brakes, the stiletto-shaped craft shot forward and was airborne within ten seconds. Ann was pushed back into her chair. *I wonder if this is what Dallas experienced when he flew his F-35?*

By the time Ann thought to look out her window, her home in Pismo Beach was long behind them. In another ten minutes, the Hawker leveled out. Jessica appeared through the galley door, pushing a service cart bearing two sterling silver cloches and a matching champagne bucket. Again, Agent Gilmore anticipated her question. "Part of the contract."

Dinner was a Cornish game hen served over a bed of saffron couscous, freshly julienned green beans in truffle sauce, and a fresh arugula salad with a balsamic vinaigrette. Ann was unable to read the label on the champagne bottle, as it was covered by a white serving towel. But it was undoubtedly expensive. She had certainly tasted nothing like it at any of the New Year's Eve parties she had ever attended.

When she was done, Ann daubed the corners of her mouth with her white linen napkin, then placed it on her plate. The napkin had barely settled into place before Jessica whisked the plate and empty champagne flute away.

After dinner, Ted Gilmore looked at his tablet. "Our agents should be in place right now. I expect they'll be kicking in the doors momentarily. It will take longer for us to drive to the scene after we land than the amount of time spent there identifying Mr. Porter."

He leaned his recliner back and closed his eyes. "It's about forty-five minutes until we land at King County Airport. If you'll excuse me, I'd like to catch forty winks before we touch down."

Ann leaned back into her recliner, too. She was reeling from the events of the day. She had just gotten confirmation that Randy Porter was indeed behind all the cyberattacks on the Prospector 1 mission, and now here she was, on her way to confirm his identity. She was wired at the prospect, the effects of the champagne notwithstanding. But she forced her eyes shut. She wanted to be absolutely fresh when she confronted and identified her nemesis.

CHAPTER 43

The Hawker's glide path took it over the Kent Valley and Tukwila before dropping into King County Airfield. The coastal fog had begun to settle in, not thickly enough to affect visual flight rules, but enough to give each streetlight its own halo. After touching down, the pilot engaged the thrust reversers, throwing Ann forward into her seat belt. The aircraft decelerated to taxi speed and turned toward a bank of hangars on the east side of the runway, where it came to a stop.

Ann unfastened her seatbelt, following Ted's lead. They stepped out of the cabin and onto the wing just as a ground attendant pushed steps up to the leading wing edge. An AV silently pulled up beside the jet as they stepped off the wing. Ted once again led Ann to the front passenger seat of the waiting AV. As they walked, she noted the continuous loud hiss of traffic on I-5 on the hillside immediately east of the runway. She had glanced at the time display on the dash screen—10 p.m., but I-5 was still choked in traffic. Unbroken strings of headlights and taillights streamed to and from downtown Seattle, just five and a half miles to the north.

Ann scanned in vain to see Seattle's most famous landmark. "Where's the Space Needle?" The dense collection of skyscrapers to the north shielded it from her view. Ted ushered her into the front passenger seat, then walked around the rear of the vehicle and took the driver-side seat beside her. After he settled in, he called out the address of their destination.

"333 Pontius Avenue North."

The AV rolled off airport property and turned north on Airport Way toward downtown. Within 10 minutes, Ann was gawking at the skyscrapers as they slid past on either side, the AV maintaining its northbound course. The AV turned right, then left, confusing Ann as to her whereabouts until she made out the Space Needle to her left down the cross streets. They were in the South Lake Union district, north of downtown and east of the Seattle Center. For his part, Agent Gilmore texted nearly the entire drive.

Their AV turned down what seemed to be a deserted street. They pulled to the curb in front of a massive edifice of black-shaded glass and polished black granite, the two materials nearly indistinguishable in the dark. A series of low, angular concrete steps and landscape beds led upward from the sidewalk to what she presumed was the front entrance.

"We're here, Ann. We're cleared to enter immediately. Randy is in custody and cannot pose a danger to you."

Agent Gilmore exited the AV and led Ann up the stairs to what appeared to be a blank wall, except for a security pad with an iris scanner. Ted stopped at the device and bent forward. The wall to the left of the keypad revealed a pair of rectangular doors that parted and slid into the wall to either side. Light from a lobby spilled out onto the landing, partly dazzling Ann's eyes. She squinted as she stepped through the doors, her eyes adjusting slowly.

Gilmore led her past an empty reception desk to an interior door. He bent forward at another iris scanner and guided Ann through the door into an equally brightly lit hallway that terminated at an elevator door at the far end. She noted more security pads mounted on each wall denoting access doors to the various side rooms. Ted stopped at the third pad on the right and bowed again. To Ann's relief, this room's lighting was dimmed. Ted ushered her inside. The door closed behind them.

The room setup was a software engineer's dream. The walls were lined with workstations, each with an assortment of PCs and electronic equipment. All were vacant save one against the wall opposite the door. A hooded figure sat with his back to her. Pizza boxes, takeout boxes, and assorted aluminum cans littered the floor and workstation surface. He conversed with a handsome man standing to his side, who was reviewing the seated man's work.

The seated man—Ann judged him a software engineer—wore jeans and a hoodie pulled up over his head, his back to her. He typed furiously as he spoke. The standing man was immaculately dressed in an expensive Italian suit and shoes. His silver hair was thick and combed back, complementing a flawlessly tanned forehead and face. When he reached out to emphasize a point, Ann caught the glint of gold, from an expensive watch. Ann had to wonder whether these were more confiscated effects gathered from some FBI case; they certainly didn't speak of a government service salary.

"It's settled, then. You'll oversee the startup of our cyber espionage group." Without breaking the cadence of his conversation with the seated tech man, he turned toward them briefly, nodding at Gilmore and ignoring Ann. "Operations will begin here tomorrow morning."

The men continued to converse, but Ann couldn't make out anything else they said. She couldn't place the tall man, but he looked familiar to her.

Agent Gilmore walked past Ann into the room and strode toward the seated man. Without breaking stride, he reached inside his suit jacket out of her view as he moved.

The handsome man continued his conversation but slowly backed away from the techie as Gilmore walked closer to the workstation. "No, we'll start with six. Once you're comfortable with the team dynamic, then we'll staff up."

Agent Gilmore now stood behind the seated man. Suddenly, the room echoed with a loud hiss, like the rapid release of compressed air. The typing stopped. Agent Gilmore returned whatever he had pulled from his suit, then turned and addressed the other man. "The cleanup crew will be here in an hour."

The man nodded. "Like he was never here." He then turned and walked toward Ann. But he continued past her without acknowledgement and out the door into the hallway. Ann turned her head back and forth, unable to focus her attention between the closed door and Agent Gilmore. He beckoned her silently. Unable to tell herself *no*, Ann approached the agent. He still blocked her view of the engineer, who had not resumed typing.

"Well, this is an interesting turn of events, Ann. It turns out that the Bureau won't be prosecuting Mr. Porter after all." As he spoke, he reached once more into his suit jacket, retrieving and opening a small ziplock baggie. It contained what looked to Ann like a wet washcloth.

Ann huffed, "Why isn't Randy Porter going to be prosecuted? What—" She stopped mid-sentence as she caught sight of the seated man beyond Agent Gilmore. The tech slumped over his keyboard, hands hanging limply at his sides. A small hole surrounded by a growing halo of blood marked the back of his hood.

A cold shiver raced down Ann's spine—it was Randy Porter. Bile rose in her throat even as her mouth ran dry. She spun to flee, but Agent Gilmore's strong hand clamped over her mouth and nose, the other snatching her tightly at the waist. Ann gagged as a strong, ether-like smell invaded her nostrils. She thrashed to break free of his restraint, but a sweet aftertaste thickened in her mouth, and then everything went dark.

CHΛPTER 44

Malcom McDowell woke to the sound of his phone ringing beside his office couch. He glanced at the time—only 10:38 p.m. *Ugh! I had just fallen back asleep.*

Checking the caller ID, he took the call. "Malcom? This is Steve Coleman."

Malcom sat up, fully alert at the urgency in the FBI field director's tone. "What's up?"

Malcom heard a heavy exhale on the other end of the call. "Field Agent Gilmore was found murdered in our parking lot two hours ago. We believe it was connected to the investigation into Randy Porter."

The mission director sat forward, about to utter his condolences, when Steve Coleman continued, "There's more to it, which is why I didn't wait until the morning to call you. Agent Gilmore spent the afternoon reviewing evidence gathered at your IT department. He left our office at 4:38 p.m. to collect another batch of evidence at EPSILON. He never made it. The ME says preliminary time of death was between 4:45 and 5:00 p.m. We also—"

Malcom blurted out. "Wait. What time?"

"Five. Why?"

Malcom furiously scrolled through his phone log. "No, Steve, he called me at 5:45!"

Steve paused briefly. "You're certain it was Gilmore?"

"It sounded like him."

"Malcom, what did he say?"

Malcom recounted how Agent Gilmore had called to announce the raid on Randy Porter was imminent and asked for Ann Waters to accompany him and identify the man.

Steve Coleman's response surprised Malcom. "Well, that explains things. Gilmore's badge and security card were missing. Following a hunch, we found that he signed in and out of EPSILON's campus at 7:49 p.m. and 8:18 p.m., only according to your security video, it wasn't Agent Gilmore. Malcom, check your phone. I just sent you a video showing the individual posing as Agent Gilmore. When he left your campus at 8:18, he wasn't alone."

Malcom opened the file. The hairs on the back of his neck prickled. He clearly saw a man wearing a suit and tie seated in the driver-side seat. Beside him was the unmistakable image of Ann Waters. She wore the same raspberry-colored blouse she had worn that afternoon. "Oh my God. Steve, who is this guy?"

"We believe his name is Gary Lefebre. He started out as a contract killer in New Orleans fifteen years ago. In recent years, he moved out west, taking jobs for various Mexican drug cartels. His portfolio includes a few high-end corporate jobs. This guy is a ghost. We've been searching for his whereabouts for years. If Ann Waters is with him, her life is in extreme danger.

"There's one possible lead we're following. A corporate jet left Santa Maria airport at 8:30. The flight plan was filed under a false name. The destination was listed as San Francisco International, but the transponder shut off at the first air traffic hand-off to the north. We're hoping the Air Force will share their radar records, but it may take some time."

Malcom's heart pounded, his breathing labored. "This guy kidnapped Ann?" His voice sounded hollow in his own ears.

"I wish I had better news, Malcom. We're doing all we can. But he has a considerable head start. We didn't find Gilmore's body until after Lefebre and Ann Waters had already left your campus But I can promise you this. Gary Lefebre has the full attention of the FBI. The FBI director mobilized the full resources of the Bureau to catch this monster. In the meantime, I'm sending agents to your campus. If Lefebre's intentions are anything but murder, he'll be in contact with you. We intend to intercept and monitor those communications."

Malcom struggled to speak, his mouth was so dry. "Steve, you have EPSILON's full cooperation. Whatever you need from us to find Ann, you've got it."

"Thank you, Malcom. We'll leave no stone unturned to get this guy and bring back Ann Waters."

Malcom set his phone down after Steve Coleman disconnected. His head swam. He reached for the trash receptacle beside the couch, pulled it between his legs, and vomited.

CHAPTER 45

For the past ten years, Gary Lefebre's clientele had consisted of cruel, depraved individuals. Ruthless and efficient, Gary was deemed by his employers a sort of feral cat. Something to be turned out of a cage to solve a rat problem, then prodded back into the wild, out of sight, out of mind. His skills were so highly regarded that several of his contracts involved eliminating prior paid assassins after they had fallen out of favor with their benefactors. The money, of course, was good. He maintained a beachfront house in Malibu, attending parties with the Hollywood glitterati who also chose to reside there.

Gary Lefebre relied on the close-range ambush. He carefully selected his hardware for maximum concealment. Most others in his line of work preferred a .38- or .45-caliber weapon. The higher muzzle exit velocity ensured deeper penetration and a clean kill. However, Gary had found that the slower muzzle exit velocity of a .32-caliber pistol, combined with the lightweight hollow-point rounds, virtually guaranteed no exit wound, while turning his victim's brains into bloody pulp. His success ratio for his close-in surprise shots was virtually 100 percent. Only once had he needed to shoot a second round to drop his target.

Like a cat, Gary Lefebre was indeed a skilled killer. And like a cat, he found playing with his victims irresistible. His contract was to kill Ann Waters, to break continuity in EPSILON'S mission leadership during a time of crisis. But the terms of the contract said nothing about how much he could play with the mouse before it was time to eat. And his client had no interest in when she was killed—immediately or later.

Gary had arranged to have a local trusted "cleanup crew" transfer Ann to his designated location once they removed all trace of Randy Porter from his workstation. But he had an hour before his crew arrived, and at least half an hour before she regained consciousness from the chloroform.

He planned to rape her, repeatedly, once she was safely stashed away in his lair. But an early start had been on his mind since he first met Ann in the EPSILON parking lot. She was as beautiful as the Malibu starlets and housewives he routinely mingled with. He planned to be in Seattle for a week, until he had fulfilled his contract. In the meantime, the cat planned to play with its food.

Gary laid the unresponsive Ann down on the floor. He jerked her pants down over her feet, then quickly removed his suit jacket and tossed it aside. He dropped his own pants to his knees and positioned himself over her helpless form. Then, in a sublime release of power and domination, he thrust himself into her.

CHAPTER 46

Ann slowly regained her senses as her pants slid down her legs. Terror threatened to jolt her upright, but instantly her mind screamed, *Don't move!* She kept her eyes shut tight, heard someone rustling with clothes. Tried to think.

When Gary Lefebre had clamped his chloroform-soaked cloth over her mouth and nose, Ann had held her breath. She hadn't inhaled the full dosage this monster had intended. She'd been unconscious briefly—not as long as he assumed.

She heard the unmistakable unzipping of pants.

Visions floated in her mind of the dead Randy Porter at his keyboard. Of Agent Gilmore, or whoever he was, reaching under his jacket before killing Porter. Of the tall man who ignored her—she was dead in his eyes already.

Ann heard the excited breath of Gilmore as he loomed over her, between her legs, preparing to plunge himself into her. Ann had one chance. He thought she was still unconscious. His sole focus was on raping her.

Ann cracked her eyelids as Agent Gilmore arched his head back, planting his arms outside of Ann's shoulders to support his torso. She caught a glimpse of a shoulder harness strapped over his shirt.

As he painfully thrust into her, Ann snatched the exposed pistol butt, jerking it free. Her index finger slipped inside the trigger guard and pulled the trigger. The report jerked the gun toward her chest, involuntarily causing a second shot.

The first round grazed Gary Lefebre's ribs, collapsing his left arm. The second round caught him square in the sternum.

As his body fell toward her, Gary Lefebre's favored weapon performed again as it had before on countless victims. The hollow-point expanded to a one-inch diameter by the time it penetrated his sternum cartilage. The slug expanded to an inch and a half diameter by the time it slammed into his heart, centered on the septum between the left and right ventricles. The outer walls of both ventricles exploded out into the surrounding pericardial sac, but the denser tissue of the ventricle wall resisted the force enough to push sharply backward toward the spine. Unable to resist the strain, the aorta separated from the left ventricle, immediately draining blood away from his brain. After smashing against the spine, the heart—or what was left of it—rebounded to its original position, where it fibrillated feebly for thirty seconds. Gary Lefebre was dead by the time he collapsed onto Ann's chest.

Pinned under his body, Ann desperately worked to extract her index finger from the trigger guard, terrified she would shoot herself. She pulled her finger free only to feel warm blood pooling on her chest. Her dinner welled up in her throat. She pushed against the man's right side, rolling over with him until he was fully off her.

She scrambled to her knees as he flopped onto his back. Ann screamed and pummeled the lifeless body of her attacker, stopping only after she collapsed back onto her heels and sobbed, her hands shaking uncontrollably.

A crimson splotch six inches in diameter stained the front of her blouse. Blood and powder residue stippled her hands. She was naked from the waist down, a faint streak of blood smeared across her inner thigh.

Ann looked around—she was alone now with two dead bodies. She recalled the man's words, *cleaning crew*, and wanted to be long gone by the time they arrived. She stripped off her blouse and removed her blood-soaked bra. Then Ann wiped the residual blood off herself as best she could, dropping her blood-stained blouse on her attacker's body. Quickly, she pulled on her underwear and pants and retrieved her shoes. She looked around the perimeter of the room, needing something to cover her naked torso.

Randy remained slumped forward. The blood stain on the back of his hood stretched down to his neck. Ann pulled the hood back. The blood had not reached his T-shirt. Pulling his sweatshirt off, she wrapped it around his bloody head. Then his shirt slid over his wrapped head, blood-free.

The shirt was a men's large; it fit loosely over Ann's much smaller frame. But it was better than nothing.

She grabbed her would-be killer's jacket and slung it over her shoulders to wear like a cape. But as she lifted it off the floor, it felt heavier than she'd expected. She fished in the outside pockets and found two smartphones—hers and his. Her phone was still turned off. His was still on. She stuffed one phone into each back pocket of her pants.

Reaching into the breast pocket, she found the ziplock baggie with the chloroform-soaked cloth sealed inside. Ann returned the baggie to its pocket.

She stopped at her assailant's body, stooped, and unclipped the holster from his shoulder harness. Then she grabbed the Kel-Tec pistol off the floor and holstered it, relieved that it sat deeply enough to cover the trigger guard. She slipped the holstered gun inside her pants against the small of her back, placed the jacket over her shoulders and headed out the door.

Her pulse quickening, Ann dashed toward the empty lobby, sprinting across but stopping short at the exterior door. She wheeled around and returned to the reception desk. Ann pulled on drawers. All were locked until she reached the receptionist's workstation. In an unlocked drawer there, she found several visitor badges and janitor's key cards. Ann grabbed a keycard and headed back for the exit, her pace quickening as she went. She broke into a full run as the motion detector activated, sliding the doors open.

Ann burst out into the chill Seattle night.

CHAPTER 47

Ann paused at the landing edge above the stairs. In spite of the audible hum of city life, Pontius Street in front of her was deserted. To her south, a lone couple crossed Thomas Street, heading for a café on the opposite corner.

She closed her eyes, lifting her face skyward, the damp chill cooling her flushed cheeks. Ann breathed deeply, with purpose, arms hanging limply at her side. Her racing heartbeat slowed. The calamities of the past two weeks paraded before her mind's eye. *This has to stop. I have to stop them.*

Ann breathed deeply one final time, lowered her head, and opened her eyes. She quickly walked down the steps to the sidewalk, pulling her cellphone out of her back pocket as she went. Ann's index finger hovered over the power button. *If Randy was the only hacker trying to sabotage Prospector, why was he operating out of a room with a dozen outrageously equipped computer stations? Randy couldn't be the only one working for that cold-blooded, well-dressed man. He'd been part of a larger group.*

The words echoed in her mind: *"It's settled, then. You'll oversee the startup of our cyber espionage group. Operations will begin here tomorrow morning."*

Ann looked back at the black edifice behind her. There was no identifying business sign, no logo on the door she had just emerged from. She examined the key card in her hand—nothing to identify the company, just block lettering that said JANITOR. *What is this place?*

She looked back at her inert phone, contemplating the consequences of turning it on. Based on the look the boss man had given her, it was obvious that he expected her dead, or at least captive somewhere else. He also expected Gilmore—or whoever he was—to be alive. Based on the equipment she saw in the computer room, both phones that she held could be monitored, or at least tracked. If she turned her phone on, it might start alarms blaring and lights flashing announcing her escape. Ann tucked her phone back into her back pocket and pulled out Gilmore's phone.

To her surprise, it was not locked. The arrogant asshole had assumed that whoever stole it would not live long enough to compromise any information that it contained. Ann scrolled through the apps and located a ride-hailing service. She opened the app and pushed a button labeled RECALL.

Ann leaned against a street sign pole and waited for a rideshare to pull up. She checked the time—11:01 p.m. Next, she looked up store hours for several nearby department stores. Most were open until midnight. She searched for open bars and coffee shops in the shopping district. Most were open until 2a.m. It occurred to her that—with apologies to New York— Seattle should change its moniker from The Emerald City to The City That Never Sleeps. With tens of thousands of software engineers filling the surrounding condos, it was no wonder that the seemingly hundreds of local coffee shops stayed open to the wee hours in competition with the bars.

A driverless AV pulled to the curb. She quickly located a digital wallet app on Gilmore's phone to pay for the ride, then seated herself in the driver seat. Sure enough, there was no steering wheel. Not that she would have used it. She was only vaguely familiar with Seattle and would have driven around in circles if left to her own devices. Ann examined the large console screen. The mapping showed all street and business names within a four-block radius, except the building she had just left.

"Drive around the block to Minor Avenue North." The car silently pulled away from the curb into the traffic lane. The interior of the AV pulsed red. Ann turned to see a Medic One emergency medical truck pull to the curb below the steps. As she rounded the corner for the first of two right turns, four emergency medical technicians raced up the steps with a gurney and several large medical kits in tow. *The cleaning crew?* Ann could think of no other reason so many men would respond to an empty office building so late at night. At any rate, *she* had not dialed 911.

Ann was mid-block traveling northbound on Minor Avenue when she commanded, "Stop! Pull over and wait."

Ann stepped out onto the sidewalk and looked up only to be disappointed. Still no company sign. Then she looked in a well-manicured landscape bed to the right of the main door.

BMAC
Administrative Support Services

BMAC was one of several aerospace corporations competing with EPSILON to reach Mars. Ann recalled that BMAC had suffered a major setback a year and a half ago when a first-stage booster blew up on lift-off. The payload, a Mars Command Module, was lost. The flight was unmanned, but it set back BMAC's Mars timetable. A replacement Command Module was scheduled for liftoff in another three months.

At the time of the accident, EPSILON's owner had tweeted condolences to BMAC's board regarding their financial loss. He had even offered EPSILON resources to help BMAC get back on track. To Ann's knowledge, the offer was never taken up.

Ann walked up to the main entrance. It was locked. Then she walked over to a security pad mounted to the right of the door. She waved her JANITOR card across the pad, and the door slid open. Ann stepped into the vacant main lobby, pistol drawn. She was extra vigilant at the thought of encountering the cleaning crew—if that was who she had seen.

The Minor Avenue lobby was much more spacious and richly appointed than the Spartan version around the block. Off to the side, she found a building map and directory. She looked on the second floor, the floor she had entered from Pontius Avenue. The schematic did not look at all like where she had been. There was no exterior door, no reception lobby. Half the floor was occupied by the Financial Services Division, the other half by Logistics. A total of eight floors were listed. The penthouse was listed as occupied by secondary offices for the CEO, CFO, and several other executive officers. Ann knew that the corporate headquarters was located across Lake Washington in the city of Bellevue.

Next, Ann walked over to the reception desk. Half a dozen portraits lined the wall behind the desk. The center portrait caught Ann's attention. *Ellis Pierpont, Chief Executive Officer*—none other than the standing handsome man.

Ann walked to the bank of elevators at the back of the lobby and pressed a call button. The doors to her far left opened with a soft chime. She waved her keycard over the security pad beside the floor buttons, then pushed the buttons for floors two and three.

The doors closed. When the elevator began to rise, Ann counted silently. The doors opened to the second floor. With her hand on the door open button, Ann looked out onto a vast open floor. Rows of support columns on either side of her field of view were the only thing obstructing her sightline to the exterior windows. Ann dashed out of the elevator to look at the part of the floor behind her, only to see more columns and exterior windows. She hurried back into the elevator just before the doors closed. She resumed her silent counting as the elevator rose to the third floor. The doors opened once more to a scene nearly identical to the one on the floor below.

Ann remained in the elevator and pushed the lobby button, counting silently to the second floor and again to the lobby. After reaching the lobby, Ann stepped out. The ride to and from the second floor had taken twice as long as the ride from the second to the third floor. Apparently, the elevator was skipping a floor between the lobby and the listed second floor—the floor where Ann had entered from Pontius Avenue.

As Ann stepped out into the empty lobby, Gilmore's phone pinged, announcing an incoming text message. Ann's hands shook as she pulled the phone from her hip pocket to read the message.

WTF??? We agreed to clean up one body!!!

Ann swallowed hard. The last thing she needed was a group of jilted criminals pinging her location and chasing her around town. She quickly typed a response message and sent it off.

Last minute change. I'll double your fee. We good?

She waited a moment for the expected response.

This is BS. Make it triple.

Ann paused a moment. Would Gilmore accept being gouged like that? She typed a response.

2½ X. If it happens again, you get triple. Deal?

The response came back so quickly, it startled Ann.

If it happens again, we'll be cleaning YOU up!!!

Ann fired off her final response. She smiled wryly as she pocketed Gilmore's phone.

Agreed. It won't.

She quickly made her way back out to her waiting AV and hopped in. Ann's next priority was a change of clothes—anything other than the dead hacker's T-shirt that reeked of sweat and hamburgers. Then she needed a place where she could sit down and think.

CHAPTER 48

Ann emerged from a department store on Sixth Avenue in the retail district of downtown Seattle, a shopping bag in each hand. The bag in her right hand contained Randy Porter's smelly T-shirt and Gilmore's oversized suit coat. In their place she wore a light blue short-sleeved V-neck under a dark blue fleece jacket. The bag in her left hand held a prepaid burner phone she had purchased from the electronics department, plus assorted toiletries.

She turned south on Sixth Avenue, walked half a block, then turned west on Union Street. She turned north at the mid-block alley, wrinkling her nose at the smell of vomit and urine. Ann paused long enough at a dumpster to drop the bag of clothing inside. When she came to the north end of the alley, she turned east on Pike Street, then entered a coffee shop after crossing Sixth Avenue.

The aroma of coffee greeted her before she opened the door. Inside, half a dozen twenty-something men huddled around a table near the front windows. Those facing Ann gave her a passing glance. Their animated discussion about a recently released video game flowed through the space. The service counter was set against the left wall. Ann walked over and perused the ridiculously complicated espresso menu. She settled on a quadruple-shot venti latte with almond milk. She added a couple of biscotti to her order, then headed to a table in the back corner opposite the coffee counter.

Ann removed the burner phone from its packaging, plugged the charger into a nearby outlet, and turned on the device. The phone came with talk and text, and even included a modest data plan. Ann scrolled through the preloaded apps. She found an email app and an e-wallet. She set both up under an alias,

Julia Smith. Next, she dialed the only phone number besides her best friends' that she had committed to memory. After several rings, the call went to voice mail. "Malcom, it's me, Ann. I'm okay, but I need your help. Please call me back at this number. And for God's sake, don't tell the FBI about this call."

Ann hung up and set the phone down on the table. She barely got a sip of coffee down before the burner phone rang. Malcom McDowell gushed when she answered, "Ann! Thank God you're okay! Where are you?"

Ann considered her answer before she responded, "Malcom, are you alone?"

"Yes. I'm in my office. The FBI are monitoring our corporate lines, but not my personal cell. Ann, Agent Gilmore was found murdered. Our security video showed that you left with a man named Gary Lefevre, who used Gilmore's credentials.

"Ann, I feel so responsible for what's happened to you. When Steve Coleman told me Agent Gilmore was dead, he also told me they had no idea where Randy Porter was. This whole thing about a raid and needing to have you identify Randy Porter was something this Lefevre guy cooked up. After you left campus, you just disappeared. The FBI assumed that you were kidnapped. They're waiting for a ransom demand."

"Malcom, I don't think this guy intended to demand any ransom. It doesn't surprise me that the real Agent Gilmore was murdered. Let me guess. He was shot in the back of the head?"

"Yes. How do you know that?"

It was a legitimate question. Once again, Ann carefully weighed her response.

"Malcom, I completely believed the man I left with was Ted Gilmore. He had the right credentials. He flew me to Seattle to identify Randy Porter. But after we reached Porter, this guy shot him in the back of the head."

A veritable torrent of questions flowed from Malcom, "Holy shit! You're in Seattle!? You're sure Randy Porter is dead? Are you hurt? How did you escape from Lefevre?"

"Malcom, slow down!" Ann interrupted. "Yes, I'm in Seattle. Yes, I'm certain Porter is dead. No, I'm not hurt."

It was not entirely true. Or rather, she did not know, having not sought medical attention. It occurred to Ann she should be tested for STDs. "I … but I got away. I'm fine, really."

"Ann, I've been so worried about you. I'll make arrangements to get you back to Santa Maria."

"Thanks, Malcom, but not just yet. I don't think that Randy Porter's death solves any of our problems with sabotage. I've seen the place where he was working. It's a black hole located in BMAC's Administrative Services building. The room he was in was set up with maybe a dozen computer stations. The computers and ancillary equipment are top of the line. Before Porter was killed this evening, he was talking with Ellis Pierpont. I overheard Pierpont talking to him about a cyber espionage group that's supposed to start using that very room tomorrow morning … I mean, *this* morning!

"Whatever it was that Randy started, it seems that Ellis Pierpont is determined to continue. I'm certain that our landing party remains in grave danger. Are we still exclusively using MGPS for communications?"

"Yes, Ann. Prospector Base's S-band link is still offline. So far, the landing crew is unaware that you went missing. Ann, if what you say about BMAC's involvement is true, we need to inform the FBI right away."

Again, she carefully weighed her thoughts before responding. "Malcom, I agree that the FBI should be brought in, but not just yet. I've seen Pierpont in action. This guy's a pro. He's having Porter's body and any evidence removed. By the time the police or the FBI arrive, it will be like nothing happened. It likely has already been swept clean.

"If this cyber saboteur group is smart enough to cover up a murder, I'm sure they're smart enough to cover their digital tracks. Remember how Porter was able to disappear without a trace? The FBI would have to monitor BMAC's black hole activity online for weeks, maybe months, collecting evidence before they could shut them down. I'm worried we don't have that much time."

"Ann, Prospector Base is safe. The only link to the mainframe is via the S-band, and that link is severed. Plus, Dallas took the extra step to take the base computer offline. Prospector Base is operating manually."

"I don't know. Malcom, these guys have managed to find a way to get at us every time. There's no way I want to give them more time to figure out ways to hurt us."

"Maybe you're right, Ann. But what can you do that law enforcement can't?"

"Good question. And the short answer is, I don't know—yet. But I have certain advantages. I know the physical location of the black hole. Ellis Pierpont doesn't know I'm alive and freely roaming Seattle. And he is unaware, at least for now, that I have access to his building. If I play my cards right, I have the element of surprise.

"What I need is a hotel room where I can get a little sleep and plan out what to do next. And I may need to obtain additional supplies. I've deliberately left my phone off so I can't be tracked. I shouldn't access any of my existing bank accounts or e-wallets for the same reason.

"Malcom, I know this is a huge favor to ask of you, but could you transfer five thousand dollars to a new e-wallet I set up on this burner phone? I'll repay you as soon as this is over."

"Ann, I'll send you the money, but it won't be a loan. Give me your wallet codes, and you'll have the funds right away. And please, keep me informed of your plans. If something goes wrong, I want to be able to send the police to get you out of trouble. I'm so worried about you. Be careful."

"Thanks, Malcom. I'll keep you informed as best as I can. I suspect that things could unfold pretty quickly once I set plans in motion."

Ann shared the necessary information on her new e-wallet. After confirming the transfer, they said their good-byes and

Ann hung up. The barista served a thirty-something couple. The six young men were still arguing over the merits of their video game.

The newly funded Julia Smith searched on her burner phone and made a reservation for a nearby hotel. Then she dropped the phone and its charger into the shopping bag with her toiletries and headed for Sixth Avenue. She walked the two blocks south to the hotel and picked up her room key from the front desk.

Her room was on the sixth floor. It overlooked the alley where she had dumped the shirt and jacket a block to the north. She drew the shades, undressed, and headed for the shower. She had not been completely honest with Malcom. Her priority was not a good night's sleep. It was getting a good shower. She felt compelled to wash away every trace of this evening.

Stepping into the steaming water, Ann let it flow over her face and began to tremble. More than anything, she wanted her mother, or Dallas—someone who would hold her, someone to ease her fear and pain, someone to comfort her. Ann crouched down, hugging her knees tightly, and sobbed for forty minutes.

After she dried off, Ann sat down on the edge of the bed, her blond hair wrapped in a towel. She picked up the burner phone and resumed searching.

CHAPTER 49

Ellis Pierpont observed the computer monitor over the shoulder of his black hole supervisor, Pang Xianjing. Pang had immigrated to the US from mainland China on a student visa to attend UCLA. He was a brilliant computer science major, unsurpassed at hacking code. After his student visa expired, Pang had gone underground, making a living on the dark web.

It had taken Ellis six months to track down Pang. For this particular position, Ellis weighed discretion equally with code-writing skills. Pang was endowed with both.

He and his team were paid out of a blind research and development account under Ellis's control. That same account funded the black hole both men now occupied.

Corporate black holes were common. Companies used them to shield research related to top-secret government military contracts or highly sensitive private R & D. Ellis's use of his black hole was less pedestrian. He intended to ensure BMAC's dominance of the Mars resources market, from extraction through processing to shipment and distribution. Trillions of dollars were at stake. That is, once BMAC's Mars program was back on track. Ellis schemed to ensure that BMAC did not lose market share to its competitors while BMAC remained crippled and Earth-bound.

"Mr. Pang, has your team completed debugging the RBI instructions I provided the other day?"

"Yes, we completed the work last night and uploaded the file to the optical laser transmitter. The code should have downloaded on Mars three hours ago. We should know by noon if we were successful."

"Excellent work. I have another task related to the RBIs I'd like to discuss with you before the rest of your team arrives."

Pang suppressed a smirk when Ellis pulled a paper notepad out of his suit breast pocket. He set the pad on the workstation surface beside Pang and wrote on it with an engraved executive pen. "Can we direct the RBIs to do this?"

Pang picked up the notepad and examined it carefully. He handed it back to Ellis Pierpont as he responded, "The coding in support of Asimov's three rules of robotics was already disabled with last night's upload. This should be pretty straightforward."

Ellis tore off the used sheet and handed it back to Pang. He pocketed the pad and pen, then turned to leave. "Please inform me when your team is ready to upload. I'll be working in my suite upstairs for the remainder of the morning."

Ellis left the room, then turned right toward the elevator at the end of the hall. The elevator led down to a secure room on the main floor of the building. From the secure room, Ellis made his way to the main lobby, where he caught the public elevator to his executive suite on the top floor.

Five minutes later, the first of Pang Xianjing's hand-picked team of hackers began to trickle into the black hole. They gravitated to a conference table Pang had set up off to one side of the floor. On the table rested a spread of coffee and donuts, the mother's milk of software coding.

CHAPTER 50

Ann woke early. She dressed quickly and went downstairs to the small coffee shop attached to the hotel lobby.

She emerged from the hotel lobby at 7 a.m., a mid-length ponytail bobbing from the back side of an adjustable Seattle Mariners baseball cap. She had just purchased the cap and a pair of sunglasses from the hotel gift shop, where she had also used the ATM to get some cash.

Ann hailed a rideshare using Julia's phone. The AV took her to the small café she had seen at the corner of North Thomas Street and Pontius Avenue North. She selected a small table against the front window. From there, she could clearly see the back side of the BMAC building and anyone who entered or exited from the secure door. Ann ordered a cup of coffee and the scrambled egg special, mentally rehearsing the plan that she had devised during the night.

After breakfast, Ann pulled Julia's phone out to check the shipping status of the items she had rush ordered. Five micro HD 1080-pixel nanny cams were on their way. When paired to her phone, they could download video and audio. The units were so small and light that they came with adhesive pads. They could literally be placed anywhere. Ann's order also included a roll of duct tape. The stuff was so useful it was standard equipment for the Prospector EVA packs. She set her phone down when she saw someone ascend the concrete steps to the back door of the BMAC Administrative Services building.

From her seat in the corner café, Ann observed a total of six men and one woman enter the back side of the BMAC building. The woman entered first, at 9:25 a.m. She wore a security uniform, so she likely occupied the reception desk.

The six men trickled in between 9:30 and 10:00. They were all casually dressed. *Like software engineers headed for a black hole.* Ann smirked.

At 10:30, Julia's phone chimed. The order was delivered to the hotel front desk. Ann tossed $20 on her table and left.

Half an hour later, Ann walked back in carrying her nanny cams and duct tape. The morning waitress cocked her head to one side. "Weren't you just in here for breakfast?"

Ann scowled. "My boyfriend is cheating on me. I intend to catch him with that bitch when they come out of her condo." She noted her breakfast table had been cleaned and was still empty. "Mind if I take that table again?"

"Honey, you take whatever table you want. Coffee?"

"Yes, please."

Ann seated herself. Pontius Avenue north of the restaurant was vacant. As she sipped her coffee, she mentally inventoried, *Pistol, check. Julia's phone, check. Gilmore/Lefevre's phone, check. My phone, check. Five nanny cams, check. Duct tape, check.*

At one, a group of men emerged from the black hole entrance. Ann counted them. ... *five, six. Techies are so predictable.*

She turned her phone on for the first time since Lefevre had kidnapped her. Scrolling through her contacts list, she called Malcom at his business number. He answered on the first ring.

"Malcom, I'm putting my plan into motion."

"Ann, please reconsider. You're going to get yourself killed." Malcom sounded harried.

Ann guessed he hadn't slept a wink since she had called him. She felt awful knowing what she was putting him through. "Malcom, I don't have time to debate. Just stand by for my download sometime this evening." Ann hung up, leaving the phone on.

She opened Lefevre's burner phone and hailed a rideshare. Then she pocketed both phones in her fleece jacket. Julia Smith's burner phone remained in a back pocket of her jeans, the roll of duct tape in a breast pocket of her jacket.

Ann walked out of the restaurant door just as six men walked in. *So predictable.*

As Ann reached the sidewalk outside, an AV pulled up to the curb. She typed in the Bellevue address for BMAC headquarters using Lefevre's app, then tossed both her phone and Lefevre's on the front seat. The AV pulled away after she closed the door.

Ann crossed an empty Pontius Avenue and walked north.

CHAPTER 51

Ellis Pierpont turned from his desk atop the Seattle Administrative Services Building and looked out his north-facing office window. The Bellevue headquarters office tower featured a breathtaking south-facing view of snow-covered Mount Rainier and the south half of Lake Washington. The view from his Bellevue office drew the most responses from office visitors. But Ellis preferred the view from the Seattle building. He was surrounded by the twenty-four-hour-a-day bustle of the larger municipality. To the north lay Lake Union, completely surrounded by the city. Sailboats plied the waters during boating season. The east shore was lined with houseboats. Pontoon planes took off and landed year 'round. On a clear sunny day, Mount Baker's snowy south face blazed in the sunlight eight-five miles to the north.

But this late September mid-day, Gas Works Park on the north shore of Lake Union was obscured behind a bank of fog. I-5's Ship Canal Bridge looked as if it were resting on a soft gray pillow. Mount Baker floated above the haze like a faint specter.

In spite of the tranquil view, Ellis was not at ease. He had achieved the pinnacle of success by trusting his gut. Today, his gut bothered him. And Ellis listened to discern the message his gut wished to convey.

Ellis had employed Gary Lefebre often enough that he perceived a certain pattern to Gary's actions. After performance of a contract, Ellis deposited payment to an offshore account. Within five minutes, Gary transferred the funds out, leaving the original account empty. Ellis knew this because a snooper program monitored all account activity. But the funds from this most recent job had remained in the account untouched since last night. Ellis had even texted Lefebre's burner phone an hour earlier but received no response.

Ellis spun around in his chair, then grabbed and dialed his desk phone.

"Mr. Pang, where are you?"

"I'm at my desk. I was just heading downstairs to the hole."

"Might I accompany you? I'd like to have you search for someone when you get down there."

"Of course. When can I expect you?"

"I'm on my way now."

Ellis hung up and quickly made his way to his office door.

CHAPTER 52

Malcom immediately scrolled through his contacts after Ann hung up. He called Steve Coleman.

"Steve, it's Malcom. Ann just called. Her plan is a go."

"Yes. My technician just alerted me her cell is active. We can track her location now. We'll take it from here."

As he hung up, Malcom contemplated his record-setting concern. Never before in human history had a man worried about the safety of two sets of people some 200 million miles apart. Ann was only 1,200 miles away, but he felt as powerless to help her as he did the Prospector 1 landing party on Mars.

CHAPTER 53

Unlike the hackers that he supervised, Pang Xianjing maintained a cubicle two floors down from the executive suite. Randy Porter had never known of Pang's existence, but Pang intimately knew everything about Porter and his freelance work for Ellis Pierpont.

Pang positioned himself at the elevator doors, anticipating the boss's arrival. He waited barely thirty seconds before the doors opened. Pierpont held the doors and Pang stepped in. "Mr. Pang, I fear that something untoward has happened to Gary Lefebre. What's more, I am concerned that he may not have tied up a loose end related to a contract."

"Would you be referring to that woman from EPSILON he dragged up here you told me about? Ann Waters, I believe?"

"Precisely. I'd like you to find their whereabouts. Here are their phone numbers." Ellis handed Pang a slip of paper torn from the notepad that he kept in his breast pocket. The elevator doors opened to the Minor Street lobby. Pang quickly pocketed the slip of paper. Both men walked to their right down a hallway adjacent to the lobby. They stopped at a secure door, where Pang leaned forward into an iris reader.

Both men stepped into the secure room and turned left toward another set of elevator doors. The elevator conveyed them up one floor, where they walked down the hall to the secure room four doors to the left.

Once inside, Pang examined the phone numbers on the slip of paper, then walked over to his computer station. He quickly logged in and pulled up a program to trace the GPS signals emitted by both phones.

The program quickly identified their locations and zoomed in. They appeared to be in a single vehicle heading eastbound on I-90 between the Central District and Rainier Valley. The signals blinked out when they reached the Mount Baker Tunnel.

Ellis positioned himself behind Pang so that he could view the monitor. "Mr. Pang, can you determine their destination?"

The signals reemerged from the east tunnel portal and began crossing Lake Washington on the floating bridge. Pang drilled into both phones and determined that the rideshare app on Lefebre's phone had hailed the vehicle. He entered a few more keystrokes and found what he was looking for. "The vehicle is on its way to your Bellevue headquarters."

Ellis pointed to the downtown Bellevue address displayed on the monitor. "This is not what I would have expected. No good can come from those two reaching our headquarters building. Please divert them."

Pang looked squarely at him, an eyebrow raised. Ellis nodded, eyes cold, mouth determined.

Pang typed furiously. "We're in luck. They're in an EPSILON AV." The signal blinked out as the rideshare AV traveled under the First Hill Lid on Mercer Island. Pang continued typing. The signal blinked on and off as the AV passed under the downtown Mercer Island overcrossings. Pang finished just as it blinked out at the Luther Burbank Lid. He held his finger above the ENTER key, waiting for the signal to reemerge. When the signal reappeared, Pang struck the key with the authority of a god determining the fate of wayward mortals.

The AV continued on its eastbound course, crossing under two more overcrossings before leaving Mercer Island. The vehicle was a third of the way across the East Channel Bridge over Lake Washington when it suddenly accelerated and swerved into the far-left lane. Then it turned sharply to the right, crossing all lanes until it slammed into the bridge railing at ninety miles per hour. The front end crumpled into the passenger compartment on impact. The momentum was so great, the car flipped over the barrier and cartwheeled the eight-five feet down to the Lake Washington surface. It landed upside down with a splash, then quickly sank to the lake bottom. Both phones' GPS signals on the monitor winked out.

Ellis's shoulders relaxed. "Thank you, Mr. Pang. I am much more at ease, now. By the way, has there been any use on these two phones in the past two days?"

Pang resumed typing and called up two phone logs. "Lefebre's has been used sporadically. Ann Waters used hers one time only. It was a twelve-second transmission, made only ten minutes ago. The number called was at EPSILON."

Ellis stroked his clean-shaven chin. "Interesting. Long enough to give a general location, but too short for much detail."

Pang responded without looking up, "But the FBI has the same capabilities to track the phones that we do. I'm certain they're monitoring EPSILON's incoming calls. They might even discern their intended destination, even as we did."

Ellis paced the floor behind Pang's chair. "Mr. Pang, did your team finish coding the instructions for the RBIs to depressurize the EPSILON base?"

"Yes. There's just one detail we need in order to complete and send. When do you want the program to execute?"

Ellis responded quickly, "Immediately upon completion of the meltdown of the reactor array."

"Got it." Pang opened another program and typed briefly, striking the ENTER key one final time. Then he closed the programs and logged off. "It's done, Mr. Pierpont. Between melting down the reactor array and decompressing the base, EPSILON's presence on Mars is finished."

CHAPTER 54

Ann arrived at BMAC's black hole entrance at 1:10 p.m. The security guard had not walked out. She was probably still at her post. Ann's stomach was all butterflies. She tasted acid at the back of her tongue as she arrived at the exterior door. She tried the JANITOR card on the card reader above the keypad. To her relief, the door opened.

Ann walked briskly across the lobby to the reception desk, pulling the bill of her Mariners cap as low over her face as possible. "Which way to the janitor closet?" she addressed the female guard.

The guard responded without looking up from her magazine. "You're the third janitor this week. You guys need to get your act together. End of the hall, then left." She jerked her head sideways toward the secure door that led to the hall.

Ann waved the card over the readers at the hall door and the computer room door with equal success. She immediately placed her nanny cams in discrete locations around the empty room. Opening the app on her phone, Ann confirmed that all five cameras operated. She adjusted one angle to capture the faces of the engineers as they entered the room.

Ann had just finished adjusting it when she heard voices in the hall outside the door. She scanned the room for a place to hide. A nearby workstation in the corner against the hall wall seemed her best option. With her heart pounding, Ann crouched down under the work surface and pulled the rolling chair against her. She felt exposed, but it was the best she could do in the open room.

Two men entered the room. She only saw their feet from her position but recognized the Italian shoes. Ellis Pierpont, CEO of BMAC. As they walked to a workstation at the far wall they came into full view. The other man was shorter, with straight black hair, casually dressed, showing ripples of muscles under a tight shirt. His manner of walking reminded her of a professional athlete.

The shorter man seated himself and opened up programs on his computer monitor. Ellis stood behind to observe the monitor over the top of the seated man. It was difficult to tell from her position, but it appeared that they were tracking something. She strained to hear their conversation. With their backs turned to her, the echoes off the hard surfaces garbled individual words.

"… determine their destination?"

"… Bellevue headquarters."

"… No good can come … Please divert them."

The seated man typed furiously, finishing with a furious strike of a key. Both men watched the monitor intently for half a minute.

"Thank you, Mr. Pang. I am much … has there been any use on these two phones in the past two days?"

The seated man resumed typing. Ann realized that they were tracking and had hacked the AV she sent to BMAC's Bellevue headquarters. She allowed one corner of her mouth to curl upward. Her intended diversion had brought Ellis Pierpont and his hacker almost directly on top of her.

"… FBI has the same capabilities … monitoring EPSILON's incoming calls."

Ann smiled more broadly. This was almost too good to be true. Her nanny cams were mining the mother lode of info on Pierpont's illegal activity.

"… finish coding the instructions for the RBIs … EPSILON base?"

"Yes. There's just one detail we need …"

"… immediately … array."

The seated man opened another program and typed briefly, striking the key one final time. Then he closed the programs and logged off.

"It's done … melting … array … EPSILON's … Mars is finished."

The seated man stood and both men walked out of the room together. Ann was no longer smiling. She looked at her cell phone. No service. She had to get out of this secure floor to get reception—she had to call Malcom and warn him about the impending sabotage by the Prospector Base RBIs.

Ann quickly crawled out from her hiding place and downloaded the video from her hidden cameras to the burner phone. When the download was complete, she sprinted to the door. As she extended her hand for the door handle, she heard the electric solenoid actuate the bolt. She threw herself against the wall behind the door as it opened. This time, she reached for the pistol tucked against the small of her back.

CHAPTER 55

Ann's heart pounded so hard she thought her head would burst. The thump, thump, thump in her ears was the loudest sound in the room. She tried hard to swallow, but her mouth was too dry. Even though she gripped the Kel-Tec P-32 with both her hands, they shook so strongly she was certain she would miss any target, no matter how close.

A single engineer entered the room. Ann recognized him from the group that had entered the restaurant. He walked directly to a workstation on the opposite wall, allowing the door to close behind him without glancing back. Ann stalked him step for step as he walked. He pulled out a rolling chair and plopped down heavily, still without looking back.

Ann pressed the gun against the back of his neck. "Don't move. I don't want to shoot you."

The feel of cold steel and the sound of a strange woman's voice convinced the man this was not a coworker's practical joke. He froze, hands hovering over his keyboard.

"Roll your chair back away from your desk. No sudden moves!" She pressed the gun a little harder against his neck for emphasis. The engineer extended his legs, pushing himself backward three feet.

"That's far enough. Here, take this roll of duct tape." Ann fished the tape out of her jacket. "Tape your ankles together, then tape them to the post of your chair."

Again, the man did exactly as he was told.

"Okay, hand me the roll of tape. Keep your eyes forward." Ann's confidence rose as her victim offered no resistance. "Clasp your hands together behind your chair. Keep your eyes forward!"

Ann quickly holstered the pistol and taped his wrists together. Then she bound them to the chair's height adjustment bar. Ann tore off a six-inch length of tape and used it as a gag. She stepped back to admire her handiwork. *One down, five to go.*

She rolled her captive to the room corner so he would not be visible by the next engineer as he walked through the door. Ann positioned herself where the door would again block her from view and waited.

The next time the door opened, two men walked in. Though they outnumbered and outweighed Ann, they weren't about to challenge the pistol in her hand. This time, Ann forced the smaller man to tape the larger man to his chair and gag him. Then she repeated the same steps on engineer number three that she had used to bind the first one.

Ann had just finished rolling the third man into the corner when the door opened again. The hapless engineer walked four steps into the room before the muffled cries of his coworkers caught his attention. He saw Ann's pistol trained on him just as the door clicked shut. His eyes widened when he realized he had no quick escape.

"Hands over your head. Now walk to this chair over here." Ann indicated a nearby chair with a sideways nod of her head. After taping engineer number four and gagging him, she repositioned herself behind the door before the final two men entered the room. They, too, were quick work for her.

Ann hoped that the hallway had enough reception to call or text Malcom. She had to warn him that the Prospector RBI units had been hacked. Ann walked over to the door and pulled it open.

She froze at the sight of a pistol aimed directly between her eyes. The pistol in her left hand was pointed harmlessly at the ceiling. Ann was so focused on the 9-mm NP42 pistol barrel she did not recognize who was holding it.

Without taking his eyes off Ann, Pang Xianjing reached out and pulled the Kel-Tec pistol out of her left hand. He stowed it in a back pocket, then braced his left foot against the door so that it wouldn't close on him. "Back up into the room, Ms. Waters."

The mention of her name shocked Ann back to reality. *How did this man know I was in the room? He was positioned at the door like he'd expected me to walk out.* She kicked herself mentally as she realized that each of the computers set up around the room came with a suite of cameras.

"That's far enough." Pang Xianjing released his grip on the door and allowed it to close behind him. "Your phone, please."

Ann fished her burner phone out of her back pocket and held it out for Pang. He took it from her and immediately shut it off, stuffing it into another pocket. "Now turn around. Stand with your hands on your head and your feet spread apart."

Ann had no sooner complied than she felt a hand against her crotch. Pang Xianjing quickly frisked her, pulling items out of her pockets as he encountered them. Soon, everything that Ann had brought was piled on the floor off to one side.

"I see you have some work to undo before I move you to a more suitable location." Pang nodded his head at the six restrained engineers in the corner. The pistol remained trained on Ann. Without speaking, she walked over to the corner and unbound one of the engineers.

Picking up the roll of duct tape, Pang followed her. "Jacob, untie the other five. Ms. Waters and I have business elsewhere.

"Ms. Waters, please give me your jacket before we leave." Pang took the jacket and folded it over his right hand, hiding the pistol from view. Then he directed Ann out into the hall. Instead of turning left to the lobby, he directed her to the right, to the elevator at the end of the hall. Once inside, he made Ann stand in the corner opposite the control panel. Pang positioned himself at the panel, gun trained on Ann, hidden beneath her blue fleece.

To Ann's surprise, they exited the elevator into a closed room. They quickly left the room, then turned left down a short hallway to the Minor Avenue North lobby that Ann had visited her first night. In the lobby, they made a hard left and took another elevator up to the top floor.

The elevator doors opened to an executive suite. The interior walls were a mixture of glass and walnut panels. The exterior windows revealed a sweeping view of downtown Seattle and the surrounding neighborhoods. Pang directed Ann to walk down the hall and into the CEO's office.

Ellis Pierpont stood between his desk and the north-facing windows. He faced outward toward the view, his hands clasped behind his back.

"Where would you like her, Mr. Pierpont?"

Ellis Pierpont remained motionless. "Put her in my conference room. I've made arrangements to have the cleaning crew move her to a more secure location for disposal after we close for the night."

Pang remained expressionless, uncertain if Pierpont had obtained contact information from Lefebre about the cleaning crew, or the other way around. Either way, he was impressed with Ellis's ability to compartmentalize his black operation. Pierpont was the equal of any Triad leader Pang knew of.

Pang led Ann to a room paneled all around with walnut. Even the door was solid. Ellis used it for meetings requiring more privacy than his open office. He forced Ann into a chair. She taped herself up, the role now reversed. Pang finished up taping her wrists together. But because the conference chairs lacked an adjustable back, Ann held her hands to her chest, then he wrapped tape around her torso and the chair back to restrain her. "This room is soundproof. Scream all you want."

When he was finished, Pang left the room, pulling the door shut behind him.

CHAPTER 56

Ann struggled to free her wrists. She could get a fingernail against the upper edge of tape, but there were too many layers to start a tear. She stopped when the door opened.

Ellis Pierpont entered the conference room and stared at Ann in silence for what felt like an eternity. His eyes conveyed—regret? *That I'm still alive? That his hired gun is dead? That he had scrambled eggs for breakfast instead of Eggs Benedict?*

Presently, he spoke to Ann, "Ms. Waters, I'm afraid that you are a liability to me. You should have been dead yesterday. Your continued presence in Seattle is jeopardizing client relations with certain long-term contracts. You will remain here until this evening, at which time you will cease to trouble me."

He dropped her burner cell on the conference table, the back open and the battery removed. He reached into a pocket in his suit coat and pulled out the phone battery and the memory card, then set them back in his pocket after he was certain that Ann had seen them. Almost imperceptibly, the corners of his mouth upturned in a measured display of pleasure. Ann returned his condescending smile with a fierce glare.

Ann knew that Dallas Gordon and his landing party had survived against all odds. But given the damage the mission equipment and facilities had sustained so far, they simply couldn't withstand any more assaults. With the RBI units hacked, the landing party's very existence on Mars hung by a thread. "I know that you're the one responsible for hacking the Prospector 1 mission. I know that you intend to hack the RBI units. You won't get away with this!"

Pierpont spread his hands in resignation. "Please understand, Ms. Waters. I have responsibilities to BMAC's shareholders. I have responsibilities for the long-term stability and success of this company. I simply cannot allow EPSILON to grow its market share for Mars resource extraction at the expense of a BMAC monopoly."

"You're murdering innocent people!"

"Unfortunate collateral damage. You have my profound sympathies."

Ann loathed everything about this soulless corporate ghoul. Exertion reddened her face as she struggled vainly against her restraints. She stopped only after her fury was spent, her head bowed in exhaustion. Satisfied she could not break free, Ellis Pierpont exited the room, his shoulders visibly more relaxed than when he had entered.

Ann sat in the silent conference room for what seemed like an hour but was really only minutes, her heart thumping, her mind racing. She heard no sound from the office outside after Pierpont's exit. She eyed the mahogany conference table three feet in front of her. *Round ends. No good.* A coffee service table caught her attention. The top was lower than the conference table—and it had sharp corners. Ann's ankles were taped together and to the center post of the chair. *If I can scooch close enough, I might be able to tear the tape around my wrists on the sharp table corner.*

By rocking her torso and pulling with her toes, she scooted over. The tape around her torso constrained her movement, but she positioned her wrists just above the corner of the table. As she leaned forward, the tape edge caught. She pulled downward with all her strength and was rewarded with a brief ripping sound. Ann repositioned her hands and repeated pulling down, the tape tearing a bit more with each effort. After a few minutes, she had torn through the whole thing.

Next, Ann focused on the tape that pinned her arms to her torso. With her wrists free, she pressed the remaining tape against the table corner. She tore a third of the tape width on her first try and tore through completely on her third.

Ann leaned back, pulling the tape off her arms. She pushed back from the corner and freed her ankles. As she stood up, she realized how much her limbs had stiffened up while immobile. She walked around the table a few times, restoring her circulation and stretching out the worst of the cramps. Then she placed her ear against the door and listened. The faint susurration of city traffic eight floors below was all she detected.

Ann cautiously opened the door and peered around. The entire floor was vacant. She sprinted to the landline phone on Pierpont's desk, where she quickly dialed Malcom's cell number and waited for a reply.

"Hello?"

Ann realized Malcom's caller ID might not identify this phone's number. She spoke in a breathless torrent, "Malcom, it's me, Ann. I'm in Ellis Pierpont's office in BMAC's Administrative Services Building. Malcom, they've hacked the RBI units. I couldn't hear exactly what they intend to do with them, but I've got it all on video. I'm certain their goal is to expel EPSILON from Mars. The landing party is in grave danger. You've got to warn them!"

Malcom sounded concerned. "Ann, are you alright? Your phone has been off the grid since you first entered the building."

The elevator doors open at the end of the hall. Pang Xianjing stepped out. He walked five steps, then noticed Ann holding Pierpont's phone. His pace quickened.

"Malcom, I don't have time to explain. Just warn the landing party!"

Pang pushed through the door and ran toward Ann, his NP42 drawn. Ann stepped back from the desk and dropped the phone. She stopped when she backed into the windowsill. Pang skirted around the desk and grabbed Ann by the arm as she turned to run, pistol-whipping her before she could react. Her thoughts fled as the room swirled. She crumpled unconscious to the carpet.

CHAPTER 57

Pang picked up the receiver and listened.

"Ann! Ann! What's happening? Are you still there?"

Pang quietly hung up the receiver and pulled out his cell phone. "We have a problem."

When he ended the call, Pang turned toward the bleeding woman at his feet. He pulled the bundle of zip ties out of his back pocket, wishing he hadn't gotten caught in the Seattle traffic. Mere seconds would have made all the difference. First, he bound her wrists together behind her back. Then he bound her ankles together. Finally, he created a short chain of zip ties and bound her wrists to her ankles.

With one hand under Ann's left upper arm, Pang half lifted, half dragged her limp body across the carpet and back to the conference room. He dumped her unceremoniously on the floor and closed the door.

CHAPTER 58

Dave Caraway tested his rappel brake, then leaned back over a twenty-foot-high rock face. He had studied the outcrop of Yttrium from below. It looked like moss with a dull metallic luster growing on the exposed rock. He had concluded the easiest way to reach the ore-bearing vein was to rappel from above. This was Site One. It was identified during the unmanned prospecting by EPSILON RBIs over the past five years.

The outcrop disappeared into the ground a hundred yards west of his current position. Dave had walked to the end of the outcrop, then returned along the top to his present position. His RBI unit had backed an open half-ton capacity trailer into position below the vein, so he could drop samples from his perch into the trailer below. The RBI functioned as a smart tractor, towing the trailer along behind Dave as he walked.

Dave chipped away surface spalls until he exposed a suitable sample, then pried the prized ore free with the pick end of his geologist hammer. He looked down between his legs and realized the trailer was off to his right. "Number One, center the trailer below me."

The trailer remained stationary. He looked down again but did not see the RBI unit stationed at the tongue as he expected.

"Number One, what's your location?" He got no response. Dave tossed the ore sample toward the trailer only to watch it bounce out of the bed and come to rest on the ground beside the trailer tongue.

"Dammit! Number One, respond! What's your location?" Still no response. Dave shifted his footing and looked off to his right. He clearly saw the track left by the RBI unit where it had positioned the trailer into place. A second track headed at a diagonal away from the cliff, more or less oriented toward Prospector Base. A tell-tale dust cloud roughly four hundred yards distant betrayed the location of the AWOL RBI unit.

"Number One, return to me!" The dust cloud faded into the distance.

Dave tapped his smartphone, switching to the base frequency. "Allie, why the hell are you recalling my RBI back to base? I'm roped in on this outcrop, and the damn thing just disappeared over the horizon. How the hell am I supposed to collect my samples?"

"Dave, I didn't recall any RBIs. Lemme talk to Luis. Maybe he called it back for service or something." Allie pushed her chair back from the communication console in the common room. Luis had informed her earlier that day that he would be in the shop fine-tuning the ore smelter controls for Dave.

She poked her head into the shop. "Dave is whining that his RBI left him. Are you pranking him again?"

Luis looked up from the smelter control panel. "Tell him he needs to treat his RBI better. It probably couldn't take any more of his abuse."

"Luis, get serious. Dave is out at Site One. He says his RBI just left him there and is heading back this way."

Luis cocked his head to one side, wearing a puzzled expression. "It really just left him there? Are you sure he's not pranking *me*?"

Allie rolled her eyes and huffed, "Would you come talk to him?"

"Yeah, gimme a sec to close up this controller." Luis set a cover panel in place and tightened two screws. "There! I'm all yours."

Luis stood up and followed Allie back to the common room, patting her on her behind when he caught up to her. She feigned disinterest. "Later, Luis. Right now, you have a crisis to solve."

He pulled up a second chair to the communication console. "Dave, this is Luis. We haven't given any commands to the outside RBI units. What's your status?"

"Luis, my RBI backed my trailer into position for me so I could drop samples into it from above. By the time I rappelled into position, it was hightailing it back to base in a cloud of dust. It didn't respond to commands to stop or give me its location. It should be back to base by now."

"Lemme check on its location and get back to you." Luis pulled up the RBI control application on a nearby laptop. He punched up the RBI location command. A map of the base and the surrounding hundred meters came onscreen.

"That's odd. I don't see either RBI. At a minimum, Number Two should be stationed just outside the shop airlock in standby mode." Luis expanded the map area to a two-kilometer radius. A label identifying Site One appeared in the far northwest quadrant. He called up status bars for both RBIs. Both indicated OUT OF RANGE.

He rolled back over to the communication console. "Dave, I think something is wrong with the RBI control program. I've expanded the location map to include your position, but I don't see either RBI unit. I don't even see the one positioned outside the shop airlock. I think you'd better head back to base. Follow the RBI tracks if you can. Report back if you sight Number One. I'm going to suit up and EVA to see if Number Two is outside the shop where it belongs."

"Roger that. I'll leave my climbing gear here so I can travel light. Besides, I have to come back for the trailer anyway."

Luis got up and walked back to the greenhouse, where Robbie was assisting LaDonna Pleasant in setting up a hydroponics station. "Hey Doc, can I borrow Robbie?"

"Sure Luis. I'm almost done here anyway. What's up?"

"We've lost contact with the RBIs. I want Robbie to help me locate them."

He turned to Robbie as the AI unit inserted lettuce seedlings into foam blocks for LaDonna. "Robbie, are you in contact with the two exterior RBI units?"

Robbie continued planting seedlings. "No, Luis. I detect no chatter on their intercom channel."

"Robbie, please contact them and ask them their whereabouts."

Robbie paused for a moment, then resumed planting. "Neither RBI unit is responding. I detect no transmission carrier waves."

"Robbie, I'm suiting up for an EVA so I can get a visual on Number Two. I want you to accompany me."

"Certainly, Luis."

Robbie followed him into the hall. Dallas stepped out of the crew quarters as they passed by. "Luis, am I hearing correctly that we've lost communication with our RBI units?"

"It's probably nothing, Flash. Robbie and I are going to EVA to confirm Number Two is stationed outside the shop. Hopefully Number One is parked there, too."

"I thought Number One was at Site One with Dave."

"Dave called to say Number One abandoned him and headed back this way."

Dallas scratched his forehead, his brow furrowed. "Let me help you into your suit. Dr. Pleasant may have cleared you for light duty, but I want you to take it easy on that arm."

Luis patted the cast on his left forearm. LaDonna had pinned his collarbone together the day after their arrival at Prospector Base. Other than exercising care with the stitches, it didn't bother him. "I'd appreciate the help getting the suit sleeve over my cast. Still can't quite grip as tight as I want, but it feels pretty good." He opened and closed his hand several times to demonstrate.

Dallas and Allie helped Luis into his pressure suit. Robbie opened the airlock door once Luis had completely suited up, then closed it behind them. He activated the decompression cycle. They both stepped outside after the cycle completed.

Luis walked around to the shop side of the base. "We got a problem, Flash. Number Two is gone too."

CHAPTER 59

PROSPECTOR BASE
MSD: 57488
MTC: 11:42:03
FROM: Commander Dallas Gordon
URGENT!

Both extra-base RBI units are missing and unaccounted for. Number One abandoned Dave Caraway during a prospecting EVA to Site 1. RBIs not responding to commands on MGPS frequency. Location app ineffective. Please advise.
ANMHE

Malcom McDowell stood beside Roger Wheeler at the Autotronics representative station in the SaMMCon Flight Control Room. "Roger, this communication disturbs me. Not only for its content, but also because Commander Gordon didn't bother coding it per current practice."

"Malcom, just before you walked over here, I was puzzling over the sudden lack of telemetry from the two extra-base RBI units. My first assumption is that they initiated an auto shutdown. Has there been a recent solar storm?"

"Solar activity has been nominal. Commander Gordon's message would indicate that the RBIs are active and actively evading detection."

Roger reread the message from Prospector Base. "I see that Gordon hasn't attempted to use normal surface-to-surface UHF channels. For all we know, there's simply a malfunction with the MGPS transceivers."

"Maybe, Roger, but that doesn't explain the absence of telemetry. Telemetry is still being transmitted via the S-band. Or at least it was up until just now."

Roger Wheeler squinted at his monitor in concentration. "Malcom, I'm very troubled by this suite of behaviors. I've never seen anything like this before. Here's what I propose. For the sake of time, let's send a reboot command followed by a shutdown command directly from SaMMCon via the S-band. That should stop the RBIs in their tracks, and re-enable the MGPS tracking app.

"Then, as a failsafe, send a return message to Commander Gordon with instructions for a hard shutdown. If their S-band transceivers aren't functioning either, this might be the only way to stop them so that they can be properly tested and repaired."

Malcom inhaled deeply. His recent lapse in judgment over these very RBIs stung. "Roger, I'm not aware of an external switch on the RBIs. How exactly would the landing party effect a hard shutdown?"

"They'll have to remove the anterior access panel and pull the memory card."

Malcom was incredulous. "On a moving RBI?"

"I didn't say it would be easy. It's either that or wait for the fuel cells to deplete in five sols."

Malcom sighed. It had been several hours since the GPS signal from Ann's phone had gone dark, and now this. Managing EPSILON personnel and equipment on two planets at once felt like trying to paint the ponies on a moving carousel while standing on the ground. "Roger, how quickly can you get the necessary code and messaging over to Evan at CapCom?"

"It should only take me a couple of minutes. The code is a quick copy and paste from the digital command library. And I'll copy and paste the memory card access instructions from the operations manual."

"Good. Please proceed." Malcom turned to return to his workstation. Then his phone rang. He pulled it from his pocket to view the caller ID, hoping it was from Ann, but instead only saw an unknown number. He could tell from the area code that the call originated from the Seattle area. Knowing that his calls were being monitored by the FBI, Malcom accepted it and held the phone to his ear.

"Hello. This is Malcom McDowell."

CHAPTER 60

SaMMCon
MSD: 57488
MTC: 12:26:57
FROM: CAPCOM

SaMMCon has issued a shutdown command to both extra-base RBI units. Confirm ASAP status and location of RBI units with MGPS app.

If the shutdown command was ineffective, an EVA is authorized to track down and hard shutdown both RBI units. Use Procedure 3.15.6(A) Memory Card Removal from the RBI 3.0 Operation Manual, as copied here.

1) Locate anterior access panel.

2) Grasp recessed release handle and rotate 90 degrees counterclockwise.

3) Pull upward on release handle to remove access panel.

4) Press release button beside each memory card to be removed.

5) Pull memory card straight up and out, being careful not to torque or bend the card.

An emergency test was performed on an RBI 3.0 in the engineering lab. The unit shut down after the memory card release button was pressed. Full removal of the card is only advised if the unit does not shut down after the release button is pressed.

Dallas shook his head as he read the reply message from SaMMCon. He dialed into the base MGPS transceiver on his smartphone. "Robbie, you received this message from SaMMCon, too, right?"

"Yes, Commander Gordon."

"Will a hard shutdown as described permanently damage the RBI units?"

"It is possible, Commander. At a minimum, there will be a substantial loss of short-term data. Worst case, the operating system could be degraded."

Concern registered in Dallas's voice, "Robbie, won't this shutdown damage you, too?"

"No, Commander. I'll be quite safe. The extra-base RBIs receive their commands from SaMMCon via the S-Band carrier frequency. I do not possess an S-Band transceiver."

Relieved, Dallas spoke to Luis, who was still outside searching the perimeter around the base for Number Two, "Luis, have you read the message SaMMCon just sent?"

"I just did, Flash. I hope the remote shut down command worked. If not, we could be without the services of Number One and Number Two for the duration of the mission. Do you have their location on the Tracking App?"

Dallas glanced up at the monitor. "No. It's still blank. Robbie, are you picking up any UHF communication from them?"

"No, Commander. I am not receiving a signal from either of them, which is unusual."

"Luis, do you have any idea which direction Number Two might have gone?"

"Affirmative, Flash. I found one set of tracks heading southeast away from the shop. The imprint is on top of every other track they left around the base."

"Luis, start following that track. Robbie will join you shortly."

"Aye aye, Flash. I'm on my way."

"Robbie, accompany Luis. Assist him in any way that you can."

"Yes, Commander." Robbie immediately scanned his surroundings and located Luis about 150 meters to the southeast, walking away from the base.

Luis focused on the tread track. It was not easy. Tracks laid down over several years crisscrossed in every direction. Number Two followed the path leading to the Descent/Ascent Vehicle and the reactor array. The RBIs frequently tended to the vehicle and the portable fuel generator, so the path was a myriad of parallel tracks and drag marks.

Luis looked up when he sensed motion in his peripheral vision to his right. At first, he thought it was Robbie, en route from the base. "Flash, I've got eyes on Number One. He's heading past me toward the DV."

"Copy that, Luis. Can you catch up to it for a hard shutdown?"

"Negative, Flash. It's moving too fast. I'm still following Number Two's tracks bearing in that same direction."

"Keep following Number Two's tracks, Luis. I have a hunch that when you find Number Two, you'll also find Number One."

Dallas rubbed his eyes and sat back in his chair to stretch his back when an alarm sounded. "Allie, what's the alarm for?"

"I'm looking it up now, Flash. The alarm is related to the electrical system."

Allie drilled into the electrical system control software. "Here it is. There's a spike in the incoming voltage at the base voltage regulator. The voltage is already into the red zone."

"Allie, this is Luis. I overheard. Your mike is open. Listen, open up the reactor array display. Tell me what you see."

Allie scrolled through a menu until she found the correct display. "It's open, Luis."

"Now tell me, what's the current operating temperature of the reactors?"

"They're all different. Number one is 2,105° F, number two is 2,067, number three is 1,926, number four is 1,774, and number five is 1,615."

Luis blurted out, "Oh my God! The max operating temperature for the reactor cores is 1,200! No wonder the voltage is so high!"

Allie exclaimed, "Luis, the temps and the voltage are climbing higher! Flash or I need to EVA and throw the switch on the voltage regulator before it arcs out and fries the base electrical circuits."

"Luis, this is Dallas. It may take us some time. The airlock has to go through a complete cycle before we can EVA." Dallas turned to Allie. "Is there something that Luis can do out there that will be faster?"

Allie's eyes danced across the screen. "Negative, Flash. It's all direct connections from the reactor isolation switches to the voltage regulator. Luis would have to isolate each reactor individually, and it's too far for him to return to base to reach the voltage regulator. Either way, he doesn't have enough time!"

"Wait a sec," Luis broke in. "I have a visual on the reactor array. Goddammit, the RBIs have pulled the heat dissipaters out of the reactor cores. They're just lying on the ground. And it gets worse. I can see that the control rods have been manually withdrawn and locked out."

"Can you release the control rods?" Dallas urged him.

Luis's response became ragged as he broke into a run. "Negative, Flash. … At the temperatures that Allie gave … the reactors are too hot to touch. … I might be able to drop … the heat dissipaters back in … but I'm still two hundred yards away. … I can't get there in time … to save the voltage regulator! Aughhh!"

At that moment, a metallic object streaked away to Luis's right, startling him. Robbie raced over to the power cable running from the reactor array to the base. Before Luis could react, Robbie grasped the cable in a claw and crushed it in a brilliant blue flash, blinding Luis.

The power to the base was cut, enveloping Dallas, Allie, and LaDonna in darkness. The backup fuel cell restored power two seconds later. The ground fault Robbie had created simultaneously initiated the reactor control rods' failsafe. The control rods dropped back down into the cores, dampening the runaway neutron cascades. The core temperatures began to drop toward a more reasonable 1,400 degrees.

"Robbie!" Luis ran to his stricken AI assistant, but stopped short. Small blue arcs played over the now-inert automaton.

Fearing the answer, Luis asked, "Flash, are you guys okay?"

"We're okay, Luis. The backup power kicked in just like it's supposed to. I'll be EVA momentarily. What happened?

"Flash, Robbie is gone. He shorted out the main power cable to create a ground fault. I can see that the control rods dropped back into place. And I can see the two extra-base RBIs. Uh oh. They're heading toward me now!"

Both RBIs crested the crater rim above the reactor array and headed straight at Luis at full speed. A cloud of rust-colored dust billowed behind them. Luis flinched just as they reached his position, expecting to be struck. But they passed by on either side, leaving him standing bewildered in a cloud of dust. "Flash, they just raced by me. They're heading your way."

"Luis, leave them to me. I'm in the airlock now. You get down to the reactor array and reset the heat dissipaters if you can. We've got a week of backup power, but it won't do us much good if we can't get the reactors back online."

"Understood." Luis turned back toward the array, rehearsing in his head how he would balance the ungainly umbrella-shaped heat dissipaters long enough to drop into the receptacle above the heat engine—all without burning a hole in his pressure suit on the red-hot nuclear core.

Dallas waited outside the airlock hatch. He saw the dust cloud before he saw the two autonomous machines that generated it. As they neared the base, Number Two headed back toward the shop airlock, where it had been on standby. Number One followed behind and to the right, like it was headed toward the greenhouse.

Dallas moved to intercept Number Two as it paused beside the shop airlock, facing the exterior wall. To his horror, the

RBI unit closed its claw, the end of its arm now resembling a spear tip. It extended its limb into the carbon fiber and resin wall, the interior pressure forcing air out like a rocket blast. The heavy RBI remained motionless in the stream of air. Dallas braced himself against the gale to maintain his position, quickly grabbed the RBI's access plate handle, twisted it, and pulled the plate away from the main body.

Just as he reached for the memory card release button, Number Two pivoted to its right and rolled past the shop airlock. Dallas grabbed the open edge of the access port, dragged along by Number Two. His air pressure alarm sounded as small holes tore in the knees of his pressure suit. Mustering all his strength, Dallas pulled himself forward. He blindly punched inside the access port with his fist. On his third try, he connected with the release button and felt the memory card pop upward against his gloved hand.

Number Two stopped so abruptly that Dallas's face shield banged against the back side of the RBI. Still on his knees, he leaned against the inert RBI unit, collecting his wits. Then he sprang to his feet, intent to run to the greenhouse before Number One breached it, too.

As Dallas stepped around Number Two, he saw a pressure-suited figure holding an access plate aloft with one hand. Number One rested motionless against the greenhouse wall. Dave's unmistakable Canadian accent came over his helmet speakers: "Bet you're glad I took that course on RBI maintenance!"

Dave dropped the access plate in the dust. A small cloud puffed out and quickly settled back down. Dallas walked up to his planetary geologist, and they exchanged a high five. "I'd kiss you if I wasn't wearing a helmet."

"Now Flash, don't you be gettin' my wife all jealous, now. How about I get extra rations for a week instead?"

"Deal. Now help me patch up the pinholes in the knees in my suit before I pass out from hypoxia."

Dave pulled a roll of duct tape out of Dallas's EVA pack and wound several passes around each knee. Dallas's helmet alarm silenced as his suit pressure rebuilt.

The two men walked back to the main airlock, where they met Luis. "Did you know that those reactor heat dissipators are held in place by a single cotter pin? And yet somehow, they're rated to withstand an F5 storm?" Luis eyed Dallas, whose suit was covered head to toe in rusty dust. "So, I take it that you two gentlemen managed to shut down Number One and Number Two?"

The airlock was still depressurized. Dallas pulled open the hatch and the three men walked in.

Once inside the Common Room, LaDonna and Allie helped the three men remove their helmets and pressure suits. LaDonna tended the minor cuts on Dallas's knees.

The four crew members seated themselves around the galley conference table, looking to Dallas. "Allie, prepare a status report for SaMMCon ASAP. We're all alive, and the two extra-base RBIs are shut down, but Robbie is lost. The base is on backup power. Luis, assist Allie with a damage assessment to include in the status report."

CHΛPTER 61

"Director McDowell, this message just arrived from Prospector Base. Sir, it was transmitted via the S-band channel."

Malcom McDowell looked up from his console toward his CapCom in the first row of Flight Control.

"Evan, are you certain it's from Prospector Base?"

"Yes, sir. The transmission is fully authenticated. Sending you a copy."

> PROSPECTOR BASE
> MSD: 57489
> MTC: 14:56:24
> FROM: Commander Dallas Gordon
>
> All personnel are alive. No significant injuries to report.
>
> Prospector Base is operational on backup power. Exterior hull breach in the shop module. Minimal disturbance to shop contents. Breach repair is underway. Repressurization remains on hold pending redeployment of portable electrolysis unit from DV.
>
> Repair of damaged primary power cable from reactor array planned for tomorrow. Primary voltage regulator is operational within a reduced voltage range. Mission robotics/mechanical engineer is on site at reactor array opening isolation switches to prepare for repair of damaged power cable.

Nuclear reactors have been restored to safe operational temperature ranges but will remain offline until clearance by SaMMCon engineers.

All RBI units are currently offline. Extra-base units required hard shutdown per procedure 3.15.6(A) Memory Card Removal per the RBI 3.0 Operations Manual. Electrical/Software Engineer and Planetary Geologist are removing S-Band transceivers prior to evaluation and restoration of memory cards from mainframe backup.

AI Assistant Robbie is lost and not recoverable. Robbie's quick action to ground fault main power cable saved the primary voltage regulator from catastrophic failure and the reactors from imminent meltdown. His actions saved Prospector Base and are hereby commended.

We have received no messages from FOD Waters in two sols. What is her status?

I have authorized the one-time use of S-Band for this transmission to make it clear to the sons-of-bitches who launched this attack that they failed. Prospector 1 mission personnel are alive. And if Earth authorities have not found you by the time we return to Earth, I will hunt you down myself.

Malcom pushed his chair back from his workstation and silently bowed his head. Then he sat up straight, grabbed his desk phone, and dialed. "Steve, this is Malcom. I'm forwarding our most recent communication from Prospector Base. Please tell me your Seattle team has Ann."

CHAPTER 62

Ellis Pierpont ducked his tall frame as he entered his Beechcraft Hawker corporate jet. "Please close the door, Jessica. It's just me today."

He settled into a leather captain's swivel chair back at the mahogany conference table. He brought no work with him. His laptop and cell phone lay on a workstation in his black hole, both having been wiped clean by equipment installed there for that very purpose.

All top-tier Fortune 500 CEOs had an exit strategy. Ellis Pierpont now executed his. It grieved him to abandon his golden parachute. He was literally leaving 150 million dollars on the table. But once the Board found out how he had been utilizing his discretionary research and development fund, they would strip him of his retirement anyway. He deeply regretted his agreement to those ridiculous morality clauses.

Ellis applied the same foresight to providing for personal contingencies that he applied to his corporate management. He had wisely diverted much of his accumulated wealth into cryptocurrency. Plus, he had siphoned off tens of millions from his R&D fund to create a comfortable retreat where he could live in blissful anonymity, far from the searching eyes of those pursuing him.

"Jessica, please deliver this flight plan to Captain Garrett. He is expecting it."

"Of course, Mr. Pierpont. Shall I bring you a cocktail on my way back?"

"That would be delightful. But make it bourbon, neat, two fingers."

"As you wish, sir."

Jessica brought Ellis his drink as the jet began to taxi. Ellis sipped thoughtfully, recalling the events of the past hour. He had been returning to his Seattle office from lunch with the mayor, and literally bumped into Pang Xianjing as Pang exited the elevator into the lobby.

"Mr. Pierpont, could I trouble you to accompany me?" Pang's concerned expression convinced Pierpont to do so. Pang immediately headed for the hallway to the secure room. Once both men were inside, Pang stopped and turned to Ellis. "I just came down from your office. Ann Waters managed to free herself. I caught her on your desk phone speaking to someone. I'm certain it was Malcom McDowell from EPSILON. I'm also certain that the authorities traced the call, even if she did not have time to provide her whereabouts.

"We also intercepted an S-band transmission from Prospector Base. The RBI hack damaged the base, the reactors, and the RBIs. But everyone survived, and they'll be able to repair the damage. If the authorities had not been tipped off about the black hole operation, I'm certain that we would have had time to finish the job on Mars. But we don't have much more than an hour before the feds overrun this building. It's time for me to disappear. I recommend that you do the same."

Ellis absorbed the full implication of this unwelcome news. For the briefest of moments, his thoughts scattered like loose papers in a gale. But his logic soon collected them. He recognized the strategic value of an hour's head start on the authorities. It was then that Ellis noticed that Pang held the laptop Ellis normally kept on his desk.

Pang looked down at it. "We need to scrub all evidence of black hole activity from your SSHD. The same goes for your cell phone." Pang held out his hand.

Ellis reluctantly handed his phone over to Pang. Both men entered the secure elevator to the black hole floor.

"Mr. Pang, I need to make one more phone call."

"Use the phone app on one of the computers in the hole. The call will be untraceable."

"Of course. Good thinking, Mr. Pang."

By the time they finished their conversation, Pang and Pierpont were inside the black hole.

CHAPTER 63

Ann woke as gentle hands laid her out flat on her back. She struggled to free herself, the memory of her last encounter with Pang returning to her. She tried to scream, but the air she breathed felt as thick as molasses. Opening her eyes, Ann found that nothing was in focus. *The cleanup crew!*

"Ms. Waters, please lie still. You have a head injury, possibly a concussion. Keep your eyes closed until we finish with the dressing."

Ann was puzzled. *You're bandaging my head?* Despite her terror, she relaxed until her head was bandaged. Then she reopened her eyes. Two men stared down at her as they kneeled beside her. She made out the letters "FBI" stenciled on their jackets. She struggled anew. "Let me go!"

Ann sat upright before she could be restrained. A pair of hands pressed down on her shoulders to prevent her from standing. A door near her opened and a woman stepped into the room, also FBI.

"Ms. Waters, I'm Special Agent Debra James of the Seattle FBI Field Office."

She flashed credentials, similar to those of Ted Gilmore. Ann recoiled in terror.

Agent James kneeled and gently placed a hand on Ann's shoulder. "It's okay, Ann. You're safe now. Do you know where you are?"

Ann gently touched the bandage on her temple. She could feel the goose egg beneath the bandage, and blood soaking through the gauze. "Am I in Ellis Pierpont's office?"

Debra James spoke soothingly, "Yes, you are. You're a lucky woman, Ann. The FBI has been monitoring your phone calls to Malcom McDowell. You've been through hell, haven't you?"

Ann nodded. Then she remembered why she had reentered this building in the first place. "Did you get them? Did you get Ellis Pierpont and the black hole supervisor?"

Agent James raised an eyebrow. "You know where the black hole is?"

Ann struggled to get to her feet. Agent James and one of the paramedics helped her up. She supported Ann under one arm as Ann steadied herself.

"It's on a hidden floor. BMAC hacked EPSILON using the equipment down there. I managed to hide five nanny cams there to document their activities. I saved the video on my phone, but they took out the memory card before I could send the file to Malcom. Please let me show you where it is. The files should still be on the cams."

"Yes, please do. But take it easy. I don't want you to fall again and hurt yourself further."

Agent James led Ann through the conference room door into the larger office. Ann estimated there were a dozen men and women, all wearing FBI jackets over Kevlar vests, and all armed. One approached Agent James as she led Ann.

"Agent James, we've found no weapons and no electronics anywhere. We did find this in a wall safe, though. The door was left ajar. Whoever opened it last must have been in a hurry."

The man handed a clear plastic evidence bag to Agent James. Inside was a sheath of paper stapled at the upper left corner. She held it with gloved hands, skimming through it quickly. Ann was able to read the title.

CONTRACT FOR TRANSMISSION SERVICES

BY THE PEOPLE'S REPUBLIC OF CHINA

ON BEHALF OF BMAC CORPORATION

Agent James looked up from her reading. "Have you found anything else?"

"Just this." The man held up another clear evidence bag. This one contained the janitor card that Ann had used to access the building. "Otherwise, the place has been sanitized. We're dusting for fingerprints, but so far, nothing."

"Tommy, stay here with Robert. Keep searching. The rest of you come with me and Ms. Waters."

Ann interjected, "Can I take that with us? I've been able to access the black hole with it."

Agent James traded evidence bags with Tommy and proceeded for the office door with Ann in tow.

Ann began to feel more clear-headed as she walked down the hall to the elevator accompanied by Debra James and her entourage. When they reached the lobby, the room was filled with flashing red light as a Medic One truck slowly drove past the main door. The sight reminded Ann of the night before when she had fled the black hole. She shivered at the thought of the one-way ride Pierpont had planned for her. *If the FBI hadn't shown up today when they had ...*

Ann turned left and walked down the hallway toward the secure room. Agent James held the card to the detection pad. The door unlocked with an audible click. The group made their way into the elevator, up to the secret floor, and down the hall to the black hole door. Ann and Agent James entered the black hole. The remaining FBI agents piled in behind them.

Ann walked to the center of the room, slack-jawed. All the workstations were vacant. No computers, no monitors, not so much as a network cable remained. Ann slowly circled the perimeter, searching for the nanny cams she had placed earlier that morning. Even they were gone. She fought back tears. "Agent James, I don't understand it. This room was crammed with computer equipment this morning. I hid five nanny cams in here. Even they're gone!"

Agent James again placed her hand on Ann's shoulder. "Don't worry, Ann. That contract we saw upstairs ties BMAC to the Chinese transmitter used to launch the cyberattacks on your facilities. It's only a matter of time before we link electronic traffic from this BMAC facility to the laser transmitter. And it's only a matter of time before we locate the men who were behind all of this."

Ann's eyes widened. "You mean that you haven't caught Ellis Pierpont, or the supervisor?"

"Or Gary Lefebre. They're all still at large. But don't worry, we *will* get them all, I promise."

Ann hugged herself, unable to stop trembling. She had been raped. She had killed a man. How would she explain that? Worse, the men who intended to kill her were still at large, possibly in this very building.

Agent James noted the color leaving Ann's face and pulled over a chair for her. "Once you're rested up, I'd like you to accompany me to the Seattle Field Office for an interview. It would be helpful for us to reconstruct your activities over the past forty-eight hours. Our last direct knowledge of you was when you were coerced away from Santa Maria."

Ann vacantly nodded her assent, then snapped back to full focus. "What about the Prospector landing party? Are they all right? Were they able to shut down the RBI units in time?"

"As far as I know, your landing party is all alive, though I don't have any details. But let's take it one step at a time, Ann. I need your statement first, then I can put you through to Malcom McDowell. He can answer all of your questions. Now please, come with me."

CHAPTER 64

Malcom McDowell sat alone in the conference room, conversing with the image of Special Agent Debra James from the Seattle FBI Field Office.

"Hello, Director McDowell. Ann Waters will be touching down at Santa Maria Municipal Airport in about an hour. I know that you and Ann had an extensive conversation after her debriefing here at our office, but I think it's important to discuss with you, as someone she trusts, some of the things that she left unsaid."

Malcom shifted uncomfortably. "Please go on, Agent James."

"What Ann didn't tell you is that on the first night that she was abducted to Seattle, she was chloroformed and raped by the man posing as Agent Gilmore. Somehow, she managed to get the assailant's gun, shooting and killing him."

"Oh my God!" Malcom's hand involuntarily covered his mouth.

"Just between us, Director, I've also spoken with the local District Attorney. The scant evidence that we have supports Ann's version of the events. The DA sees Ann's action as a clear-cut case of self-defense. No charges will be filed. I informed Ann before she boarded her flight for Santa Maria. I hope that gives her one less thing to worry about." He raised his eyebrows. "She's a resourceful woman, Malcom. After she escaped, she spent the following day repenetrating the BMAC black hole."

Malcom's response was a mix of pride and concern. "Yes, she and I spoke about her intent to collect evidence, using a diversion to allow her to reenter the building."

"Which, of course, we monitored. And which she successfully pulled off. Unfortunately, after she got back inside, we lost contact with her due to the building's electromagnetic shielding. She was recaptured. Then she briefly escaped again. That's when she called you from Pierpont's Seattle office."

"And you mobilized her rescue. I can't thank you enough, Agent James."

"But she was pistol-whipped for her trouble."

Malcom closed his eyes at the news for a moment before responding, "Agent James, Ann never mentioned any of this to me when we spoke!"

"She's been through a lot of trauma, Director. Ann is a strong woman, but her recovery may take some time. I can tell she's used to being in control. That can make it difficult to accept when events spiral out of control for her as they just have."

Malcom smiled at the FBI agent's accurate assessment of his strong-willed flight director. "Yes, of course. But knowing Ann like I do, she'll open up when it's right for her to do so. And not a minute before." Malcom made a mental note to discuss Ann's abduction experience with Rebekah Gradwahl. If Ann ever requested counseling, he would see that she got it. And if she didn't, he still wanted to support her as best he could.

"There's something else that I want to discuss with you, Director. We at the Bureau have collected evidence that BMAC was behind all of the cyberattacks directed to your Prospector mission. We know based on Ann's eyewitness account that Randy Porter is dead. We also know that the man who abducted her is also dead. Our forensic technicians have found minute traces of blood in the two locations that she described where these deaths took place.

"We have solid documentary evidence linking BMAC to the Chinese lunar transmission site that was the source of the hacking signals. According to the contract we found in Ellis Pierpont's office safe, the optical uplink and lunar S-band transmissions were in support of BMAC's Mars missions. As expected, China claims no knowledge BMAC used those same facilities to launch their attacks.

"But there's something about this case that niggles me. We don't know the whereabouts of Ellis Pierpont, or the hackers who staffed the black hole. There's disagreement internally within the Bureau. Did they remove the equipment to destroy evidence, or do they plan to set up somewhere else? Time will tell.

"Given all that the FBI now knows about how the attacks were perpetrated, it will be difficult for them to relaunch. But in the meantime, and out of an abundance of caution, your company needs to protect itself from any future cyberattacks."

Malcom nodded. "I can't thank you enough for all you've done for Ann, and for EPSILON. I hope that one day I can introduce you to the Prospector 1 Flight Control staff and the landing party."

"It's a date, Director."

Malcom looked down at his watch. "But I really need to be going. I plan to meet Ann when her flight touches down."

"Then I'll sign off. Best of luck to you and the Prospector 1 team, Director."

"Thanks again, Agent James."

The screen went blank. Malcom pushed himself away from the conference table and headed for the door.

CHAPTER 65

"Oh Miss Ann, I was so worried for you while you were gone!" Ann Waters found herself in a bear hug as soon as she stepped through the door into the flight control room. Monica Gonzalez was in full-on surrogate mother mode. And now, the entire flight control staff took on the role of family.

Ann awkwardly brushed back the tears that welled in her eyes. Monica showed no such inhibition. Tears streaked her cheeks. Many others wiped their eyes with sleeves and tissues. Several were so excited they bounced up and down like five-year-old children crowding around an ice cream truck.

As Ann worked her way through the crowd toward her flight control station, she continued to receive hugs and back slaps. When she arrived, Malcom gestured for the crowd to quiet down. "Like you all, I am so happy to have Ann back with us, safe and sound."

Malcom cast a quick glance at Ann. He knew she was uncomfortable as the center of attention. "I have even more good news, but I wanted to wait until we could all be together before sharing it. As you know, BMAC indefinitely suspended their Mars landing program pending the completion of the ongoing criminal investigation."

Scattered boos could be heard around the room.

"NASA declared BMAC in noncompliance with their lease agreement for a DeepStar nuclear ion propulsion unit. They have given BMAC two weeks to remove their Command Module and surrender their DeepStar back to NASA. EPSILON has assumed the lease agreement and may take possession of the DeepStar in fifteen days. EPSILON now controls both DeepStar boosters available for Mars exploration. This means we don't have to wait for the

Prospector 1 Command Module to return for fitting with a new DV. Now we can send the Prospector 2 replacement crew in our second Command Module with a new DV and bring back the Prospector 1 flight crew. We can get help to Prospector 1 six months earlier than previously thought."

Cheers filled the flight control room. Ann turned and smiled at Malcom. "You really know how to work a crowd."

"I couldn't have done it if you hadn't forced the FBI's hand, getting them into BMAC's Seattle building. By the way, I have a little welcome home gift for you." Malcom opened a desk drawer and pulled out a smartphone identical to Ann's original company-issued phone. "With your old phone lying at the bottom of Lake Washington, I figured that you might like a replacement. You'll once again have direct contact with the landing party when you're not at your flight control station."

He winked at Ann as he handed her the phone. She blushed as she took it.

CHAPTER 66

Dallas Gordon opened the personal message from Ann Waters on his mission command monitor in the common room. There was less privacy here than in his crew quarters, but he was so relieved to see her name as the sender that he opened it immediately.

SaMMCon
MSD: 57491
MTC: 22:43:51
FROM: Ann

Red, I have so much to tell you I hardly know where to start. First, I'm so glad that you and the crew are safe. Ever since the crash landing, the thought of losing you forever is more than I can bear. I love you and can't wait to hold you again.

Malcom told me he did not inform you of my whereabouts for the past three days. I agree with that decision. You had enough on your mind already. But I owe it to you to explain what happened. Before I start, I want to assure you that I'm OK.

I was abducted from the SaMMCon parking lot and taken to Seattle. It was there that I learned that BMAC was behind all the Prospector 1 cyberattacks. I managed to escape and then infiltrated BMAC to get more evidence. That's when I learned about the cyberattack on the RBIs. But I was recaptured.

I managed to get word out to Malcom and the FBI and was finally rescued.

Two of the men responsible for the attacks are dead, including Randy Porter. But many more who were involved escaped, including the CEO of BMAC, who was the mastermind behind the scheme. There is so much more I want to share with you about what happened, but it will have to wait until we're together.

The FBI has collected enough information that if another attack happens in the future, they'll be able to detect and stop it. But to be safe, Malcom has ordered the IT department to develop a security patch for the Prospector Operating System. Autotronics is doing the same for the RBIs. Once they have the patch, you can reactivate the extra-base RBIs and use the S-band again.

Better news is that we have the second available NASA DeepStar. With that, we can have you off Mars and back on Earth six months sooner. I can't wait to give you the welcome home that you deserve.

ANMHE,
Sprite

Dallas pushed himself back from his workstation, oblivious to the audience of four that had peered over his shoulder as he read.

"Damn, Flash. I knew you two had the hots for each other. I could see the sparks fly whenever you looked at each other back on Earth."

"Actually, Luis, we had the 'hots' for each other a long time ago. Ann and I were a couple for the year after she graduated from Stanford. We were both climbing instructors at the time."

"What happened?"

"What often happens when two people fall in love too soon. She went her way to graduate school at Stanford, and I went into the Navy and learned to fly. I have to admit that I didn't think that it was even possible that she still had feelings for me after all these years."

Allie walked up to Dallas and gave him a long hug. "I hope that you two find happiness together again. But can you answer why she always signs off with the letters ANMHE?"

Dallas grinned sheepishly. "It's the initials of a song title we heard one day on an oldies radio station in Lander, Wyoming. Afterward, she always played it when we climbed together. It's the title from an old Marvin Gaye song, 'Ain't No Mountain High Enough.' I guess it's our song."

"Aww, that's sweet, Flash," Luis piped back up with a mischievous glint in his eye. "But maybe you should have her change the letters to ANCDE."

"ANCDE?"

"Yeah, 'Ain't No Crater Deep Enough.'"

Four yellow foam balls pummeled Luis.

CHAPTER 67

"Lieutenant Pang, welcome back to China."

Pang Xianjing stood stiffly and saluted his old recruiter and mentor, General Aiguo Zhang. Aiguo had recruited Pang shortly after the promising youth graduated from high school in rural Qinghai province. The general was a colonel back then. Pang expected his own rank of lieutenant to be changed as well. He stood stiffly, ready to accept his demotion.

"Your assignment for the People's Liberation Army Cyber Cell 457 was enormously successful. I have recommended you to the Strategic Support Force Command for a commendation for your work, in addition to your promotion to the rank of Captain."

Pang cast a puzzled look at his commanding officer. "Commendation? Promotion? My mission was a complete failure. Prospector Base is still operational. I failed to penetrate NASA's DeepStar design plans. I couldn't even deliver Ann Waters when she landed in my lap after killing that bumbling assassin. I called the cleaning crew early, but the FBI beat them to her." Pang suspected his mentor knew that Ann was the one who had alerted the FBI while he was delayed, but said nothing about it.

"Yes, accomplishing any one of those objectives could have advanced our Mars program a full ten years. But the extensive diversion your chaos created allowed the placement of our assets without detection. Our long-term interests have been served well indeed by your patriotic actions."

"Thank you, General Zhang." Relief washed over Pang's face. He remained within his mentor's good graces. Then an afterthought occurred to him. "What of Ellis Pierpont? I searched in vain for him after we decommissioned the black hole. I nearly missed my own extraction looking for him."

General Zhang laughed and gave Pang a hearty slap on his back. "Our operatives reported that Mr. Pierpont suffered a tragic accident. It seems that while sailing on his yacht en route to his secret South Pacific island, he fell overboard into shark-infested waters. Such a pity.

"Leaving only the one paper copy of BMAC's transmission agreement was a stroke of genius. The contract provides us with plausible deniability. The Strategic Support Force Command, of course, claims ignorance of BMAC's intentions. The American FBI is convinced BMAC was behind everything."

Stepping away, the general turned back to face Pang.

"Rest assured. Both you—and my intentions for Mars— remain undetectable."

AFTERWARD

Ann Waters is a fictitious character. Like so many real women, she is talented, driven and resilient. But unlike real women, the consequences of her sexual assault are brief.

In real life, as in fiction, bad things happen to good people. But in real life, most survivors of sexual assault cannot simply shrug off such a traumatic event. The scars, both physical and emotional can be deep and long-lasting.

If you are one of the estimated 431,840* women in the United States who endures sexual assault each year, there is help and hope. If you need help, please reach out to any one of the fine organizations that offer counseling, medical and legal assistance.

- National Sexual Assault Hotline, 1-800-656-HOPE (4673)
- Rape, Abuse & Incest National Network, https://www.rainn.org/
- Your local Rape Crisis Center
- Your local Emergency Room

Guys, understand that forcing any woman into sex without consent can have life-long negative consequences for her. Adopt the mantra that it's never OK. Then make the effort to tell your sons. We need to get this right.

* National Crime Victimization Survey, 2016.

ACKNOWLEGEMENTS

While my name may be on the cover of Crimson Lucre, the development and publication of this novel was definitely a team effort.

Developmental Editor, Sandra Haven. I can't thank you enough. You made me a better writer and made Crimson Lucre a much better book.

Copy Editor, Dylan Garity

Cover Designer, Daniel Schmelling

The Wednesday Writers. The collective wisdom of this (very informal) group guided and supported me as I navigated the unfamiliar world of writing and publishing. I am so grateful to you all.

- o   Bethany Brengan, Editor, Poet
- o   Michelle Chappel, Creativity Rock Star Consulting, Singer, Author
- o   Susan Furlong, Author (Kensington Press)
- o   Danielle Gomes, Author (ANJO One-Eleven Press)
- o   Anne Greer, Author
- o   Jim Harvey, Author
- o   Kiera Mayock, Author
- o   Bridget McQueen, self-published author

Lastly, thank you to my wonderful wife, Karen Brozovich. Your support and astounding patience allowed me to pursue this, my long-suspended dream. I love you.

A Note from the Author

Thank you for purchasing Crimson Lucre! Like all indie authors, my success depends on good reviews (Think five stars, hint, hint!), either at the point of sale (Amazon.com) or at book review sites (Goodreads, Bookbub, Reedsy, etc.).

If you enjoyed this book and look forward to future installments of the EPSILON series, leave a review, then go to my author website, https://BrianHRoberts.com to sign up for my monthly newsletter, Just Over the Horizon. You'll receive up-to-date info on future book release dates, musings about what the near-future holds for us, and my schedule of virtual and public appearances. I'll also introduce other Sci-Fi Thrillers by up-and-coming authors in between my own book launches.

As a newsletter subscriber you'll have exclusive access to free interquels (short stories published between two books in a series).

A few months after Crimson Lucre is published, I'll release the interquel between Crimson Lucre and Red Dragon (book 2). Each interquel is free, and available only to newsletter subscribers.

Connect with me on…

Facebook: https://www.facebook.com/bhrauthor/

LinkedIn: https://www.linkedin.com/in/brian-h-roberts-792b15212/

In his first life, Brian worked as a contractor and civil engineer in bustling Seattle. Desiring a change, he and his wife traded big city life for the outdoor adventures of Central Oregon. His writing draws deeply on his lifelong loves of science/technology and adventure sports. Crimson Lucre is his first novel.

Follow him at

https://brianhroberts.com
https://www.facebook.com/bhrauthor/
https://www.linkedin.com/in/brian-h-roberts-792b15212/

Made in the USA
Monee, IL
07 July 2021

72430983R00173